This book
belongs to

Director's Cut

DIRECTOR'S CUT

a

Moses Wine

novel

ROGER L. SIMON

ATRIA BOOKS

NEW YORK   LONDON   TORONTO
SYDNEY   SINGAPORE

ATRIA BOOKS

1230 Avenue of the Americas
New York, NY 10020

ISBN: 0-7434-5802-8

First Atria Books hardcover edition June 2003

10 9 8 7 6 5 4 3 2 1

ATRIA BOOKS is a trademark of Simon & Schuster, Inc.

For information regarding special discounts for bulk purchases,
please contact Simon & Schuster Special Sales at 1-800-456-6798
or business@simonandschuster.com

DESIGNED BY LISA CHOVNICK

Manufactured in the United States of America

For my mother,
Ruth Lichtenberg Simon

JUST AT THIS MODISH MOMENT, everybody under thirty and his idiot brother wants to be a film director. And why not? Let it be whispered that film directing (the very job itself) is often grossly overrated. Good paintings don't come from a bad painter, but good motion pictures are often signed by directors of the most perfect incompetence. Writers, editors and actors do his work for him. His only task is to speak the words "action" and "cut" and go home with the money. Such a man can, as we have seen, wing his way through fifty years of film directing and never be found out.

ORSON WELLES

Director's Cut

1

I KNEW I WAS IN TROUBLE when I was starting to agree with John Ashcroft—me a lifelong card-carrying left/liberal and graduate of the University of California at Berkeley, who had espoused every so-called progressive cause from anti-nuke to pro-choice to saving the West Indian manatee, arrested at a half dozen demonstrations and bashed over the head by at least as many cops, nodding approvingly at the utterances of our Attorney General, a man who, a mere decade or two earlier, would have delighted in locking me in the slammer and throwing away the proverbial key. And I wasn't even embarrassed by it.

Of course I wasn't the only one. Nearly everyone I knew had done a political about-face as sharp as a class of prize plebes at a West Point graduation ceremony. It was a symptom of the times in which we lived. Like others I wanted to help, be Rosie the Riveter or even Clarence the Computer Chip Maker, but I didn't have the skills for any of that, and besides we were told just to go about our normal work, that simply being vigilant would be enough to fight terrorism, whatever that meant. Nobody could explain.

Certainly being a private investigator in Los Angeles didn't have much to do with battling Al Qaeda in the mountains of Tora Bora. In fact my job didn't appear to have much to do at all with the successful pursuit of this conflict, which promised to go on in some form for the rest of our natural lives and possibly beyond, as if we had embarked on a re-upped version of the Punic Wars. It was a depressing prospect indeed. I shuffled around my offices in downtown LA's warehouse district—my collection of vintage Joplin and Hendrix posters decorating the walls seeming oddly self-indulgent in the new era—feeling distinctly irrelevant and going through the motions of the few cases we had.

Samantha, my wife and business partner, ordinarily would have criticized me for my inattention to our work, but I knew she was feeling the same way. She was sleepwalking as much as I was, relying on her methodical FBI training, which she had previously disdained as uselessly bureaucratic. We were just trying to make it through the day. I felt worse for her than I did for me. She was younger and had had fewer years to enjoy the dream of a better world now being decimated by more racial and religious hatred than you could find in a galaxy of skinheads. I was also guilty for having dragged her into a professional alliance with me, urging her to quit the feds and join up with some ex-hippie dick who, in his more feckless youth, had been profiled as the "People's Detective" on the cover of a then newly minted *Rolling Stone* magazine with a photograph by Annie Liebowitz, a Bogarted joint dangling from his lips and a Mao button pinned to the band of his tilted Borsalino. "On the case with Moses Wine, the stoned Sam Spade!" said the headline plastered across his weathered leather trench coat. Like many of my generation, I had gone through what felt like several dozen fads and lifestyles since, ending up marrying someone who worked for the very organization I had once reviled—the federal government. At least with her old employers, however inept they might have been recently, she would have been at the center of things, would have more reason to get up in the morning. On top of that she had wanted to have a kid, but now, in this insane world?

So it was with mixed emotions—half excitement, half suspicion—that I received a phone call early one Tuesday morning from the Los Angeles branch of the FBI asking me to come down to their headquarters that day and speak with Fiona Lucas, the SAC, or Special Agent in Charge, for anti-terror investigations.

The local bureau HQ was in the Federal Building on Wilshire Boulevard in Westwood and I remembered when I drove up that I had been there relatively recently, December 2000 in fact, when Samantha and I had participated in a protest against the Supreme Court decision in the Florida election. Of course we were standing *outside* then as cars whizzed past, the vast majority of them honking their horns in support of several thousand of us demonstrators who held placards excoriating Bush and the Supremes as thieves or worse—the alliance of Jews, Latinos and blacks having long ago made Los Angeles almost as solidly a Democratic city as New York.

This too seemed like ancient history after all that had happened and now I found myself on the *inside*, suite 1700, the second largest branch of the Federal Bureau of Investigation outside of D.C., showing my ID to the front desk. I was then led down several corridors to a small conference room where I was met by Special Agent Lucas, a squat woman in her early forties wearing a floral print blouse and a younger man with a trendy spiked haircut identified as Agent Michael Sudsbury. They were polite but businesslike, skipping the small talk and getting right down to asking questions the minute I was seated across the table. Lucas conducted the interview while Sudsbury made notes on a legal pad.

"Mr. Wine, we understand you're a private investigator here in Los Angeles with your own agency."

"That is correct."

"And that your wife Samantha Faber was an agent at our National Domestic Preparedness Office in Washington. . . ."

"Correct."

"And that she now works with you."

"Yes."

"And that your services include serving subpoenas, collecting evidence and testifying at trial."

"Yes."

"Have you met Mohammed Atta?"

"Mohammed Atta?" I stared at her with incredulity. The interview had just veered off in the most extraordinary direction. "You mean *the* Mohammed Atta who flew the plane into the World Trade Center?"

She nodded.

"What makes you think I would know *him?*"

"Just answer the question, please."

"Of course I don't know him."

"Have you ever seen him?"

"No . . . except on television of course, like everybody else."

"When were you last in the Czech Republic?"

"I've never been to the Czech Republic."

"What about the Radio Free Europe headquarters in Prague?"

"Prague? How could I have gone to Prague when I've never been to the Czech Republic? Last I heard it's the capital of the country. Would you mind telling me what's going on here? Why are you asking me these questions?"

"Have you ever met any agents of the government of Iraq?"

"What?" I looked back and forth at the two stony faces in front of me, feeling as if I had suddenly dropped down in some whacko Southern California version of *Darkness at Noon,* palm trees and cell phones replacing dank walls and plates of gruel with stale bread. "This is absolutely unbelievable. Why in the world would you think I have met Iraqi spies? I'm a Jewish-American from New York City, as I'm sure you're well aware. Not exactly a candidate for Islamic jihad."

"These are just questions that we've been told to ask you, Mr. Wine," said Lucas.

"By whom?"

"Our superiors."

"And why would *they* want to ask me these questions?"

"We don't know."

"I see. Well, the answer is no."

"Very good."

"Anything else they need to know?"

Lucas and Sudsbury looked at each other. For a moment I wondered what I could possibly expect next. Was I a friend of Yasser Arafat? Did I know Osama bin Laden? Was I planning a trip to Mecca? But she answered simply, "Not for the moment. Thank you for your time. We are sorry if we inconvenienced you."

And with that they escorted me out. I didn't know what to think. I drove back on the 10 with my eye cocked on the rearview mirror. Nothing out of the ordinary. A half hour later I was in my office telling Samantha what had happened. She was as non-plussed as I was and phoned an old friend of hers at National Domestic Preparedness in Washington to try to find out why I was dragged into this. A couple of hours later the friend called back. Indeed there was an ongoing investigation of Mohammed Atta's trip to Prague last April to meet with an Iraqi agent. The Americans weren't convinced it actually happened, but the Czechs insisted it had.

"But why me?" I asked.

"She says she's not exactly sure," said Samantha. "But they've been having computer problems and evidently you're on a political watch list from the old days and your name came up on a search engine."

"You mean they typed in Atta and Prague and Radio Free Europe and Iraq and up popped little old Moses Wine, boy radical?"

"Who knows? She told me you shouldn't worry about it."

"Great," I said and tried, after a day or two, to push the whole thing into the back of my mind, but it wasn't easy. And it wasn't exactly reassuring that the FBI was having "technical difficulties," although it was scarcely surprising. I had read somewhere that the previous director, the less than charismatic Louis Freeh, was such a Luddite he had his personal computer terminal removed from his office. But this still didn't really enlighten me about why I had been brought into the LA offices that day. But in the natural course of life, even this strange event began to recede, only to come back full force one night two weeks later when we were at a Lakers game.

It was one of those dull matchups early in the season when the one-time champions were struggling to stay awake against the chump-of-the-day, in this case the Memphis Grizzlies. This night they were making such a hash of it they had fallen eleven points behind. Phil Jackson sat there with his arms folded while his team glanced over in embarrassment, waiting for him to signal a time-out, which of course he didn't. Then the whistle blew and Shaq was called for charging, accidentally running over one of the smaller Grizzlie guards, who looked as if he needed to be carted off on a stretcher to the ICU. It was at that point that my phone rang.

"Hello," I said, attempting to balance my orange chicken from the Staples Center Panda Express on the rail in front of me while answering the call. The crowd was starting to come alive, responding in a desultory way to the words DEE-FENSE! flashing on the giant monitor over center court.

"Moses, hi, it's Arthur Sugarman. Where are you?"

"Lakers."

"Sounds it. Where are you sitting?"

"Row sixteen, visitor's side."

There was a funereal silence on the other end as if I had cited a location several light years beyond Alpha Centauri. Arthur was a completion bondsman, a kind of insurance man for movies who provided investors financial guarantees that their films would be finished, and no self-respecting member of the entertainment industry would be caught dead sitting further back than row three at Staples. It was a public humiliation equivalent to forgetting Tom Cruise's name in a story meeting. "Oh," he said finally. "Then you can't see Peter's seats."

"Who?" His voice was fading in and out and I could hear what sounded like a satellite bounce on the line.

"Peter Farnsworth, our director. They're in the second row, section 101. Just behind Dyan Cannon. Anyway, it doesn't matter. He's not there. He's with me."

"Where are *you?*"

"Prague."

"What . . . did you say Prague?"

"Yes."

I glanced over at Samantha, who, until then, had shown little interest in my conversation but was now reacting to the astonished expression on my face. "Hold on." I cupped the phone and turned to her. "It's Arthur Sugarman. He's calling from Prague."

"No kidding!" She sounded as startled as I was. Arthur lived around the corner from us in the Hollywood Hills but he was calling from the very city six thousand miles away that had been the inspiration for my interrogation. "What does he want?"

"Beats me." I had known Arthur for several years. But he had never called me from out of town, not even from as far away as Santa Barbara, let alone Eastern Europe. In fact, he hardly ever called me at all.

Kobe swooped in for a tomahawk dunk and suddenly the crowd was wide awake, yelling and screaming for Grizzlie blood. The Lakers were coming back.

Samantha looked at me. "Better talk to him where it isn't so noisy."

I nodded and slipped out of my seat, walking into a part of the colonnade near a window for a better connection, which amazingly turned out to be clearer than I usually got calling the local pizza delivery. By the time I returned it was halftime and Samantha was standing in the aisle waiting anxiously. "It's the weirdest thing. He wants me to go over there for a few weeks," I explained. "Help out on this film he's bonding."

"Did you tell him about what happened to you?"

"Of course. What I could on a cell phone anyway. He didn't seem to know anything about it. All he cared about was this threat to his movie. It's driving him crazy. Some members of the cast and crew . . . the leading lady and the director . . . have been finding plastic snakes in their hotel rooms."

"Plastic snakes? Sounds like more of a practical joke than a threat."

"I have a feeling there's more to it, something he didn't want to talk about."

"What about the Czech police?"

"He says they're not taking it very seriously."

The whistle blew for the start of the second half and we both went back to our seats. Samantha eyed me cautiously.

"What'd you tell him?"

"I'd call back."

"Do you want to go?"

"What about you?"

"We can't both. Someone's got to finish Harrison." Harrison was a child custody case we had been working on for Sheldon Dichter, a family lawyer. It was the kind of ugly business I normally avoided, but there wasn't a lot of work around now and we had to take what we could get. "You go ahead. I'll come over when I'm finished. You've been complaining about not being in the thick of things. This will sure put you there . . . And I don't want to be the one who stopped you from going."

This woman sure knew me. "The FBI didn't say I couldn't leave the country."

Samantha smiled. "If it turns out to be nothing, you still might find it amusing. You're always complaining about how movie people get what we do all wrong. This is your chance to set them right."

"This isn't a crime movie, Sam. It's a love story about the Holocaust . . . an art house film."

✛

THE FIRST PLACE I WENT the next morning was to see the morning gang at the table at LA's old Farmer's Market on Fairfax and Third. That was where I had first met Arthur when I had been taken there several years ago as the guest of a screenwriter friend who has since moved to Montana. I didn't think I'd be able to stand it, but I went back and for a while now I had been dropping in to have breakfast under the same umbrella with Arthur and his film industry buddies at what some local rags had taken to calling, with some exaggeration, "The Algonquin Roundtable West." The group that hung out there was a cranky lot at best. All more or less successful, some even famous writers and directors, they acted as if the world, usually personified by philistine movie executives, was a conspiracy to deprive them of their creativity. Every time I stopped by over the years it was as if I had interrupted the same conversations, bemoaning the state of the cinema or the decline of the culture in general. It was a tad repetitive, but they could be funny. And that was the reason I came—not to mention the flattery of being asked, as an "actual, bona fide private dick," for advice on what would happen in real life for somebody's screenplay. After I gave it, they would reply with a chorus of "Ah, what does he know?" or such like, but I often saw one or the other of them scrawling a note under the table.

I wanted to find out about Arthur and his movie before I boarded a plane to Prague. It was early and the only ones there were the director Harry Chemerinski, his sometime screenwriter Douglas Corfu and Dorothy Windham, a shrink who was one of the other "civilians" who turned up at the Market on occasion. "Well, look who's here," said Chemerinski as I sat down with them. "We haven't seen you in months. What happened? With this new war, husbands can't afford to have their wives followed anymore?"

"What do you call that . . . tracking errant spouses?" said Corfu. "You have a term for it."

"'Peace of Mind Insurance,' " I said.

"Right 'Peace of Mind Insurance,' " said the writer. "I like that. You should use it as your advertisement on a bus bench or something."

"Who do you think Moses is?" said Chemerinski. "A real estate agent? A gumshoe's a classy occupation."

"Don't mind those two," said Dorothy. "HBO just turned down their script."

"Bunch of retarded blood leeches from Hell," said the director.

"Speaking of insurance," I said. "I just got a call from Arthur Sugarman. He wants me to go over to Prague to help on some film he's bonding."

"Peter Farnsworth's movie," said Chemerinski.

"What's *he* like?" I asked.

"Sitcom writer trying to make up for his sins," said Corfu. "Surprised you don't know. He used to come here all the time before he got married for the third time." I shook my head. It didn't ring a bell.

"Hey, where's *your* new wife?" said Harry. "Why don't you bring her around? We'd like to meet her."

Just then Douglas's wife, a Swedish grad student in her twenties, showed up, pushing their two-year-old son in a stroller. A few years ago, Corfu had made himself the butt of the usual midlife jabs about seeing too many Bergman movies by marrying Ingrid, a woman thirty years his junior, but that quickly disappeared and she soon became a welcome member of the group. It had to be that way. Aging was the last frontier for the Hollywood Boomer and, although no one was getting a facelift yet, it was an unspoken agreement that anything you could do to stay, or at least look, young was fair game, especially in the movie business where one's livelihood depended on the illusion of youth. So no one ever made jokes about Harry's intermittent dye job, to his face anyway, and, despite the fact that I was only a part-timer, no one so much as batted an eye when I married someone twenty years younger. They only wanted to know when I was having a kid. But I had two already. Grown ones.

"So what gives with Peter's movie?" said Corfu.

"Plastic snakes in the hotel room," I said.

"Donna Gold's the leading lady," said Harry. "She could have my snake in her room any time she wants. And only part of it's plastic. . . . Hey, he can save us some bucks on FedEx charges." He winked at the others. "We made a birthday present for Peter. We were going to mail it, but you can carry it over. They won't keep you too long at customs. It's just one of those little razor gizmos you use to slice cardboard. Box cutters I think they call them." Nobody laughed. The director had started his career as a standup comic and the compulsion to crack wise was embedded in his DNA. "Okay, okay," he continued, "you didn't like that one. What is this—the good-taste police? Here's the real present. Let's hope they have Mini-DV format in Prague. Otherwise he'll have to wait to get back to see it." He reached into his pocket and handed me a small videocassette.

I ran my eyes over the label: "Happy Birthday, Peter—Just because you married a Jew, doesn't mean you have to make a movie about the Holocaust. The market's already saturated. Ever heard of *Schindler's List?* Your pals at the FM!"

I stuffed it in my jacket and stayed around for a while, hoping to glean a little more information about the film before I left. A few other members of the group, some screenwriters and a producer, a journalist or two, came and went. But no one seemed to know much about the movie, other than it was written by Farnsworth's wife, a woman named Ellen Feig, who had been his assistant when Peter was the writer/producer of a TV series called *His Name Is Herman* about a family living in downtown Seattle with a pet goat. And when Chemerinski started launching into his old stories about the glory days of the seventies and eighties when the auteur was king and he almost won a couple of Oscars, I knew it was time to leave. Even I, an interloper, had heard them too many times before.

"Watch your back in Prague," he said as I started off. "Isn't that where those Iraqis met with that Twin Towers guy? What's his name? Mohammed Atta?"

"That's bunk," one of the journalists chimed in. "Never happened."

There was that name again. "I doubt I'll be running into *him*," I said, waving good-bye and wondering, for a split second, if Harry or one of the others in the group had been the one to tip off the FBI. But I realized immediately that was impossible. Until this morning, they hadn't even known I was going to Prague. I hadn't stepped on the airplane and I was already in a paranoid state of anxiety and dread.

Samantha drove me to the airport but she wasn't allowed to come with me past the gate. We had to say good-bye at the long line in front of the x-ray machines. Under the watchful eye of a trio of National Guardsmen, she gave me a world satellite phone as a going-away present. "Call me three times a day," she said. I gave her another kiss and joined the line. An hour and three quarters and two and a half security checks later, I was on the plane.

2

"THAT'S THE OLD TOWN SQUARE. Quite something, isn't it?" said Arthur. He was pointing out the window of our Soviet-era Tatra limousine, which looked something like an oversized Studebaker circa 1957, a back-to-the-future mobile. He and a driver named Tomas had picked me up at Prague's Ruyzne Airport and were taking me to the production hotel by the scenic route. The square outside was indeed "something," a stage set-like agglomeration of four centuries' worth of meticulously preserved European architecture, its well-scrubbed rococo facades illuminated with klieg lights for the tourists, who were out in droves, despite the lateness of the hour. One side of the giant plaza was dominated by a spiny black Gothic church, the other by a mosaic clock tower with zodiac signs and a death skeleton chiming the hour as puppets of Christ and the Apostles skittered through a bronze door. A street vendor just beneath it hawked T-shirts of the city's favorite son, Franz Kafka.

"It is all rather magnificent," I said, "but it seems like a long way to come because of some toy snakes."

"Well, there's more to it than that," said Arthur who *had* seemed extremely nervous and distracted since I arrived, alternatively drumming on his knee and patting his ample belly nearly the whole way in the car while taking shallow breaths. In fact he had seemed so desperate he snatched my hand the moment I passed through the airport gate as if he were a drowning diver grabbing for his scuba buddy. "Thank God, you're here!" he had said. It was flattering but disconcerting all at once.

"Naturally I assumed there was more," I said, sitting in the back of the Tatra, waiting for him to explain.

Arthur frowned and nodded at the driver. "He speaks some English. We better wait."

Ten minutes later we pulled up at the Hotel Forum, a pretentious seventies edifice outside the city center that seemed a cross between an overblown midwestern Holiday Inn and a Brezhnev epoch Moscow mental hospital. Whatever the case, considering the beauty of what we had just driven through, it was depressing in the extreme.

"Who picked this place?" I asked Arthur as we followed Tomas through the revolving door into a garish lobby with a blinking multicolored chandelier.

"The Czech production company. They have a deal with the hotel management. Everyone here has a deal with someone or other. Only now I understand the management is changing."

"Good. Maybe there'll be an improvement."

"I doubt it," said Arthur, leading me toward the concierge's desk, "considering who bought it."

"Who's that?" I asked.

"The government of Libya."

At least it wasn't Iraq. I left my passport with the concierge and accompanied Arthur back to the raised island bar in the middle of the lobby. Arthur sat there a moment, catching his breath, then anxiously scooped up a handful of Brazil nuts and stuffed them in his mouth. "Do you want a martini? They're passable. Or some of the local plum brandy? It's just like slivovitz. In fact it *is* slivovitz."

"What's going on, Arthur? I'm pretty jet-lagged here."

"Okay, okay," he said, opening his attaché case and handing me a manila envelope that was tied with a string. "Go ahead. Look inside." I untied the envelope and took out a piece of paper, which had been folded in half. On the outside was a crude drawing of a coiled snake next to the Star of David; on the inside were the words PREPARE TO DIE. YOU HAVE DOMINATID THE MEDIAR FOR TO LONG! written in green ink with a backhanded cursive scrawl.

"Charming," I said. "I guess someone ran out of ideas for Hanukkah cards." On the other side of the fountain, I could see two women in chadors crossing toward the elevator. One of them carried a bulging Versace shopping bag. Polished crimson toenails peeked out from under her long gray cloak.

"Who do you think would do this?" said Arthur. "Are the misspellings on purpose? You're a professional."

"Not a professional psychic. How come you didn't tell me about this on the phone?"

"Why?" He suddenly looked alarmed. "Do you think it has something to do with Mohammed Atta?"

"He's dead."

"Right." He sounded relieved, but I don't know why he was. "Anyway the letter came after I phoned you. Someone left it at the concierge's desk this morning with the director's name on the envelope."

"Peter Farnsworth? He's not even Jewish."

"They probably think he is. He is by marriage. I don't think they know the difference."

"I suppose." I looked at Arthur carefully. "So did you show *this* to the Czech police?"

Suddenly he froze up.

I looked at him and pointed firmly to the envelope. "Did you or didn't you, Arthur?"

Reluctantly he shook his head.

"Why not?"

He looked away.

But I had already figured it out for myself. "Because they might not take *this* as lightly as a bunch of plastic snakes. And if they shut down the production, your company has to pay."

The completion bondsman started drumming on his knee.

ROGER L. SIMON

"How much would it cost you?"

"Eight million."

"That's a fair amount," I said, knowing that by movie standards it wasn't particularly grand, but Arthur's company was less than a year old and such a sum would probably bankrupt them. "What about this Farnsworth guy? Did *he* want to tell the cops?"

Arthur stopped drumming and looked at me as if I had lost my mind. "He's the *director* of the film, for crissake! It's his baby. He and his wife have been working on it together for four years, ever since *His Name Is Herman* got canceled. Neither of them wants to give up now, a couple of days before the start of principal photography." He sat back in his chair and reached for another handful of nuts. "Anyway, they think it's some kind of hoax. So do I, frankly."

"Really?" I asked. "Nowadays?"

"Really," he repeated, but he didn't sound totally convinced. "God I'm glad you're here," he continued to himself in a voice so low I almost couldn't hear him.

Against my better instincts, I scooped up some of the nuts myself and shoveled them in my mouth. "Listen, Arthur, I don't want to do your business for you. I certainly don't know much about it anyway. But isn't there some way your company can back out of this . . . declare *force majeure* or something? There's no way you could have anticipated what's going on now."

"Of course, of course. You're right," he said nervously. "Only I can't. They bought the rider."

"What rider?"

"The special security rider that protects against terrorism. Nobody ever bothers . . . except these producers. They bought it two months ago, before everything happened." He shook his head in bewildered despair. "They must have been the *real* psychics."

"Who are *they*?"

"A Japanese guy and a German guy."

A Japanese and a German financing a movie about the

Holocaust made by a gentile director from his Jewish wife's screenplay in the era of Mohammed Atta. That about covered the neighborhood. I sat there thinking maybe I *would* have a martini. Or a slivovitz. But suddenly my eyes started to shut almost irrevocably, as if someone had slipped me a Mickey Finn on the plane. But I knew it was only jet lag. "I better call it a night," I said, staggering to my feet. "Flying's not exactly a pleasure these days. I feel like I haven't slept in a week."

"Sure. Fine. We'll sort it all out tomorrow." He stood and shook my hand. Now it felt limp. "But Moses, please, in the morning, don't tell anyone you're a detective. Otherwise they'll be suspicious. Especially since we don't know who we're dealing with yet."

"What do I tell them then?"

Arthur hesitated. "Tell them you're a reporter for *Variety*."

"Sounds like a promotion."

Arthur laughed. "See you here in the lobby at seven-thirty. We're going location scouting."

"You want me there for that?"

"Peter Farnsworth wants you. As their bodyguard."

I felt a quick tightening. "Arthur, that's not really what I do."

He shrugged and forced another laugh. "Hey, somebody has to. If you don't, who will?"

⊞

WHEN I CAME DOWN the next morning, a group of six or seven was already waiting by a Volkswagen van parked by the hotel entrance. They were wearing ski parkas and sipped gingerly at takeaway coffee cups. It was easy to guess which one was Farnsworth. He was the tall American, extremely handsome in a blond, blue-eyed, ramrod-straight, preppy sort of way and, most conspicuously, he had one of those directors's scopes I didn't think anyone used anymore dangling from his neck, fingering it pretentiously as if the whole world was waiting with baited breath to be chosen as part of his artistic vision. I could see what Douglas Corfu meant by a sitcom writer making up for his sins. No way this dude was prepared to go to his grave known as the creator of *His Name Is Herman.*

He walked directly up to me with a confident smile "You must be Moses Wine . . . the, um, *Variety* reporter." He shook my hand. "I'm Peter Farnsworth. Great to see you, though I must say I'm surprised your paper would be doing a piece on a humble little art film. You're usually too busy covering studio musical chairs or *Lethal Weapon 25.*"

"We're not always as crass as you creative people think. Besides, I hear they're not doing any more *Lethal Weapon*s. The leading men have arthritis."

"Very good," he said with an amused nod. "I see you'll do this quite easily. . . . Why don't I introduce you to the crew?" He took me to the others who were standing by the van, pointing to a tall man in his sixties with kind, intelligent eyes. "This is Jiri, our cinematographer. He speaks some English so don't insult him. . . . And Jan, our production designer." He nodded to a courtly man who looked even older than the cinematographer. "He *doesn't* speak English but he worked on *Amadeus* so we excuse him. And this is Ivan, the location manager."

"How's it going?" said Ivan, a pleasant younger fellow in a down vest from J. Crew. "I read *Variety* a few times. There's not much in it, but I'm sure that's not your fault."

"Ivan obviously speaks English better than I do, as does Eva, our first A.D." He nodded to an attractive blonde near forty who saluted smartly. "Eva's working on being the most indispensable woman in Eastern Europe. And this is Jana, our translator." An even more attractive but somber girl in her twenties shook my hand. "She just broke up with her boyfriend, so she's in mourning . . . and this is my wife, Ellen, the instigator of our masterpiece." He put his arm around a surprisingly plain woman with a

pallid complexion and a narrow, pointy chin who looked particularly unappealing next to her Adonis-like husband.

"Thank you for coming to our rescue," she said, fixing me
intently in her gaze.

Farnsworth gave her a sharp look.

"What am I supposed to say?" she continued, lowering her
voice. "That's what he's doing."

"We don't need to broadcast it," her husband hissed back and
then he gestured to Arthur. "And I gather you know our friend
the completion bondsman from the Farmer's Market. . . . Okay,
everybody, *andiamo!*"

The driver slid the side door of the van open and everyone
but Farnsworth got in. He climbed into the front passenger seat.
"I have to sit up here," he explained, motioning to me to sit
behind him. "Formal film hierarchy for reckies. Not very egali-
tarian, I'm afraid. I hope you're not offended. The guys at the
Market tell me you're one of those sixties people."

"Most of us at *Variety* are," I said. The director grinned.
"Speaking of the Market, the gang asked me to give you this." I
reached into my jacket and handed him the tape.

Farnsworth looked at it and frowned. "Mini-DV format?
How am I going to replay this around here?"

"We'll find it for you, sir," said Eva.

"Sir?" he said. "The last time anybody called me that was
when I got my diploma from Swarthmore. What about you,
Wine?"

"Cub Scouts," I said. "Then I got kicked out for singing
Hound Dog over the Pledge of Allegiance."

Farnsworth laughed and the location manager said something in Czech to the driver, pointing off into the distance. The
van pulled out. Arthur, who was sitting in the back row, leaned
over to Ellen. "Everything's going to be okay," he said. "Trust
me."

A few minutes later we parked on a wide shopping street

called Parizska with posh Art Nouveau buildings and tree-lined sidewalks that did, as its name indicated, resemble Paris, at least for a block or two. But we didn't stop long. Ivan, the location manager, directed us around the corner, down a narrow street heading into Josefov, the old Jewish Quarter. Farnsworth looked impatient. "Don't we have other places to go?" he said. "I thought we had the cemetery locked up."

"It is just a formality," said Ivan. "The Grand Rabbi wants to speak with you personally before he signs off. . . . He writes screenplays himself, you see."

"The Grand Rabbi of Prague is a *screenwriter* too?" said Farnsworth.

"I hope he didn't take one of those weekend classes at the Airport Marriott," said Ellen.

"He is my old friend. From school," said Jiri, loping along next to us with a limp. "Perhaps he has read the script and would like to share his views with you."

"Great, great," said Farnsworth who looked over at his wife and rolled his eyes. We were threading our way through a crowd of tourists now, heading toward the wrought-iron gate of the Old Jewish Cemetery. Outside Israel, this was supposed to be one of the most important memorials of historical Jewish life, a highpoint on the itinerary of any self-respecting *bubbe* from Great Neck.

Just then a stocky bearded man in his fifties appeared in front of us and embraced Jiri. "My friend Shmuel Herzog, the Grand Rabbi," said the cinematographer, introducing him to all of us at once. Despite the fact he was wearing a yarmulke, Herzog looked more modern than I expected in wire-rim glasses, a teal cardigan and matching Jerry Garcia tie. "I am his only gentile friend," quipped Jiri.

"You and my sushi chef. Which one is Farnsworth?" he asked. The director cautiously raised his hand. "Very interesting project," said the rabbi, "if a little derivative of that Costa-Gavras movie *Music Box*. But I did enjoy reading it, nevertheless. Very

American. Quick, perhaps too quick in parts, but I understand. The audience is so impatient. But I'm sure you know that." Farnsworth didn't make a comment and the rabbi looked a little disappointed. "Anyway, I understand it is your wife's screenplay, Ms. Feig. She is the one to be congratulated."

"For the script. Yes," said the director, patting Ellen on the back. "She did a great job."

"And she is fortunate to have a director for a husband. Perhaps I should marry one. . . . And who is this gentleman?" he added, looking at me.

"A reporter for *Variety*," interjected Arthur.

"Ah, publicity, that most necessary of evils. Perhaps you would like an exclusive interview with the only screenwriter in Eastern Europe who gives kabala classes to foreigners on a riverboat cruise ship with catered kosher dinners in the style of the Vilna ghetto."

"It definitely sounds like a first," I said. "I'll keep it in mind."

The rabbi nodded and signaled to a guard who opened the gate for us and we followed him around the waiting line of tourists. Soon we were inside the cemetery itself, a hodgepodge of centuries-old gravestones jumbled up on top of each other like an image out of Chagall, brilliantly colored autumn leaves carpeting the ground around them. I could see why the spot would be attractive to filmmakers.

The rabbi escorted us further away from the tourists, who were watching with curiosity as we crossed through a cordoned-off area to an isolated, hillier part of the graveyard that was filled with even more-picturesque stones. "It is because of the artistic integrity of your film that we have decided to let you be the first to shoot in this restricted area," he said to Farnsworth. "But you must be out by nine in the morning, the very latest. We have certain people in our community, the more Orthodox of course, who might object to your filming so close to the tomb of our revered ancestor Rabbi Loew, who, as your wife's screenplay indicates, you know to be the creator of the magic Golem himself. Or itself—there is considerable controversy about the gender of mythical creatures."

"I understand. As you know, we only have a few lines of dialogue by the rabbi's tomb," said Farnsworth.

"Also, if you would like some feedback on your script, I would be glad to talk with you at your convenience."

"Thank you. That's very kind of you to offer." Farnsworth was trying, as far as I could see, to restrain himself from taking the guy by the throat.

"No charge. You don't even have to read *my* script."

Farnsworth smiled politely. Jiri laughed and said something to his buddy that I assumed to be Czech for "Relax, the Yankee bastard thinks you're a pompous ass." But I was wrong. "He is asking if there was a party in the cemetery last night," Jana, the translator, explained to Ellen, who had come up beside her. "But the rabbi is saying that the gate is always locked at night and there is a watchman. So Jiri says the watchman must have been drunk." The rabbi was now laughing too as his friend escorted him around the back of the tomb. But then the rabbi stopped short. His expression went from amused to horrified in an instant and he appeared to lose his balance for a second, steadying himself on one of the gravestones. Jiri came over and said something to him in Czech. The rabbi said something back, then just shook his head, looking down at the ground before addressing Farnsworth in a gravelly voice that was almost a whisper.

"Please find another location for your movie, Mr. Farnsworth. It has been a pleasure to meet you. Good luck with your project." And then, abruptly, he started off.

Farnsworth, startled, took off after him. "Rabbi Herzog," he said. "Is something wrong? Please tell us. If there's anything you'd like us to change we . . ."

"This is impossible," said the rabbi. "There is nothing you

can do about this." And with that he disappeared through the gate, shutting it behind him.

The director, dumbfounded, walked back to his cinematographer who shrugged ironically and nodded toward the graves a few feet off. Someone had built a large fireplace just behind Rabbi Loew's tomb. It looked new, with freshly cut stones arranged in a neat circle. "He said this was not supposed to be here," said Jiri.

"It's just a campfire," said Farnsworth, throwing up his hands in dismay. "Probably vandals. He's canceling for *that?*"

The cinematographer shook his head. "He is going to have it removed."

I crouched down and looked at the stones. The largest had some Hebrew writing on it, beneath the symbol of a snake.

"What do you make of this?" said Farnsworth, who was standing over my shoulder.

"Not a lot. I forgot my Hebrew after my Bar Mitzvah."

"I can read it," said Ellen, walking up behind me and examining the stones. " '*Eizehu chacham? Haroeh et Hanolad* . . . who is a wise man? The one who sees things to come.' I think it's from the kabala." She looked up at her husband who was staring down at her, mulling over that not entirely reassuring thought. "We don't need the cemetery," she said. "The scene's just a walk-and-talk. We can do it anyplace."

Farnsworth nodded and signaled to the others it was time to leave and we started out of the graveyard. When we crossed through the gate, he leaned over to me and spoke in a low voice. "Moses, do me a favor and don't tell Donna Gold what happened here. I guess Arthur told you she's looking for an excuse to bolt and she's got one foot out the door as it is because of her boyfriend back in West Hollywood."

"I haven't even met her yet," I said.

"You will soon. We've got a rehearsal later today."

"It's in twenty minutes, sir," said Eva.

I glanced over at Arthur, who looked like one of those

depressed characters in the comics with a storm cloud over his head. "It'll be alright," he said.

✥

THE REHEARSAL WAS TO BE HELD at the Filmovy Club, a kind of latter-day beatnik coffeehouse cum cinema near the center of the city with a restaurant/bar and a downstairs screening room, which, judging from the poster, was the only place left on the planet showing *Last Year at Marienbad* in regular rotation. A small lunch was waiting for us when we arrived, but Donna wasn't there so Farnsworth, Ellen and I cooled our heels at the bar with Goran Babic, the leading man. Goran, a political refugee from Belgrade who made his home in London, was a weathered handsome man about fifty with long pepper-and-salt hair that made him look like a Serbian Dr. John. Ellen told me on the way over that he had won the grand prize at Venice for his starring role in a groundbreaking film about the Yugoslav war and I could see how he might be a romantic figure for a love story, but right now he seemed grumpy and distinctly unlovable as he sat there with a scowl, knocking down glasses of schnapps like they were berry juice.

"Peter, my good friend, we have problem," he said. "But perhaps should not talk in front of representative from *Variety* magazine."

"No, no. It's okay," said Farnsworth, winking at me.

"Production manager says Donna has full-size American Winnebago trailer but all I get is little teardrop like KGB prison cell."

"There's only one Winnebago in the Czech Republic," said the director.

"But my good friend, I have clause of favored nation in contract. My trailer is to be equal to or bigger than all other player in movie. Also four first-class round-trip air ticket for friend and family I am owed with hotel paid at luxury accommodation. My agent say I should not work unless—"

Just then Donna Gold came bounding in, wearing a chenille cloak with her head swathed in a towel, which made her look like a fashion model pretending to be a female Taliban. "Sorry I'm late," she said. "I've been walking all over. Prague is the coolest place. Great garnets up near the Castle for less than half what you pay at home. And is that the cemetery in the Jewish Quarter where we're going to be shooting? My grandmother is going to be *so proud*. She hasn't said a word to me since I did the steam room scene in *Casino Nights*." She didn't notice Farnsworth's suddenly tense expression as she sat down on a stool next to him. "By the way, I hope you don't mind if we cut rehearsal short today. I have my first appointment at the Janak Institute at three."

The director looked at her with a frown. "That gives us about twenty minutes. What's the Janak Institute?"

"It was profiled as a hidden treasure in the June *Vogue*. Ellen will know. Right, Ellen?" But before she could answer, Donna noticed me. "Who are you?"

"Moses Wine. From *Variety*."

Suddenly the actress's face darkened. She turned to Farnsworth. "You didn't tell me the press was going to be here."

"Is okay," said Goran, stepping in. "Moses is good guy. I can tell. He will write excellent article."

"Well, he has to get permission from my publicist first. It's in my contract. And this is our rehearsal time. You should know that. It's sacred."

"Then why you give us only twenty minutes?" said the actor. "And we are supposed to rehearse cemetery scene."

"What're you talking about? I'm here."

"But you just say you are leaving for some Institute."

"No, no, no. *I'm* leaving," I said, checking my watch. "I just realized I'm late for an appointment." I stood and addressed Farnsworth "I know you won't believe it, but the magazine wants me to do a feature on the Grand Rabbi of Prague, of all people. Apparently they think it's a story because he wants to be a screenwriter."

"That *is* bizarre," said the director, beginning to catch my drift. "But I suppose everybody does these days."

"I'm going to try to find out where he gets his ideas. You know, walking in the cemetery or . . ."

"And why he changes them," said Farnsworth.

"Yes, why. . . . Who knows—perhaps he'll change back again?" I added and turned to Donna, who did not seem irritated anymore and was suddenly looking disappointed she wouldn't be the center of attention. "I hope I have the opportunity to speak with you soon, Ms. Gold. I'm sorry if I intruded. . . . Have a great rehearsal." I gave them all a wave and started off.

"Make sure he gets my publicist's phone number," I heard her telling Farnsworth as I headed through door.

"Mine too," said Goran.

⠿

ON THE WAY BACK to the Jewish Quarter, I couldn't help recalling some of the cross talk about directors at the Farmer's Market. The gang there always seemed to diss the stereotypes of the profession—field marshal in jodhpurs, Woody Allen intellectual in slouch hat, Gen-Xer in humungous earphones and backward baseball cap. Being a director to them was more like being a desperate babysitter for a group of terminally spoiled five-year-olds and about as glamorous. They didn't make much sense to me at the time, but after a couple of minutes with Donna and Goran I was beginning to see exactly what they meant.

Of course, being a private eye wasn't all it was cracked up to be either. I wondered what was. Being a rabbi? Most of the ones I had known moonlighted at something—shrinks, lawyers, accountants, lovelorn columnists, one even wrote mysteries. This one wanted to be a screenwriter. Only he was willing to throw over a possible connection to *that* career the moment he saw a makeshift barbecue strewn behind some old gravestones.

I planned on asking him that, among several other questions.

Unfortunately, when I next encountered Rabbi Herzog, he was unable to answer any of my inquiries, or anything else for that matter. He was splayed out across the frayed Persian rug in his office, his unblinking eyes staring at the ceiling and blood trickling from his open mouth. Naturally, in my line of work, I had seen a few fresh corpses before and his wasn't atypical—skin slightly colorless, pupils dilated—except for one thing: He was clutching a manuscript close to his chest, which appeared, again from my experiences at the Farmer's Market, to be of the size and format of a conventional screenplay. It had red bloodstains all over its front page, almost, but not quite, obscuring the title, which upon reading it was almost as upsetting as the dead body itself. When I stared at the words of that title, I knew my initial surmise was correct. It was a film script all right, but there was no way to extract it without seriously disturbing the corpse. I would have to find out the contents of the screenplay some other way.

I reached for my cell and dialed Samantha. "Hello," she groaned.

"Hi, Sam."

"Oh . . . Moses. Do you know it's five A.M. here?"

"You told me to call you three times a day."

"Right. What's Prague like?"

"Beautiful."

"Good. I'm going to go back to sleep now."

"Wait a minute. I need your help. It's kind of an emergency. Have you ever read *The Protocols of the Elders of Zion?*"

"The famous anti-Semitic tract? Why would I do that?"

"Someone seems to have adapted it into a screenplay?"

"Who? The KKK?"

"No. A rabbi. It's called *The Protocols of the Elders of Zion—The Motion Picture.* . . . A little long, don't you think?" I continued, looking straight down at the bloodstained title page.

"What rabbi would write that?"

"One who wears Jerry Garcia ties. Or did. Look, would you just get a copy of the *Protocols* for me? As soon as possible."

"Sure. At my local hate store . . . Where are you, Moses?" She had caught the tension in my voice and was starting to get agitated. "I know you're on a cell, but are you in trouble?"

"Not as far as I know," I said, making that assumption, although of course I wasn't entirely sure. I looked around the room. Then I glanced out the window to the street below. The building wasn't guarded at all, not like most Jewish institutions I knew in New York and LA, which were protected by huge amounts of security of all sorts, technological and human, SIGINT and HUMINT, as they say. Here, I had just walked right in the faded baroque building and followed my nose, sticking my head in various doors, smiling at people who appeared not to notice me. I continued up a spiral stairway to a long, cavernous corridor lined with dusty portraits of what I assumed were Grand Rabbis of yesteryear to the last door, a heavy filigreed affair that had been left ajar. Inside I found the rabbi.

I looked down at him again. He had been shot through the head, probably at close range. Whether he had been clutching the screenplay at the time or it had been placed in his hands, I couldn't tell. But it was likely his assailant came in the same way I had. There was no other visible entrance, not even a fire escape. Perhaps the building was too old. At that point, the rabbi's phone rang.

"What's that?" said Samantha, her voice rising when she realized no one was answering. "If you're where you shouldn't be, please get out. Or call the police. You're in a foreign country, remember?"

Normally the second option would have been the wiser. But if I did tell the police, I would certainly have to inform them of what I was actually doing there—my *Variety* disguise was far too porous—and for some reason that I was then only dimly aware of, I felt oddly protective of the movie production. There was a chance, how much I didn't know, that this event had nothing to do with it or was only peripheral, so peripheral in fact that to taint the enterprise with the rabbi's demise, which would certainly stop filming before it started, scarcely seemed fair. I took a last look at Herzog. His skin had become more ashen and more blood had oozed over the screenplay where the word "Kaprova" had been scrawled in pencil at the bottom of the title page. I wondered if that meant anything. "I'm leaving now," I said to Samantha and slipped out the door, heading down the corridor. "I love you," I added, clicking off the phone while hiding my face from a pair of Hasidim who were coming up the stairs opposite me.

3

"MOSES, THIS IS Karl Volksbruner and Hideo Takashima," said Arthur Sugarman. "Karl and Hideo, this is Moses Wine, the *Variety* reporter I was telling you about."

"I am glad you have such interest in our project," said Karl, taking my hand with a brief, clammy shake. He was a short, bullet-like man with a bulbous chest popping out of an under-sized and slightly outdated Armani jacket. "Hideo, I guess now we will have to pay for dinner ourselves," he continued, turning to his fellow producer with a nervous chuckle, "since the press is here." Takashima, a man in his fifties in a formal black suit, was accompanied by an attractive twenty-something Japanese woman in a kimono who whispered to him. He turned to me with a smile and bowed. Evidently he spoke no English.

We were all standing by a large table in the formal Intermezzo Restaurant on the tenth floor of the Hotel Forum, the city's famous castle visible, illuminated against the night sky through the picture window behind us. Peter and Ellen, looking quite uncomfortable—I imagined because of the unpleasant news about Herzog, which I had only recently imparted to them—stood with us, as did Donna, who looked bored out of her mind, and Goran, who was pacing back and forth like a hypoglycemic two hours from his last sugar fix.

"Well, let's eat," said Farnsworth, trying to be pleasant and gesturing for the group to sit. "We have a lot to celebrate—we start shooting the day after tomorrow."

"I am sorry, but is not possible," said Goran suddenly. "I am not paid and I must return to London immediately!"

Everyone looked startled. "I was told your money had been sent," said Karl, glancing at the other producer, whose girlfriend quickly started translating for him.

"My agent says escrow account empty," continued the Serb. "Was to be full two weeks ago."

More words in rapid-fire Japanese passed back and forth between Takashima and the Japanese woman, who finally folded her hands and bowed very low in Goran's direction, almost touching the table. "Please, Mr. Babic . . . Mr. Takashima beg your indulgence and to kindly bear with him patiently. There have been many bank holiday in Japan in recent month as well as religious ceremony with business closed. Money will arrive in account quite soon. Perhaps even tomorrow or next day." She smiled sweetly up at the Serb, who began to melt slightly, probably more at the sight of her than at what she was saying.

"Good, good. Why don't we all have some dinner?" said Farnsworth, seizing the moment.

"We ate here last night," said Ellen. "The Dover sole was pretty fresh. But stay away from the fried dumplings."

Everyone laughed politely and took a seat. Just then women in chadors entered with two Arab men in the kind of Italian suits Volksbruner wished he had. They were escorted to a table across from us where a bottle of what later proved to be Cristal was waiting in a silver bucket. "I guess they're not Wahhabis," said Farnsworth, referring to the extremist Muslim sect that didn't allow women to touch men or drive, let alone drink expensive champagne in fancy restaurants filled with foreign atheists.

"Not tonight," I said.

Then he looked at me and frowned, speaking under his breath. "I hope we're not being crazy."

"Who isn't?"

"You know what I mean—nothing's going to happen here, is

it? We're only making a movie, after all. It's not worth . . . ," he laughed nervously, "you know, putting anyone's life in danger or anything."

"It's not," I agreed.

He asked the same question when I was up having a nightcap in his suite a while later with him and Ellen and Arthur. But this time he sounded more rhetorical, as if he wasn't really serious about it. It was more of a casual aside aimed at discouraging the suggestion that production be derailed by anything as inconsequential as murder, particularly a murder not proven to be connected to the movie . . . not yet anyway. This all occurred when I asked him how many people had read the script and would know they were going to shoot in the Jewish cemetery. "Too many," Peter said, "A hundred or so at the studio here . . . not to mention all the others in LA, Berlin and Tokyo."

"And the French investment banker who stiffed us for the restaurant bill," added Ellen. "And the phony British lord who said he was a friend of the Prince of Wales."

Then Arthur chimed in that about a half-dozen people at his bond company had read it as well the cast insurers in Munich whose job it was to pay up if anything happened to Donna or Goran. And then there were all the people around Prague, Farnsworth explained, the myriad government bureaucrats who demanded copies of the script for even the most minuscule of requests. That came to a whole lot of folks, in the Czech Republic and abroad, with all those who may have made or received copies from them. It almost seemed as if I was the only person left on the planet who *hadn't* read it.

"Maybe I'd better take a look," I said, nodding to a copy on the coffee table in front of Farnsworth. "I'm sure you don't want any more problems, if they can be avoided."

"Just as long as we don't have to hear your feedback too," he said with a smile, picking up the screenplay and handing it to me.

"Don't worry about it. I'm a detective, not a screenwriter."

"Yeah, but you hang out at the Farmer's Market," replied the director. "You might have gotten infected."

I grinned and was about to say good night when I asked them if the name "Kaprova" meant anything to them. It didn't. Then I did say good night and headed down to my room a couple of floors below. I was still feeling a little jet lag and welcomed the chance to stretch out. So I lay there in bed, making my way through *Prague Autumn* by Ellen Feig, jotting down the locations for future references, when the phone rang. It was Samantha. "Up early," I said.

"I haven't gone to sleep yet," she said. "I've been reading *The Protocols of the Elders of Zion*. I couldn't find it in any stores, but it turns out the Internet's filled with free sites where you can download it."

"Big surprise."

"Right, but it *may* surprise you to know, it's not so badly written. Not exactly a page-turner but . . . It purports to be a secret handbook for Jewish world domination."

"Any good ideas in it?"

"Not funny, Moses."

"Okay, okay. Who wrote it anyway?"

"The *Okrana*, the tsar's intelligence service, to smear the revolutionaries as Jews. But *they* plagiarized from a French satire of Machiavelli, which wasn't about Jews at all, and a novel called *Biarritz* by a German."

"So the German put the Jews in it." I said, as if making the usual racial assumption. But I knew how outdated that was. The way the world was now, the Germans were one of the few friends the Jews had left, though even that felt as if it was turning once again.

"I guess. Anyway what seems like the most important chapter . . . the one that keys the whole book . . . is a rabbi's speech made in the Jewish Cemetery of Prague."

"Oh," I said. Now she had my attention.

"It claims that every hundred years representatives of the Twelve Tribes of Israel gather in that graveyard to listen to the Grand Rabbi review the last century and plot the control of the next one."

"And how're they going to do that? I can't even control the next ten minutes."

"The usual ways . . . politics, business, religious leaders . . . but, especially, the media."

I looked down at the screenplay in my hand written by a media Jew, in this case for her husband to direct. Was this also a plot for world domination? More likely it was a plot for a critic's prize at the Sundance Film Festival, one that at which, from my reading so far, it was not likely to succeed. But perhaps I wasn't being fair. I was only on page fifteen.

"And, by the way," she continued, "the symbol of *The Protocols* is something called the Snake of Zion. But it's not made of plastic, as far as I know."

"I better get hold of a copy for myself," I said.

"It would have made a great Oprah pick," said Samantha dryly. "No one should be without." She gave me the URLs for a couple of the sites where the book was available and I jotted them down on the back of the screenplay. Then she yawned and said she was exhausted—in only three hours she was due at a deposition for the Harrison case—warned me to be careful and then said good night or good morning or whatever it was.

I turned the script over and picked up where I left off. It was a love story between a Czech former dissident writer, one of those idealistic types who had done prison time during the Communist era, and an American woman shrink with Czech ancestry who was in Prague for a conference. She stays after the conference ends and she and the writer draw closer, much closer, until they are about to get married, when their relationship is thrown into turmoil. The American woman discovers her long-dead and cherished grandfather was a brutal guard in a concentration camp where the Czech writer's father was interned. The couple is driven apart, only to come back together, tentatively, many months later, in another country. At the end we are left to wonder if the love of these two people can overcome the horror of the past.

The conclusion of the screenplay was not on our crew's minds the next morning. Although referred to only briefly and elliptically, it was the rabbi's demise that dominated our thoughts as we rode out to Barrandov, the Czech film studio, for what was described as a last day of costume and set checking before filming began. This studio was located in a western suburb and to get there we drove out a freeway of sorts and then up twisty mountain roads through a boho neighborhood oddly reminiscent of the Hollywood Hills with white Constructivist-style houses built onto steep inclines overlooking the valley below. The studio itself was supposed to be one of the largest in Europe but you came upon it without warning—no grand palm-lined entrances here or officious gate guards looking askance at a five-year-old Toyota, but only a lonely striped barrier pole behind a rundown pilsen-and-sandwich joint like a railroad crossing in some rinky-dink border town. Still, its white Art Deco buildings were impressive, erected in the early thirties—Eva, the A.D., told me—by the family of Vaclav Havel himself, their nation's playwright-president and hero of the Velvet Revolution against the Soviets. Now, after decades of neglect by the Germans and Russians, the Czechs were trying to rehabilitate the studio as a modern facility to attract foreign production, particularly the biggest fish of all, Hollywood.

Such reconstruction, however, would not explain the presence of three police cars by the front door when we pulled into the parking lot. "I imagine that has something to do with us," said Farnsworth.

I nodded and glanced at Arthur, who had told me he saw a brief report of Rabbi Herzog's murder on CNN that morning mentioning the rabbi had only just met with the producers of an American motion picture called *Prague Autumn*. The Czech crew, I assumed, had all read about it in their own papers as well. "Perhaps it's better if they don't question me," I said to Farnsworth, who saw the wisdom of my remaining anonymous and spoke with Eva.

"I will take you in," she said to me. "You can wait in the costume department. No one could find anybody in there."

We got off first and I followed her around the building to a side entrance and up the stairs to the second floor. We proceeded down a cavernous hallway like the dank corridor in some wretched high school horror flick, but with tiny babushka ladies, remnants of communist times, scurrying about with scowls on their faces to extinguish the few dim lights the moment we passed as if we were profligate capitalists hell-bent on wasting all the electricity we could. At the end, we came to the costume department, which was indeed a vast, musty storeroom, rows and rows of what mostly looked like tattered formalware from the Austro-Hungarian Empire hanging on over fifty yards of rusty iron coat-racks. Nothing appeared to have been moved for years.

Eva deposited me in this allergist's nightmare near a couple of frumpy women at sewing machines and told me she would be back when the cops had left. I wandered off to finger the fringed epaulets of a guardsman's uniform when I heard a woman's voice behind me. "Have you talked to my publicist yet?" I turned to see Donna Gold standing across from me, holding a bright red sweater. "Just kidding. The asshole doesn't return my calls either. He's probably off in the Caribbean somewhere jumping a towel boy . . . What a hoot, huh?" She gestured to the rows of racks. "Good thing I made them bring all my costumes from home." She turned to a mirror, modeling the sweater in front of her chest. "What do you think?" she asked. "Ellen says my character wouldn't wear Gigli. But what does she know just because she wrote it? Lots of women shrinks from Michigan buy designer clothes these days. Typical Hollywood—they all think the people in the middle of the country are hicks." She pulled the sweater over her head and smiled at me, brushing back her hair. I had always thought of Donna as one of those women who could go from gorgeous to ordinary in a microsecond. One moment she could look like a latter-day Ava Gardner and the next just another Jewish girl from the Valley with a slight overbite, which she was. She always had a great body though and there isn't a straight man on the planet—married, single or engaged—who, deny it though he might, doesn't get at least a slight buzz in the presence of a movie star, even a minor one. And I was feeling one right then.

"It looks terrific on you," I said.

"Thanks. Why don't you tell it to Ellen? Oh, never mind." She started to take off the sweater, but stopped, looking at me more curiously than before. "I guess you didn't get to interview that rabbi," she said. "I saw what happened on CNN. Crazy, huh?" Now she started to take off the sweater. "Peter probably doesn't want me to know about it. He thinks I'll bolt, but I won't. I mean what does that have to do with us? Besides, Nick wants me to do this movie. He says I need a serious part, as if playing a lesbian short-order cook wasn't enough. All that got me was a lot of unwanted e-mail."

"Who's Nick?" I asked.

"My boyfriend, Nick Hodgetts. He owns the Bar Sinister on the Strip. You know it?"

"I can never get in. I guess I don't wear the right shoes."

She looked down at my ancient Nikes and laughed. "Maybe you need a raise. . . . Hey, you want to do a wild article? You've got to see this!"

She took me by the arm and led me out of the costume department into the corridor again. We rounded a corner to a giant metal door and slipped through the crack onto a sound stage as large as any I had ever seen back home. A small army of construction workers was hammering away on the interior of a mammoth period edifice replete with chandeliered ballrooms, mirrored hallways and what looked like a dozen sitting rooms with inlaid marble floors, marquetry armoires, spinets, balalaikas and giant murals with mythological scenes of unicorns, cloven-footed beasts, satyrs and fleeing virgins. "Can you believe it?" said Donna. "It's the inside of the Hermitage from St. Petersburg. Some Russian company is making a movie about the fall of the Tsar. . . . And they're reproducing the *entire thing* on this sound stage from scratch. With *real walls*." She banged on the back of the frame, which made a solid thump. "We could never afford to do that . . . but you know how they do?"

"Cheap labor?" I guessed.

Donna shook her head. "Mafia money," she said in a low voice.

"How do you know?" I asked.

She leaned closer and nodded to a squat man with a shaved head, furry mustache and shoulders a mile wide who looked like the weightlifting champ of Uzbekistan or some such place, light heavyweight division. He was standing at the corner of the set, clutching a fat leather briefcase that was attached to his behemoth-like forearm with the kind of shiny black metal chain you might find at one of the finer S&M shops on Santa Monica Boulevard.

"His name is Yevgeny. He was flirting with me and showed me the briefcase. It's filled to the brim with one thousand dollar U.S. bills! . . . He said they come from Brooklyn."

"From Brighton Beach to Moscow and back to Prague to finance a film about the Russian Revolution. That's quite a laundry."

"You should write about it," said Donna.

"For *Variety?*"

"You don't want to work for *them* the rest of your life, do you? I've got some friends at *Vanity Fair*. They love stories about money laundering."

Just then Yevgeny noticed Donna and smiled. But that evaporated in disappointment the moment he saw me, morphing into a suspicious frown. He wagged his finger with the time-honored "nyet" and motioned for us to leave. "I'll think about it," I said, escorting Donna back into the corridor again where we encountered Eva coming the other way.

"Ms. Gold," she said. "We have been looking everywhere for you. You must approve your shoes for the first day of shooting. . . . *You* can go. Those people have left," she added to me about the cops before starting off with Donna.

"Thanks," I said. "By the way, do you know someone named Kaprova?"

Eva laughed. "Kaprova is not a person. It is a street."

4

THE CREW HAD THE AFTERNOON OFF and I took the opportunity to walk Kaprova Street, crossing the Old Town Square to its starting point at the recently named Franz Kafka Square. (I wondered if one day there would be a Raymond Chandler Freeway in LA or a Phillip Roth Junior High in Newark.) Then I proceeded down Kaprova the few blocks past the also-renamed Jan Palach Square, which commemorated a student who incinerated himself to protest the Russian occupation, to the Manesuv Bridge over the Vltava River. I didn't notice anything of significance, but I retraced my steps and made the trek up and back the street twice more, not sure what I was looking for, until I wound up at the river a third time and stopped on the esplanade. As I stood there at the water's edge, watching swans negotiating their way between the tourist boats, I could see down past the Charles Bridge with its buskers entertaining crowds beneath the statues of saints to the hills of the Mala Strana beyond. For the first time I felt relaxed enough to take in the fabled beauty of this city whose buildings were miraculously untouched by the bombs of World War II, and I wished Samantha were there to share it with me. But when I reached for my cell to call her, I caught a glimpse of a sign in a second-story window not more than thirty yards back up Kaprova. "Institut Janak," it said in small, but distinct Art Nouveau lettering. The "hidden treasure" from the June *Vogue* apparently had been so well hidden, at least from me, that I had missed it coming down on the left side of the street beneath the arcade.

I walked down to the building, which housed a glass shop and women's boutique on the ground floor, and stepped inside through an ornate iron door with an eagle's crest on the front. A small brass plaque by the cage elevator indicated the institute was on the third floor. I rode up with a woman with a poodle who got off one floor below me at what looked like a private apartment. The elevator then stopped at the third floor and I walked off into a small foyer painted white in a determinedly international style. I could have been anywhere. A speaker labeled "Institute" was next to a brushed-aluminum door. I pressed the button. *"Prosim,"* came the disembodied voice.

"May I come in," I said. "I'd like to make an appointment."

I was buzzed into a large waiting room with about a dozen people, men and women, lounging on sofas, leafing through magazines and talking on cell phones. Others were visible through a wire-glass door, walking about in terry cloth robes. A tall blond woman in a lab coat came out from behind a desk toward me. "Welcome to the Institute Janak," she said. "How can we help you?"

"I'm interested in an appointment."

"For what program?"

"The one that was in *Vogue.*"

She looked at me with some amusement. "You are interested in herbal estrogen treatment?"

"I . . . uh . . . I guess not," I said. "What do you have for men?"

She walked behind the desk again and handed me a brochure in English. The front page showed a Buddhist monk floating on a cloud above the words "An Afterlife is not only for the spiritual!" Inside was a list of programs, including the herbal estrogen, with prices in Czech crowns and U.S. dollars. It was hard to tell which were for women and which for men and which for both, but they all seemed like conventional spa treatments—massages of various sorts, water and steam therapies, facials, colonics, yogic teas, herbal wraps and the like—with the familiar boilerplate about their life-enhancing capabilities. Only at the very bottom did I notice something out of the ordinary—"The Special Injection Program." It had no explanation but only a price, which was far higher than that of any of the other treatments, starting in the tens of thousands of dollars and escalating with the number of weeks. After a month, you could spend about forty grand. That was one helluva spa treatment. For that kind of money I would have to regain every hair on my head and end up looking like Brad Pitt. With the emotional serenity of Krishnamurti thrown in.

"What's the Special Injection Program?" I asked the woman.

"An interview is required."

"Yes, but what is it?"

"A patented treatment of Dr. Janak."

"For what?"

"You don't know?"

"Obviously not."

"An interview is required."

"And it is?"

"A patented treatment of Dr. Janak."

"Are we rehearsing *Waiting for Godot*?" I asked. She didn't laugh.

"Not everyone is allowed to take it," she said.

"I see. . . . So it's a kind of exclusive thing. . . . Suppose I had forty thousand dollars. Would it get any less exclusive?"

"An interview is required."

"How about if I could get the recommendation of a movie star? You know—somebody around town."

The woman stared at me. "I will speak with Dr. Janak. What is your name?"

"Miles," I said. "Darius Miles." She wrote it down while I tried to figure out what strange free association made me choose the name of the string-beany twenty-year-old forward of the LA Clippers. Maybe it was the appeal, at my age, of being able to play above the rim. I wondered if Dr. Janak's injections could do that, some shots for a jump shot. "Is it possible to have a look around the facility?" I asked.

"If you have an interview," said the woman. "Call us tomorrow, Mr. Miles. The number is on the back of the brochure." I turned it over to see a picture of Dr. Pavel Janak himself. With curly salt-and-pepper hair and a soothing smile, he reminded me of a certain type of con artist back home, the kind that tends to attract celebs like actors and rock stars. But perhaps I didn't give him credit. He had made the pages of *Vogue* after all and maybe even drawn the attention of a scriptwriting rabbi who was hip enough to sport a Jerry Garcia tie. At least the doctor's address had appeared on Herzog's screenplay. Could the rabbi himself have had one of Janak's injections?

I mulled that one over as I rode down the elevator and exited the building. But I hesitated at the entrance when I noticed a man in a doorway across the street, smoking a cigarette while banging his cell phone in frustration in that familiar way we do after having lost a connection or not gotten one in the first place. I wouldn't have thought anything of it but he was dark with the sort of bushy mustache many Muslims wear outside their home countries and looked Arab or possibly Pakistani. Yes, I knew he could have been Indian or Southern Russian or even a Mexican campesino, but I couldn't be sure. I wasn't proud of it. I was engaging in my own small-time version of racial profiling. Or maybe it wasn't so small time. But those were the times in which we lived. Anyone who said he didn't engage in racial profiling was either a liar or a saint. I certainly wasn't the latter and I was particularly good at the former.

So I continued down the block, drifted casually behind one of the columns and stopped for a longer look. The man finished his cigarette and pitched the butt in the gutter. But he didn't move. He remained in the doorway across from the Institute, watching people enter and leave the building. Then he tried the cell phone again but couldn't get through. After another moment, he started up Kaprova away from me. I followed, keeping a discrete distance, when he turned and walked down an alley. I waited for him to approach the other end, then continued quickly after him. He walked another half a block to his left and stopped at a newspaper kiosk. I edged closer as he purchased a copy of the German paper *Die Zeit*. Then he continued around the block and up another one as if he were taking a stroll until he doubled back a third way, coming along the river and winding up entering a door almost directly across from the Institute. When I reached it, I saw it was yet another shop selling the ubiquitous Czech glass. The Arab man, or whatever he was, was now behind the counter, acting as if he had just returned from a cigarette break.

"Doesn't sound like a normal cigarette break to me," said Farnsworth that evening. I was back in his suite with Ellen and Arthur.

"Just because he looks Middle Eastern?" said the bondsman.

The director shook his head. "His *modus operandi*. I think the guy went outside to check in with his handler while keeping his eye on activity at the Institute. Then he returned to work in the erratic manner undercovers use so their patterns aren't traceable."

Something about the way he said that made me think he had learned it all from a James Bond flick, but in this case it had some plausibility. When I entered the store, I noticed the copy of *Die Zeit* the man had just bought, apparently unread, dumped in a wastebasket by the counter. "His name is Latif," I said, "and he's an immigrant from Yemen. I bought four of these from him." I held up a martini glass with green spiral stems. "Not bad, huh? He even packed it in a nice Styrofoam box to take home."

"So he really *is* a salesman," said Arthur, relieved.

Then I told them about the newspaper.

"We have to tell Donna," said Ellen, alarmed.

"Just because she's going to the Janak Institute," said Arthur. "Half the Americans in Prague turn up there."

"That's a ridiculous exaggeration," Ellen responded. "Hardly anyone can afford it, especially if they go once a week for those injections."

"What are they?" I asked. "They must contain enriched uranium at those prices."

"Some concoction of B-12, ginseng, GMBH and other stuff that hasn't been licensed by the FDA. I warned Donna it could be dangerous but how're you going to keep an actress away from something that's supposed to make you look ten years younger?"

"So what're we supposed to tell her?" said Arthur, "That Moses was visiting the Institute to investigate the rabbi's murder and discovered a possible terrorist lurking next door? She thinks Moses works for *Variety*."

"I didn't say he was a terrorist," I said. "I don't know what he is."

"It doesn't matter," said Farnsworth. "We have to tell her. If something happened, we couldn't live with ourselves." He walked over to the desk, consulted a list of extensions and dialed. For the first time I was starting to like the guy. He wasn't totally an arrogant Hollywood asshole. Just partly. "It's busy," he said.

"Try the other line," said Ellen.

Farnsworth looked at the list again before dialing a second time. "That's busy too."

"Both lines in her suite are busy," said Arthur, belaboring the obvious in a worried voice.

"Maybe she's trying to get some sleep. We start shooting tomorrow," said the director.

"Her call isn't till ten," said Ellen. It was eight P.M.

Suddenly I could sense a heightened anxiety in the room. "She could be talking to her boyfriend," said Arthur. "It's five A.M. back in LA but he owns that swanky bar. He works late. . . . And what's-her-name, Tina, her makeup woman, could be on the other line. They're like sisters."

Silence. Finally, Farnsworth said, "Let's go up and see for ourselves."

So the four of us got into the hotel elevator, rode up to the eleventh floor and walked down to Donna's suite, which was the largest one at the end of the corridor. Farnsworth knocked, once, twice. There was no answer. "Donna, it's Peter and Ellen *et les autres*," he called out. "Are you in there?" More silence. "We need to talk to you! It's kind of important. . . . In fact it's very important!" Still nothing. I glanced down at the plastic card hanging from the handle; the side asking the maid to please make up the room was turned suspiciously outward. My heart started to beat a little faster and I was beginning to get a queasy feeling in my stomach, as I assumed the others were. I couldn't resist thinking about my encounter with the FBI lady at the LA Federal Building, wondering if, even though I didn't want to, Latif was connected in some way to cronies of Mohammed Atta, if the silence behind Donna's door had geopolitical ramifications none of us wanted to face.

"Don't you know how to open it?" said Farnsworth finally, gesturing impatiently at the handle and looking at me as if I were an expert. "I thought you gumshoes could get into everything." He pronounced my job title with the slightly superior tone I often heard from the gang at the Market. But I did my best to ignore him and started to rummage through my wallet for a certain fifteen-year-old Mobil card, which had sometimes fooled modern computer locks. I found it and, after a certain amount of fiddling with the card, the small green bulb suddenly illuminated on her door light. It was open. Everyone looked at each other hopefully. Pleased with myself, I started to turn the knob when a muffled voice came from within. "Please go away. I can't see anyone now." We all broke into broad smiles. It was Donna. She was alive. And better yet, since she didn't want us to come in, we didn't have to deal with telling her any uncomfortable truths about terrorists, at least for the moment. "I can't see anyone now," she repeated, gasping as she bolted the door from the inside with a chain lock. "I want to be alone!"

I didn't learn the reason for this Garbo act until the next morning, the first day of principal photography. We, I mean they, were about to start filming on a small square just north of the Prague Castle in front of an elegantly frescoed building that had once been the home of the artist Alphonse Mucha. Because it was the first day the schedule was deliberately short to get the crew accustomed to each other. The initial scene on the call sheet— like most movies *Prague Autumn* was being shot out of order to save money by consolidating locations—was near the actual finale of the film's story. Donna and Goran were to emerge from their house to be surrounded by avaricious reporters, demanding the truth about Donna's Nazi grandfather. Goran would briefly answer their questions, make an impassioned speech about privacy and the rights of man, then spirit Donna away in his car.

The camera and lights had been set. The press, most of whom were extras, was in place. Goran was there, his first week's salary having been miraculously delivered into escrow at the last minute. Indeed, everyone and everything had been ready to go for two hours. But Donna was refusing to come out of the makeup truck.

"Nerves," said Arthur, who had sidled up next to me. "She's got a zit on her left cheek the size of Yankee Stadium."

"That's why she wouldn't let us in last night," I said. "What're they going to do?"

"I told them time is money. Shoot her from the right. But Farnsworth doesn't want to compromise the first day."

"Why should he?"

Arthur rolled his eyes. "Stick to your day job, Moses. . . . Anyway, I don't think he's in a condition to shoot right now. He's gone catatonic on us." He nodded toward the director, who was bent over in his chair, staring at the ground like a man waiting for the guillotine while his wife shook him by the shoulder, yelling at him to snap out of it.

"What the fuck can I do?" he said, waving her away. "She

won't come out of the trailer. At least in television the network would have forced her out!" Behind them, sitting on director's chairs of their own with their names on the backs, Volksbruner and Takashima looked on in alarm. This was a helluva way to start.

Just then one of the extras came over to us. He was a man in his thirties in the international uniform of the hipoisie—John Lennon glasses, shaved head and earring. "You gents look like you might know something. How much longer is it going to be?" he asked in pearly cultured tones masking what I guessed was once a flat midwestern accent, but it could have been from almost anywhere. "I don't want to sound like a prig, but I don't have the time to wait around all day to play a quondam reporter in some spurious piece of cinema. I've got a poetry reading to organize for tonight. Chilean sonnets."

"I don't think I would call this a spurious piece of cinema," said Arthur, now coming to his friend's defense. "Peter Farnsworth's one of the more serious writers in Hollywood."

"I heard Farnsworth didn't write the screenplay," said Earring. "I heard it was his wife. But that's typical of Hollywood, isn't it, the director taking credit for a script he didn't write, even if it's his closest relative? Commodity capitalism at its most refined. Not that it makes any difference. It comes to the same thing. You visit Prague for a week and go home and make a movie about it. Some of us have been here for years, immersing our-selves in this culture since the Revolution of '89. Of course, you Industry people might not have the time for that." He looked straight at me as if he were sizing me up, wondering where I fit in, then turned away. "*Now* look who's here! *Quel surprise,*" he added with studied world-weariness. "The Black Prince of Moravia and his Evil Consort!"

He gestured to a shiny new Volvo, which was pulling in next to the catering truck. A pudgy gray-haired man in a loden coat got out accompanied by a taller blond woman with a sly smile that could only be described as Eastern European. He walked straight over to Farnsworth and gave the director a reassuring squeeze on the arm, saying something that sounded like "Don't worry. Be happy" under his breath while offering Farnsworth an open hip flask. "Pretty early in the day," I said. "Who's that?"

"Jaroslav Schlick, the CEO of our Czech producing company, and his business partner, Anna Rockova," said Arthur.

"Tell him what Schlick did under communism," said Earring, continuing before he could get an answer. "He was the head of the studio. And, lo and behold, he's the head of the studio now, *under capitalism.*"

"Not the head," said Arthur. "The director of one of four companies that share it."

"A distinction without a difference," replied the expat, walking off. *"Plus ça change, plus c'est la même."* He went and joined Ivan, the location manager, muttering something to him and nodding toward Schlick.

"Asshole thinks he's at a World Trade Organization protest," said Arthur.

Suddenly someone tapped me on the shoulder. "Ms. Gold would like to see you." It was Eva. Arthur gave me a surprised look and I shrugged, then followed the assistant director to the makeup truck. She knocked on the door, said something in Czech and they told us to come in. It was the first time I had ever been in a makeup truck and it reminded me, this one at least, of a rinky-dink beauty salon in Modesto with a couple of stylists working near the front while several clients, under dryers, read outdated fashion magazines, in this case with inscrutable local titles like *Mlady Svet.* It even had the same fetid smell of cheap hairspray and leftover open conditioner bottles. I did not yet realize these trucks were the seat of all gossip, one of the most important power centers on any movie set because the stars, for the most part, resided there with their closest confidants, the makeup artists.

Donna Gold was in a semiprivate cubicle in the back with *her* makeup artist from home, Tina Kerides, a tall brunette of the leggy type you associated with the 1940s. When I arrived there, the actress had the left side of her face covered by a towel with her head reclining over a basin and her eyes staring at the ceiling as if she were about to get a shampoo, which she wasn't. She was just trying to hide a zit. "Oh, hi," she said. "Is everybody hating me out there? They shouldn't. If their cheek looked like it was hit by a thirty-millimeter howitzer, they wouldn't go out in public either. I'm beginning to envy those Arab women back at the hotel, running around with those *schmattas* under their noses. Nobody *ever* has to see them. Anyway, I just wanted to tell you, I talked to my friend at *Vanity Fair* and she's really interested in a piece on money laundering at a Czech movie studio, especially if you can work in some kind of white-slave angle. You know, Russian models or something."

"Thanks," I said, suddenly feeling a twinge of guilt about the man I saw the day before as I looked down at the actress who seemed quite vulnerable with her head dangling over the basin. Her naked neck would have made an easy target for a flashing scimitar. "Would you mind if I talked with you privately?"

"Really? I think I'm going to be propositioned, Tina."

"About time," said the makeup artist, winking at me as she ducked out, shutting the flimsy cubicle door behind her. Then I sat down on a stool next to the sink.

"I'm not a reporter," I said. "I'm actually a private detective. I was hired by Arthur Sugarman to find out about those snakes and to make sure nothing untoward happens to anyone on this production."

"Wow," said Donna. She reached up to pull her towel off, then thought better of it. "I knew you were too cool to work for *Variety*."

"I wanted to tell you that you might have been under sur-veillance going in and out of the Institut Janak."

"By whom?" she said, this time sitting up, but still holding the towel to her cheek.

"Someone of Middle Eastern background. His name is Latif and he works in the glass store across the street."

"Oh shit!" said Donna. "Whatever you do, don't tell my family. They'll send the FBI over here to take me home and then bye-bye movie. . . . What a piece of fucking luck—a terrorist threat on top of *this!*" She squeezed in irritation on the towel and for a moment I thought she was going to break the zit by herself. "You know my shrink was right. I *am* terrified of real success. The moment I get a serious part all Hell breaks loose."

At that point there was a knock on the door. *"Prosim,"* somebody said.

"Prosim yourself," said Donna. "Whatever the fuck that means."

"May I come in, please?"

"Sure, sure. Things couldn't be any worse."

The door opened and Jaroslav Schlick and Anna Rockova were standing there. With them was a third person, another woman, even taller than Anna, quite beautiful, with a black leather bag in her hand. "Donna, you will excuse us, I hope," said Anna. "This is Nadia Novakova, well-known actress with our national theater, specializing in tragedies of Schiller and Racine." Rockova . . . Novakova . . . This country was filled with more ova than an egg factory. "She is also leading dermatologist in city."

Donna stared at the doctor in embarrassed astonishment. "How do you do? Sorry for the, uh . . . sometimes I've got a mouth. I don't mean it."

"No problem," said Novakova. "Would you remove the towel from your face, please?" I took that as my cue to leave.

Forty-five minutes later Donna emerged from the makeup truck with her zit, helped by some miracle medicine and the judicious application of an extra dollop of pancake, a distant memory. Farnsworth, no longer slumped in his chair like a drowned river rat looking as if he wanted to quit before he even started, sprang to his feet. Donna's finally surfacing seemed to have given him a shot of adrenaline. "You look terrific," he said, "brand new . . . absolutely sensational . . ." and ushered her inside the building from which she and Goran were supposed to emerge. Thirty seconds later he was out again, bounding up to Eva. "We've lost too much time. We'll shoot the rehearsal!"

"Yes, sir!" Eva saluted. "Quiet, please . . . *Ticho, prosím!*" She barked out orders in English and Czech. "Camera . . . rolling . . . speed," the crews responded. "Extras!" screamed Eva in a megaphone. A gaggle of would-be reporters, including our friend Mr. Earring, rushed across the street, firing cameras. "Action!" yelled Farnsworth into an intercom connected to the interior of the building. The door opened and Goran and Donna stepped out to a fusillade of flashbulbs. Goran put his hands up to the reporters and made his fiery speech. I have to admit he was good, surprisingly good on the first go-round, with a real intensity that seemed to come out of nowhere. The Serbian could act and everybody knew it. Even Donna looked impressed. Or was it jealous?

We celebrated the first day of shooting at the Café Slavia, the legendary artist's hangout where Havel and the other communist era dissidents lingered over Turkish coffee and stale baklava when they weren't in jail. Closed for the better part of the nineties, it reopened a few years ago under new owners who renovated the Deco establishment in a green theme echoing the emerald painting of a female absinthe drinker perched seductively on a tabletop that dominated the entry. With its optimum location across from the National Theatre and its polyglot crowd of local bohos, expats, tourists, jet-setters and overdressed mobsters both Russian and Czech, if there was any place in Prague that was the equivalent of Rick's in Casablanca, this was it. Only the Slavia wasn't fictional and the absinthe was legal—so legal, in fact, that a fair number at our table of a dozen had ordered some, ignoring the beverage's fabled brain-rotting characteristics as well as its very name, which was the ancient Greek for "undrinkable."

"I had this before in Andorra," said Farnsworth, sipping gingerly at his glass of the 140-proof licorice juice, "when I was a college kid hitchhiking through Europe. I hoped it would help me paint like Van Gogh or write like Poe, but all it did was make me trip over a sewer drain on my way back to the youth hostel and fracture my toe."

"Is nothing!" said Goran, waving him off. "When I leave Belgrade because of that sonofabitch Milosevic, I have no penny. All I drink is cheap Bulgarian cologne, straight from bottle. Makes me pass out for three days and almost die. Have stomach pumped in Catholic hospital in Slovenia." He chugged down his absinthe with alacrity and reached for a refill.

"Perhaps you should eat something first," warned Dr. Novakova, who had joined us for the evening at Donna's urging. A waitress was passing out menus but my eyes were on the crowd at the bar where a familiar figure was standing. It was Latif, slicked up and dressed for an evening out in a sports jacket and tie. With him was a shorter Arab man with an eye patch, who, wearing a chic brushed suede cardigan, looked like a mujahedin gone yuppie. They were leaning on the bar, not saying a word and staring across the room in our direction. I was going to tell Donna, but the waitress had come around for my order. The actress was busy anyway, engrossed in a cell phone conversation with her hand covering her free ear.

"Don't bother with the food here," said Ivan, before I could open my mouth. "It's terrible and overpriced. Unless of course this is on the production." He gestured cynically to Schlick, who was at the far end with Anna, discussing the day's shoot with Karl and Takashima. "But I've been working for him ten years and he hasn't picked up the check yet," continued the location manager only half under his breath. "He wouldn't even pay for my meal when I took the head of Miramax's London branch to lunch to show him our production facility. We are exploited now worse than under communism." It was hard to figure if he was joking or not but it didn't seem to bother the former studio boss, who, smiling pleasantly down at us, winked in our direction and swallowed his drink.

"Don't worry about it," said Farnsworth expansively. "I'm paying."

"No. I am paying," said Goran. "I insist."

"Fuck you all," said Donna, hanging up her cell phone. "I'm paying! That bastard is having an affair and I'm not going to let him make me suffer for it!"

"What bastard?" said Goran.

"Nick 'The Asshole' Hodgetts. The bastard who said he was going to come over here and propose, but now says he has to go to Honolulu on business. Does he think I was born fucking yesterday like Judy Holliday? He's going to drink Mai Tais on the beach with that teenybopper bisexual bitch from Santa Monica who used to make videos with his personal trainer. Come on, girlfriend," she said to Tina, downing her absinthe in one jolt. "Let's work the room!"

And with that the two women got up, making straight for the bar. I could see them heading in the direction of Latif when I jumped up to intercept them. "Hold off, Donna. That's the guy."

"What guy?"

"The one I told you about, who was watching the Institute."

She stared over my shoulder at the Arab who was pretending not to see us. "He's a fox!" she said. I hadn't noticed. "No, no, really. He's very handsome, a young Omar Sharif." She looked over at Tina, who clearly agreed. "He's just what I need at a time like this. Do you think it would be unpatriotic to fuck him?"

As she was speaking the front door swung open and two men wearing heavy cloth topcoats and looking distinctly untrendy for a place like this came in. One of them was short and bald while the other was taller and had shaggy red-orange hair that seemed about three inches short of a dye job. For one weird moment I thought it was 1995 and I was back home watching Detectives

Tom Lange and Phillip Vanatter on the *Geraldo Show*. But then I realized, as they handed their coats to the hatcheck girl and started for the main room, that these weren't OJ's famous nemeses but local cops on the Prague force.

I could see that Latif had realized it too. He looked from them to Donna and then to me, wondering if there was a connection. Then something registered in his brain—a set of martini glasses perhaps, green spiral stems—and he said something to his partner. Almost immediately they started to back out, dodging through the crowd. I headed after them. They saw me and began to move faster, pushing past people through a pair of swinging doors. I followed after them into the kitchen area of the Slavia, which was equally crowded but this time with employees. Apparently, the Czech Republic was well on its way to catching up to Western Europe when it came to guest workers from the developing world. And from the looks on their faces they didn't seem to cotton to a guest detective from the exceptionally or perhaps excessively developed world of California USA pursuing two of their own through their professional bailiwick. Latif must have noticed this because he shouted to them in Arabic, a language enough of the workers understood to form a blockade impeding my path. "Stop. Wait," I yelled as Latif and his buddy disappeared through the back door. I could see them running down an alley out of sight through a wire-glass window.

When I walked back into the café, the plainclothes detectives were sitting at our table opposite Schlick. Evidently they had come here because of a small break in the Rabbi Herzog murder. Two members of the Hasidic Jewish community had reported seeing what they thought might have been an American male in a brown leather jacket coming down the stairs from the rabbi's office somewhere around the time of the killing. The detectives, whose names were Josef Fule—he was the short one like Lange—and Bohumil Pisek—the gangly local Vanatter—had come to discuss the matter with Schlick, who, as Czech production chief,

Eva elucidated in a flat manner not lacking in irony, was still after all these years "the responsible leader" as they used to call it in communist times. Perhaps *he* might help them discover who this mysterious American in leather might be and whether this person could indeed have any connection to the film or indeed to the crime.

"What happened?" Donna whispered to me as soon as there was a moment.

"I lost them," I replied, thinking not just of the two Arabs but of the brown suede jacket I had bought only a month ago on sale at Bloomingdale's. Fortunately, it had been too cold to wear it that night, but now I knew I would have to dispose of it for good the moment I got back to the hotel.

❖

The next morning, from location, I dialed the glass store precisely at ten, and then again at eleven, asking for Latif. Not surprisingly, he had not arrived. He still wasn't there when I called at noon and the owner of the store, a Mrs. Vlasikova, seemed a bit miffed. She wanted to know if I was a friend of Latif's and if he was always this irresponsible. I told her that I didn't know him very well but from what I did know he seemed to be the type who took his assignments seriously. The production was filming at a park behind the Castle at the time and I watched while a crew spread autumn leaves across the grass for added color as I talked to her on a cell phone and wondered if indeed Latif had been scared away and we would ever see him again.

I continued to wonder the same thing the following several days as I sat on the set in one of the empty director's chairs or stood by the side watching them set up for the next shot. That was painstaking work by the director of photography and his gaffer, the light man, which as often as not had to be completely redone as soon as it was finished because of a passing cloud. On my few previous visits to film sets, I had quickly learned that watching movies being made could be deadly dull. I spent most of my time playing hearts with Arthur or gossiping with the crew, one of whose favorite sports was listening in on the supposedly private conversations of the actors on the sound department earphones they called "pots." I have to admit it was amusing to hear Goran swearing to his hair stylist that he *had* used the medicinal shampoo she had given him the previous day and those white things jumping around in his stringy locks were *not* lice or asking that very same stylist on another occasion to give him a prostate massage—"I tired, Katalinka,'" he said. "Healer in Zagreb say must have finger stimulation from beautiful woman in secret male energy spot"—or Donna telling a distinguished actress from the English stage who had a small part in the movie that she, Donna, had improved on certain sense memory techniques pioneered by Meryl Streep.

"I hate this job," I told Samantha one afternoon on the phone as they set up a tracking shot on a walking street near the Old Town Square where Donna and Harriet Whelan, the British actress, were supposed to be shopping for souvenirs. "The only one who has any fun around here is Farnsworth. Being a director is like being the dictator of some obscure Bavarian principality, everybody kissing your ass while you arbitrarily pick out colors for the palace bedrooms!"

"You sound jealous," she said.

"Maybe I am, but I can tell you one thing, I'm bored as Hell and I'm the world's worst security guard. I fell asleep in a chair yesterday at ten o'clock in the morning while we were shooting an elevator scene and didn't wake up for forty-five minutes. They could have blown up half the high-rise buildings in this city by then."

"*Ticho, prosim* . . . Quiet, please," said Eva.

"Hold on," I whispered. "They're filming." And then I watched them do a closeup of Donna peering in the storefront window. It was a short one and within seconds I could see

Farnsworth mouthing the words "Robert Wise . . . Robert Wise . . . Robert Wise . . ." as he frequently did, slowly repeating the name of the director of *The Sound of Music*, of all people, to force himself to wait before yelling "Cut!" in case the actors did something extraordinarily interesting or revealing in that unguarded moment after finishing the prescribed scene. It rarely worked, as far as I could tell. But what did I know? As I said before, I was only a detective. In fact, sitting around a movie set, I felt more like a blue-collar worker than I ever had in my life, what they called, in the brutally hierarchical language of film budgets, "below the line" personnel, down there with the grips and electricians.

"Is it okay to talk now?" said Samantha.

"Yeah, yeah, sure. Where was I?"

"You were bored stiff."

"Right. When're you coming over here?"

"Not for at least a week, I'm afraid. I tried to get free sooner but you know Dichter. He hasn't let anybody out of a contract since the Lakers lost. Look, stop feeling sorry for yourself. You're in Europe. You're being paid. Have an adventure. Go . . . go . . ."

"Go what? Kayaking on the Vltava River? Maybe I should I have an affair with an actress," I teased. "But it won't be Donna Gold. She's way too old for me. . . . She's thirty-nine."

"Donna Gold is thirty-nine?" Samantha sounded genuinely amazed. "I thought she was in her late twenties at the most. She really looks good. How do you know?"

"I saw her file yesterday at the Janak Institute. It was on the doctor's desk and I peeked when he went to take a personal call."

That wasn't the only interesting fact regarding Donna I learned that morning when I finally had my interview with Dr. Pavel Janak. Apparently, if my quick perusal of her file was accurate, this was not her first visit to Prague, but her fourth. The first of these visits was seven years ago, when the actress was, so it now appeared, thirty-two and, if Janak's injections were all they were cracked up to be, it was then that he put his initial interrupt into whatever portion of Donna's DNA dictated her deterioration. Like any card-carrying member of my supposedly wildly self-involved generation, the first thing that popped into my head was could he do it for me. Unfortunately, Janak had headed me off at the pass on that one only a few minutes after my arrival in his pristine office.

"I am sorry, Mr. Wine," he had said, leaning forward ever so slightly in his Aeron chair and scrutinizing me closely. It seemed as if he was staring directly into the whites of my eyes for signs of decay. "But you do not appear to be a good candidate for my treatment."

"Why not?" I said, feeling defensive as I gazed about the room, which was completely undecorated except for a tinted seri-graph of Keith Richards. Had he been a patient? If so, maybe the doctor's formula included a fifth of bourbon, a dash of metham-phetamine and a carton of unfiltered Camels along with the gin-seng and vitamin E.

"I do not want to be mystical about these things. Perhaps it is better if I explain it this way," Janak continued, now tilting back slightly in his chair without taking his eyes off me. "Many years ago, on a trip to the People's Republic of China, I was taken to a Shanghai hospital to witness an operation using acupuncture for anesthesia. A young man of twenty or so had had polio as a child and they wanted to reset his deformed leg. He was wide-awake, with needles in his arm and forehead, eating an apple, when the surgeon lifted a steel hammer and broke his kneecap like that." Suddenly he slammed his fist on the desk, shaking his penholder and causing me to sit up in *my* chair. "Most of us Westerners in the room gasped, almost passed out, but the young man simply smiled as the surgeon calmly went about repairing his twisted leg. Later, I told him how amazed we were that the acupuncture allowed the man to remain awake during such an excruciating procedure. But the doctor said it was rare even there, that only a few had sufficient faith in the teachings of Chairman Mao to endure the pain."

"So it's the placebo effect," I said.

"Not quite," said Janak. "More accurately, it is the interrelationship between the treatment and the belief. Both must be present for the chemical reaction to take place. In your case, alas, I have detected an excess of skepticism, perhaps a lifetime of cynicism which for most intelligent individuals is simply a rational response to reality. They have had most of their assumptions destroyed either by the betrayal of personal relationships or by the terrifying vagaries of history itself. I often wonder if I could benefit from my own injections. I tend to doubt it."

"I wouldn't worry about it," said Samantha, after I finished relating my encounter with the doctor to her. "It's probably a bunch of horse-hockey anyway." But what if it's not, I briefly thought. Then I'm left out and the likes of Donna Gold get—what?—thirty extra years in the bloom of youth. It scarcely seemed fair. "Besides," Samantha continued, "it's obvious he didn't want you nosing around his enterprise."

"He didn't care. He showed me his lab. Everything. Of course he wouldn't show me his formula, but that's his privilege. Maybe he's onto something. He's applying for a license from the FDA, but he says that could take years at the rate they go. The problem is it all makes me think about my own life. I know this sounds self-pitying but I really haven't accomplished anything."

"What? I always thought you were a workaholic."

"But what have I left behind? Nothing creative. No paintings, no symphonies, no movies. A private dick is nothing but a functionary. Just raw protoplasm, in and out—one minute it's alive and the next it's dead." What was I saying? Had I gone crazy? I had never talked that way before, but I couldn't stop myself.

"Moses, you really *are* sounding self-pitying. It's not attractive. There are people out there dying of cancer, starving in Afghanistan."

"You're right. You're right," I said, not sounding this time as convinced as I knew I should have. Meanwhile, Eva was waving to me. Farnsworth had wrapped his last shot and we were moving to the night location. That, at least, I was looking forward to. It would be my first experience with a camera car and the director had offered to let me ride on the truck with him, just like a kid at an amusement park. "Look, I really love you and miss you and I'm just an asshole and forget everything I said."

"I'll try," said Samantha. "But just remember when you downgrade what you do, that we're partners. Think how that makes me feel."

"I'm sorry," I said, with all the attendant lameness of that pathetic phrase, and promised not to do it in the future, although she and I both knew I would. It was one of my personality defects—I was a world-class *kvetcher*—and she would have to learn to live with it just as I had to learn to live with her less appealing foibles, which, regrettably, I could rarely remember at the appropriate moments.

I said good-bye as best I could, stuffing my cell phone back in my jacket just as Arthur came by in the Tatra, offering to give me a ride to the next set. We arrived at a lonely road along the river ahead of most of the crew, who had to negotiate the narrow streets at rush hour. He dropped me by the camera car and I climbed over its galvanized steel railing. A retrofitted three-axle truck, it had front and back camera platforms and an onboard electric generator. No one else was around when I got on except for a tech who was hooking up the video playback monitor and a grip connecting the picture car, a battered Opel driven by Goran's character, to the rear of the truck for the scene to be filmed—the couple's romantic first night out.

It was cold and already dark and I hunched up against the side, waiting, my mind drifting back to my interview with Janak again, to the more crucial part when I tried to ascertain his connection to a murder. I was wondering if he had told me the truth when I asked him about Rabbi Herzog. I tended to believe him when he said he had never met the man, that members of the clergy, even screenwriting ones who shared the doctor's affinity for classic rock and roll, didn't dare avail themselves of his services, even if they wanted to. After all, even the whisper that a rabbi, priest or minister had been seeking immortality through injection, herbal or otherwise, would have been ruinous to their reputations. But then I smiled to myself, thinking of the obvious exceptions like Tammy Faye Baker. It was hard to imagine her turning down the Devil himself if he could perform a good tummy tuck with his pitchfork.

The truck revved and we lurched forward a few feet and the camera crew jumped on, followed by the sound mixer, followed by Farnsworth wearing a pair of pots. He nodded to the video tech and the monitor popped on, the Opel fading into view in the middle of the screen. "Great toy, huh?" the director said to me and then barked some orders down to Eva, who passed them on through a walkie-talkie. He wanted the street wet down and soon what looked like a huge off-duty garbage truck rounded the corner, its yellow headlights blinking, spewing water across the pavement like some prehistoric monster taking a giant piss in every direction. "I know it's been done to death," continued the director. "But what the Hell, it looks great. . . . Where's the talent?" he shouted to Eva, who again passed the word on.

"Coming in!" yelled the second A.D., spouting another cliché of the film world that I already recognized, as if the arrival of the star or stars was akin to the Second Coming, rendering nouns and pronouns irrelevant.

Through the blackness, I could just make out Donna and Goran, accompanied by hair and makeup, approaching the Opel. Goran got in behind the wheel and Donna waited for a last touchup of blush before entering the passenger side. Then I heard a thud behind me that sounded like the driver getting into the truck cab.

"Good evening. How's it going in there?" said Farnsworth into a walkie-talkie.

"Why my character drive this shit car?" responded Goran through a speaker, his voice slurring. "Seat too small. I need Katalinka for massage."

Farnsworth rolled his eyes and looked down at Eva. "I thought I said to keep the slivovitz out of his trailer." Then, suddenly, the camera car lurched forward, throwing us all backward and knocking a lamp off its mount, sending it flying to the ground where it shattered on the asphalt. "Hey, what was that?" yelled Farnsworth. But before anyone could respond, the truck accelerated, moving at an extraordinarily rapid clip toward a bridge in front of us. "I didn't say . . . Stop! Where're we going?" The director's words were barely audible in the roar of the engine, which was now headed into overdrive. "Do something!" he screamed at me as if I could. We were all holding on to the rail for dear life. The truck swerved and shot up the ramp toward the bridge, the Opel swaying uncontrollably on its tow behind us, the tiny car nearly tipping over on its side, its wheels barely touching the ground. I could only imagine the terrified expression on Donna's face. "We're being kidnapped . . . you fucking . . ." Farnsworth gesticulated furiously at the cab, then started running toward it. I tried to stop him but he was already on the railing, climbing recklessly over to get at the driver when the truck made a hard right onto the bridge, pitching the director over the side. I stared in horror as Farnsworth bounced off the pavement ten feet below, crashing into a concrete abutment with a deadly thud, which could be heard even over the screeching tires and the roar of the motor.

I couldn't see what happened to him, because by now we were barreling across the bridge and, in seconds, were on the north side of the river, passing cars as we headed uphill in the direction of the area known as Hradcany, the Castle district. But we instantly veered away from the famous landmark, heading around a barricade into a park, which was apparently closed at night, the outlines of the cupola of what looked like a small shrine flying past us. A freezing rain was beginning to fall and I stared back fruitlessly for a police car or some help when the truck, speeding ever faster, emerged in an industrial neighborhood and then slowed. After another few seconds, it drove straight through the waiting open doors of a warehouse, which were immediately shut behind us.

Three men wearing the green-and-white hoods of the type I recognized from demonstrations in Hebron and Ramallah, holding Kalashnikovs, instantly surrounded the truck and the Opel. "Everybody down, keep hands up," said one of them. The group immediately complied, carefully climbing down from the camera car. Behind me, Donna was being helped out of the Opel while a shaken Goran stumbled out the other side. "Now on floor, face down," the speaker continued. "Don't worry, actress only. Everybody else go home." He turned to Donna. "You go van. This way, please, lady." He took her by the arm and started escorting the actress toward a windowless white van parked by the wall.

"What the fuck?" said Donna, as he shoved her inside.

"Just what do you think you're doing?" I said, walking toward him.

Suddenly another of the hooded men started pointing at me. "Martini man. You no want glasses. You liar!" It was Latif. He started buzzing away in Arabic to the other man. I couldn't understand any of it, of course, except the words *"ham Allah,"* and what appeared to be the acronym "CIA," which was the same in all languages. "You spy," he now said in English. I had gone from being investigated by the organization to being a full-scale member in less than twenty years. But in this case it would be useful.

"That's right," I said. "What're you going to do about it?"

He and the other man looked at each other for a split second, then Latif gestured toward the van with his Kalashnikov for me to climb in after Donna. She stared down at me gratefully and whispered thanks. As I clambered in behind, I reached into my pocket and pressed the speed button for Samantha on my cell phone. But the other man saw what I was doing, said something unfriendly in Arabic and pulled out my phone, hurling it across the floor in anger. Then he slammed me with the butt of his rifle and threw me into the back of the van past Donna. The van door was shut and locked behind both of us and in a few seconds I heard the motor go on and the doors of the warehouse open again.

"Where do you think they're taking us?" said Donna after what felt like an hour but was probably closer to three minutes.

"I don't know. Bosnia? Albania?"

"Bosnia? Why would they want to do *that?*"

It came as no surprise she had no clue these were countries with Muslim majorities, but it scarcely seemed worth explaining. "Don't worry about it. We'll be alright."

"What are you talking about? They're going to kill us!"

"If they were, they would have done it already."

"You mean we're going to be hostages? Why would they want us?"

"You're a movie star, Donna."

"That's not what my ex-manager says."

We sat there for a while without talking on the icy, corrugated metal floor as the van hurtled into the night. A mixture of cold air and exhaust fumes filtered up through razor-thin cracks in the vehicle's frame. We were in what was essentially a sealed storage container with no way of seeing out onto the passing countryside or into the driving compartment in front of us. I tried to figure out where we were going but it was impossible with all the twists and turns and, in truth, even if we had been going straight at this point I had no idea in what direction we were heading. Donna put her head down and started to sob quietly. I checked my watch. We had been traveling for only twenty-four minutes. When I checked it again, it was closer to an hour. When I checked it a third time, we had been on the move for an hour and forty-seven minutes. Roughly half an hour later we came to a halt.

When the door opened, I saw snow. We were up in the mountains somewhere, a crescent moon peaking through tall pine trees. I ran a map of the Czech Republic through my mind and seemed to remember a small range a hundred or so miles north of Prague, but maybe it was to the east.

"I hope ride not too uncomfortable," said Latif, who, now without his mask, was standing there in a parka with two buddies, including the one-eyed guy from the Café Slavia. They still had their Kalashnikovs, needless to say, but Latif was also carrying blankets, one of which he wrapped around Donna as she stepped down to the ground, handing the other to me. "Is chilly up here, no? But air sweet. I like it. . . . You must wear this too," he continued to the actress, passing her a scarf as the third man kept his assault rifle trained on her. "To cover hair and be modest. It is not necessary to hide face. You are Western woman. I understand."

"Whatever you say," she replied, trying to be strong, but I could see her hand shaking as she slipped the scarf over her head.

"Yes. That is better. Thank you." He smiled shyly at Donna, then nodded to the other two, who took us both by the arms and started to lead us toward a low-slung building that looked like a barracks.

"Why are we here, Latif?" I asked.

"In moment," he said, holding the door open for us. "Must have tea first." They took us inside a large room in what indeed appeared to be a residence hall in an old military compound. The walls were covered with faded murals of crudely drawn soldiers with red stars on their uniforms and flying helicopter gunships with identification markings in Cyrillic. It must have been a Russian camp from the glory days of the Warsaw Pact. Only now most of it was trashed, the few remaining chairs and tables clustered at one side of the room near where some empty rusted oil barrels were lying on their sides. A couple of cots were pushed into a corner near a nuclear hazard warning sign, which hung, unnervingly, on what appeared to be the bathroom door.

"It's the Four Seasons Love Canal," I said to Donna, trying to cheer her up.

"Sit, please," said Latif, dusting off a couple of the chairs for us. He snapped his fingers at One-Eye, who hustled over to a kettle warming on a hot plate and returned with two teas in juice glasses, placing them on a table in front of us. Latif frowned, barked out something in Arabic and One-Eye hurried off again, this time returning with two threadbare chocolate cookies that looked like imitation Oreos. "Please," said Latif, gesturing toward them. Donna and I each reached down and picked one up, tentatively putting them to our mouths. "Is good, no? American style. I think you like. Now I tell you demands. Demand one—cease immediately film about so-called Holocaust. Demand two—renounce existence of so-called Holocaust as propaganda of Zionist conspiracy. Demand three—end all racist anti-Arab movie in Hollywood. Demand four—expose CIA as agent of Israeli world domination. Demand five—withdraw all American troops from Middle East, Far East and Northern Africa." He stopped and looked at us. "Is enough, no?"

"Indeed," I said. At least he didn't ask for restitution for the Crusades or moving the Statue of Liberty to downtown Damascus.

"I believe you must think now," he said and stood. "You are tired, I am sure. In the morning we no doubt find good solution to mutual problem."

"No doubt," I said.

"Good night, my guests," he said. " I will see you tomorrow." He added a few words in Arabic to One-Eye, before starting out with the third man. I noticed Donna watching them.

"One moment . . . Latif?" she said in a suddenly lilting voice. He stopped, surprised, and the actress took a step forward, smiling at him the same way she had back at the Café Slavia. "I just wanted to thank you for being so . . . straight with me . . . with us. I appreciate your hospitality."

Latif blushed. "It is the custom of our people, Missus Gold."

"It's miss," she said. "I'm not married."

"Yes. I understand." The Arab looked flustered.

"I'm sure you do," she replied, smiling again, almost batting her eyelashes.

I could see Latif swallow. "Good night," he said and exited in a hurry with the third man as if he were afraid something truly evil was going to befall him.

"What do you think you're doing?" I whispered to Donna, as soon as they had left. "Flirting with him? You're going to get us killed."

"Just trust me. Okay?"

One-Eye then turned to us and gestured ceremoniously to an alcove, where I could see another cot had actually been made up for the night with sheets that seemed clean enough. A folding screen was hinged to some wallboard for privacy. It was obviously for Donna. She gave a shrug and walked in.

I walked over to one of the cots on the other side and lay down. One-Eye watched me for a moment before going, without looking away from me for a second, and turned out the lights. Then he came back to the other cot and sat there opposite me with his assault rifle on his lap. The situation wasn't exactly conducive to sleep, not that I would have slept anyway, given my present mood of more or less mind-boggling anxiety and the fact that the springs in my bed were so bare and pointed only the most experienced yogi would get a second's rest on them. So I just lay there with my eyes shut, pretending to sleep, but I must have gone out at some point, because I was awakened by noise from the alcove. Then I heard Donna's voice coming through the wallboard.

"Oh, Latif . . . hi . . . What're you doing here?"

"I thought to visit you, Missus."

Shit, I thought, now what?

"It's late but . . ." said the actress, "it's nice of you to come. I was having trouble sleeping."

"Would you like perhaps better bed?"

"Something. What I'd really like is to get out of here." She laughed nervously for a moment, then purred. "You're a very attractive man, Latif. Did anyone ever tell you how much you look like Omar Sharif in *Lawrence of Arabia?*"

There was a moment of silence. I held my breath, glancing over at One-Eye, who, sitting there with his assault rifle in his lap, appeared not to be paying attention to any of this. Then I heard a thumping noise as if someone was getting down on his knees.

"You are so beautiful," said Latif. "Ever since I see you in *Casino Nights*, I am in love with you. Arab women do not understand me. I am a gentle man. I do not wish to be violent person. As great artist, you must see this." What was this? We all know about the power of Hollywood, but this was beyond. Put him in front of his first movie star and even a terrorist goes gaga. "Will you tie me up?" he asked

"What?" Suddenly there was an anxious edge to her voice.

"Yes, yes. Tie me up. Now!"

"Whoa, big boy, not so fast. Maybe after we get to know each other better."

"Not later. Now. We do now." He sounded insistent.

"How about after you let us out? We could go someplace together. Just the two of us."

"I do not want to go someplace. I want you to tie me up here."

"I thought we were having a nice conversation."

"What for? We do sex game. Now!"

"Sex games are a kind of intimate—"

"You must do them now!" said Latif. He was getting angry.

"I think you've got me mixed up with Tiffany Woods, the other girl from *Casino Nights*. She's into bondage. I—"

"You are slut," said Latif, "movie star slut!" his voice rising. "You must tie me up immediately!"

"I told you. It's prema . . . hey, get back! What're you doing? If you want a dominatrix, log on the Internet!"

"What do you know about what I want?" shouted Latif. "What do you . . . ?"

But by this time, Donna was fleeing the alcove followed by the Arab, who looked furious and humiliated and was clutching a Russian Tokarev semiautomatic. She headed straight for the door when Latif trained the Tokarev on her back. "Stop! You go nowhere!" he said. I could hear the pistol cock.

Donna froze. "Oh fuck!" she said, turning to where I was now sitting up on my cot opposite One-eye who was holding his Kalashnikov in my face. "I blew it."

I nodded my concurrence as, without saying another word, the actress turned around and walked back into the alcove, shutting the screen behind her. I slumped back down on the cot again, trying not to look at Latif for fear it might embarrass him and then who knew what would happen. But through slatted eyes I could still see him standing there with his head down before muttering to himself and skulking off into the night.

The following morning Latif acted as if nothing had happened. "I have good news," he said, entering the building with the third man, who was carrying a tray with two slices of bread and cups of coffee just as Donna walked out of the alcove, looking, understandably, as if she hadn't slept all night. "The Sheik say we make too many demand. Only two demand necessary. Demand one—stop production of so-called Holocaust movie. Demand two—end all anti-Arab racist movie in Hollywood."

"Who *is* this Sheik?" I said.

The smile disappeared instantly from Latif's face. "He is great spiritual leader."

"I'm sure he is," I said, knowing that was an honorific applied to many, even to bin Laden himself, though I doubted it in this case. "But I think your Sheik should know this movie is not about the Holocaust. It takes place a half century later. It's about racial and national reconciliation. Healing."

I don't know why I felt compelled to explain Ellen and Peter's story to him, perhaps it was some unconscious sympathy for Farnsworth, whom I had last seen slamming into a concrete bridge abutment, or perhaps it was some dim hope its morality might permeate his sclerotic fundamentalist brain, but Latif's reaction was only too predictable. "This so-called Holocaust did not happen."

"Ho-kay," I said. "So what do you want us to do?"

"Provide guarantee movie not continue when Missus Gold free." He smiled politely at Donna and I realized that was the first time he had really looked at her.

"And how will we do that?" I asked.

"Sheik decide."

"When?"

"Soon, I am hoping."

"And will he also explain how we prevent Hollywood from making anti-Arab movies?"

Latif frowned. This one seemed more complicated. "I will discuss. Meanwhile I wish you pleasant morning." He gave Donna another polite smile but this time I could see the anger from the previous night seeping out. Before he turned to go he said some other words in Arabic to One-Eye, who was just waking up. The heavier man grabbed his Kalashnikov, rolled off his cot and got two pairs of handcuffs out of a drawer. Latif watched as he secured them to our wrists and then left.

It wasn't until almost two hours later that we began to hear the helicopters. Donna and I were sitting across from each other on stools, each handcuffed to opposite ends of a small iron radiator that was connected by rusted hinges to the back wall. It looked as if it hadn't worked for a decade. One-Eye remained perched on his cot, his assault rifle now seeming like an extra arm growing out of his torso.

"Is that for us?" said Donna in a low hopeful whisper that prompted our guard to stare at us suspiciously, then get up and go to the window. I crossed my fingers but in a couple of seconds the sound started decreasing again as the chopper headed off in another direction. Maybe not, I thought. But in about thirty minutes it was back. And now it sounded as if there were two of them, flying almost directly overhead, their propellers yammering so loudly the walls shook.

Latif ran inside. "You have signaled them!" he said, confronting me directly. I threw up my one available hand in ignorance. "Why did you do this? Open your pockets!" He started to pat me down frantically, finding nothing. "Or was it her?" He wheeled around and stared murderously at Donna.

"We didn't need to signal anyone," I said. "You kidnapped us in front of about a hundred people."

"And now she will die in front of no one." He continued to glare at the actress, who for the moment had completely lost her previous night's bravura and looked as if she was about to throw up from fear. "We must leave immediately!" barked Latif. He disconnected us from the radiator but kept Donna and me chained together, giving us no choice but to follow him and One-Eye out of the building and into the van. But this time they got in back with us, their partner shutting the door and jumping into the driver's compartment. Within seconds the motor started and we were off, roaring along the mountain roads again even faster than before, skidding back and forth and coming I could only imagine how close to flying over a hairpin turn. Inside Donna and I bounced against the walls, inextricably bound like a bizarre opposite sex/same ethnicity version of Tony Curtis and Sidney Poitier in *The Defiant Ones*.

"I am sorry for inconvenience, missus," said Latif with overdone sarcasm, when Donna took a particularly hard jolt on the back of her head. Then he smiled as the helicopters seemed to disappear again, their whirring sound now distant as if heard through a baffle. "There are tunnels here," he said triumphantly. "They cannot see us."

Somehow we emerged from these tunnels without being detected. Were we in some dense forest, I wondered, hiding us from overhead view? I couldn't recall the exact topology of Moravia, if that's where we were, but I remembered green patches on the map. Or perhaps we were in Slovakia. But then we would have had to stop for passport control, assuming they had it, assuming there wasn't an open border between the two countries, which once formed Czechoslovakia. Or were we going north toward Germany, home of those terrorist cells in Hamburg I had watched being profiled ad nauseam on CNN, their storefront mosques virtual petri dishes for paranoia? But wherever we were, our most immediate danger was asphyxiation from the black tobacco cigarettes One-Eye had been chain-smoking incessantly since we left.

"Can't you get him to stop?" Donna asked Latif. "You should tell him about the dangers of second-hand smoke."

He didn't answer. Donna smiled again at the Arab, who looked away in embarrassment. A short while later we pulled over. "For prayer," he said. They locked us in the van and went outside for a few moments, returning without comment and then continuing on. Occasionally I thought I could hear the whir of the helicopters, but it was far off. We kept driving for hours. Sometimes, although I couldn't be sure, we seemed to be going in circles. It must have been growing dark, but I had been unable to see outside except for the brief prayer stop.

Suddenly the van came to an abrupt halt and started backing up. Latif's cell phone rang and he started jabbering away in Arabic, knocking on the panel of the driver's compartment as he spoke. I shared a look with Donna. Something must be going wrong. Was there a roadblock? We started to hear the helicopters again. The van kept backing up. Then it did a one-eighty and made a sharp turn onto what was obviously a dirt road, pitching forward into a gully, bottoming out on some rocks and then coming up again with a sharp screech. Its frame started rattling uncontrollably and for a moment I thought the axle had broken, but it calmed down and we continued along the dirt road for about a half hour before we slowed again and came to an easy stop. Latif nodded, satisfied. "We get out here," he said. "Spend night."

It was twilight and we were in a small clearing in a thick wood. Through the close-standing evergreen trees, all I could see were a brook and a single granite boulder surrounded by pine needles. Our captors spread their blankets and prayed in a direction I now took to be southeast, toward the Persian Gulf thousands of miles away, their assault rifles held close. They also each had pistols strapped to their sides, the Tokarev and others I couldn't recognize. It would have been fruitless to try to attack them.

Later, we all sat on the cold dirt in the middle of the clearing, eating stale bread. It was freezing. Donna's teeth were chattering, despite the fact they had found an old tarpaulin in the van to wrap around her. Latif had done it himself, dropping the tarp quickly around her shoulders and jumping away quickly so they wouldn't have to touch. Now he was staring at me, rubbing his hands together anxiously as if he were washing them, but they appeared perfectly clean.

"Why CIA come here?" he asked me. "Sheik wants to know."

"I'm not in the CIA," I said. "I'm just a private eye hired by the movie company."

"What is that?" said the Arab, his suspicion suddenly doubling.

"A private dick. You know, Humphrey Bogart," said Donna.

Latif didn't lose his frown. "Why would a movie company want such a thing?"

"To protect me, sweetheart," she said. "Among other things."

She smiled at him and he blushed and looked down. I took a breath, glancing at Donna before speaking. If there was a moment, I knew this was it. "Aren't you going to build her a fire?" I asked him.

Latif raised his head to Donna whose smile had now opened into something almost Dietrich-like and lascivious I never imagined would be in her emotional vocabulary, even if it was an imperfect version at best. At least she was trying. "I'm sorry about last night," she said. "I guess I was nervous." She stretched out her legs while running her hands down the side of her tightly fitting jeans. I could hear Latif breathing shallowly. He peeked over at his buddies. One-Eye was leaning against a tree, smoking. Our driver had gone back into the cab and was studying a map in the car light. "Please light us a fire," she continued. "I would like to play some games with you. But only if I am warm and can relax." She tousled his hair.

Latif looked at me, but I averted his eyes, pretending to be arranging some pebbles on the ground. But even with my head down, I could see him struggling, vacillating between suspicion, anger and desire, and then back again, to that most insidious of emotions, and one with which I was not entirely unfamiliar, although undoubtedly in a less virulent form, self-hatred engendered by extreme lust. It was hard to believe that this strategy could work, but in a short while Latif got up and began to collect kindling. Soon we had a small fire, visible, I hoped, to the helicopters or their governing satellites, those able to detect hidden sources of heat.

Latif stood there for a while, staring down at Donna and wrestling with his conscience. When he lost—it didn't take all that long—he lay down on the ground next to her, on the opposite side from me. I closed my eyes and pretended to sleep. Latif didn't do anything but lie there and moon at Donna. Through my slatted lids I could see her tensing, fighting to stay in character. It would be a long night of waiting and Latif, if previous experience were any indication, would make it interminable for her.

"If you don't sleep, my sweetheart, I won't let you worship me," I heard her whisper to him. "You want to be my slave, don't you?" Latif bolted up. The shame was too much for him. Had she gone too far again? He reached into his pocket and for a moment, I was certain he was going to shoot her or slit her throat, but like some kinky Samson, or maybe that was the essence of Samson anyway, he relented and shrank down on the ground again. Donna, again surprising me, did not flinch. Perhaps she was a better actress than I gave her credit for. Or maybe dead-on, gut-wrenching fear made us all more than we were. "Sleep," she said, "my pet." And Latif closed his eyes to sleep. Or at least he tried to. And so we had more time for the fire to burn, to be found.

It happened at about three in the morning. I hadn't slept at all and, having never heard a helicopter or a vehicle of any sort, land or air, I suddenly sensed a stirring near the granite boulder. Some figures were moving about, wearing camouflage outfits and helmets with what must have been night-vision scopes on them that made them look like futuristic coal miners. With that apparatus no doubt they could see quite clearly our driver asleep thirty or so feet away from us and One-Eye sitting watch against the same tree, fighting to keep his eyes open, hand clutching his Kalashnikov as if it were a baby bottle. Latif was asleep with his mouth open at the instep of Donna's foot. Although her eyes were closed, the actress was wide-awake. Of that I was certain.

The soldiers drew closer. One-Eye didn't seem to notice; the driver didn't seem to hear. They edged yet nearer in shoes that were uncannily silent, almost as if they floated. Were these some new invention in the art of asymmetrical war? Computerized drones capable of assassinating enemy leaders? Or were they just arctic Air Nikes? I held my breath until they reached the perimeter of our campsite when Latif suddenly sat up. He must have sensed the Special Ops or whoever they were like I did and he stared at Donna and me as if we were responsible for their arrival, which we were. Then he looked back at the soldiers and then at us, his expression a mixture of surprise and horror. "Allah akbar," he declared, sitting up to full extension and reaching down to a bulge in his pocket I knew was no longer an erection.

"No!" I shouted, yanked on my handcuffs and jumped, flying and rolling backward about fifty feet and pulling Donna with me. She later told me she thought I had dislocated her shoulder. At that moment all I could register was the grenade exploding as Latif blew himself to martyrdom, smiling, I imagined, at the vision of a hundred leather-clad virgins with whips waiting for him or whatever other confused version of Paradise filled his climactic moment.

5

"THEY DEBRIEFED YOU?" I was looking down at Farnsworth who, for a guy with a left leg in traction and an entire right side in a cast from hip to shoulder, was sounding remarkably peppy. Maybe it was the drugs. After a short stint under U.S. Army supervision in Germany, I was back in Prague, in its most modern hospital, which was, it now seemed quite natural to me, in a suburban neighborhood once occupied by the homes of high party officials.

"Only a few hours," I said. "In some military base outside of Stuttgart, one of those places where they import the lawns intact from Newport, Rhode Island. It would have been longer, but we didn't have much to say. I never learned Latif's full name, if even *that* was real, or who the buddies were he was kind enough to take with him on his mission to God."

"Whom were they working for? Oh, yes, the Sheik, you said. Everyone's a Sheik. I'd like to be a Sheik."

"Who wouldn't? In any case, they got what they could. Then they swore us to secrecy before letting us go, which pissed Donna off because she was just dying to tell the details of the episode to her publicist, or most of them anyway. She thought it would be an amazing scoop for *Variety*, the real one. Turn her career around. "Actress Kidnapped from Location by Terrorists! Special Ops Drawn Away from Bin Laden Hunt!""

"That *would* make her hot for ten minutes," said Farnsworth. The thought of it started to make him laugh, but he stopped, in agony, reaching for his IV Demerol. "This accident is making me an addict."

"Enjoy it for now. . . . Anyway they promised to let her know when she can talk about it. Maybe it'll be just in time for the opening of the movie."

"If there *is* a movie," he said. "Speaking of which, have you considered my offer?"

"You can't be serious about that."

"I am. Absolutely. I've been giving it a lot of thought."

"Not that much thought. I've only been gone for three days. And half of that time at least you were probably in surgery. . . . And, in any case, I don't think I really want to do it."

"Of course you want to do it!" he said, straining to sit up and then, again, realizing he was making a mistake. "Everyone wants to do it. Didn't you see that cartoon drawing about ten years ago? It was on every T-shirt in Los Angeles, the one with the CAA agent sitting behind his desk interviewing a dog client with a cigar and the dog says 'What I really want is to direct.' Tell me you don't want to direct."

"Actually I've never even thought of it."

"What difference does that make, assuming I believe you? Frankly, I can't imagine anyone who comes to that table at the Farmer's Market even for a day never thinking about it at one time or another."

"Well, anyway, I'm not qualified. I've never done it before."

"Neither had I."

"This was your *first time?* I thought you ran a television series. Something about a goat."

"I was the writer/producer. I never directed. In TV the director's just a factotum, not like film where people think of him as the crown prince . . . or did . . . even that's changing. But no matter."

"You had me fooled," I said.

"That's the point. Anyway, it's no big deal. All you need is some actors and a screenplay. You don't even have to know any-thing about photography. The cinematographer does that. And then there's the editor. This *auteur* nonsense was just a bunch of self-serving propaganda made up by some unemployed French film critics. Look," he continued, holding himself up higher. I was afraid he was going to rip his leg out of its stirrup. "You've got to do it. You don't want this movie to fall by the wayside, do you? That's just what the terrorists wanted, whoever they were and whoever they were working for. We'd be giving in to them. And right now, under these circumstances, you're the only one Donna will trust."

"There must be somebody else."

"Who? We've already called LA and the only people avail-able are a bunch of warmed-over hacks who've directed a couple of episodes of *That Seventies Show*. What do they know from the Holocaust? At least, you've had some life experience. That's more important than anything."

"What about your wife?"

"That's not possible."

"What do you mean? She knows the script better than I ever will and she's obviously very smart and savvy about moviemaking."

"Can't be done."

I stared at Farnsworth who was looking away and biting his lower lip. "What's this about, Peter?"

He held his breath a moment before answering. "Do you really want to know?"

"I think I have to."

"Yes, I suppose you will in the end." But he still seemed reluctant to answer. "What if I told you I was having an affair?" he finally said, swallowing the words and pronouncing them so quickly I almost couldn't hear him.

I shrugged. It wouldn't have been the first time a good-looking guy played around on a homely woman.

"It's not what you think," said Farnsworth, as if reading my mind. "I've always been in love with my wife. But once we started working on this project, she just shut me out. I'm not sure why. Maybe because deep down she thought I was stealing something from her. And in a way maybe I am . . . her story, her screenplay, her people. . . . Anyway there was nothing between us for over a year."

"So who's the lucky lady?"

"Cindy Lemon."

"The script supervisor?" He was referring to a stocky woman from Brooklyn with dirty blond hair and a pug nose. She was nice enough and highly professional but she would scarcely have been my first pick for object of desire in a movie company, which included several Czech women who were model material as well as the seemingly globally coveted Donna.

"I know what you're thinking," said Peter. "She's no better-looking than Ellen. I guess that's my thing. In any case, if El directs this movie, she'll be working with Cindy and, if I know my wife, eventually she'll figure out what's going on. Any hope of our reconciling will be crushed forever. I was always praying that once the film was finished . . . if it came out and did well . . . things would be better with us." He exhaled and looked at me. "I'm sorry to burden you with this. It's not your business. . . . But the film has to go on. And you're the man to do it." He grabbed my arm. "So what do you say? You seem too gifted to be a detective your whole life . . . or *just* a detective, I should say. You're a person of many talents, a natural-born hyphenate. And the hippest hyphenate of them all, I might add. We've heard about writer-director, actor-director, producer-director. But detective-director? Who could top that? So just do it. I'll be here. I'm not going anywhere." He gestured to his IV and his traction device. "Anytime you have a question, just come and ask. Or phone me. It'll be a collaboration of sorts, you on location, me in my hospital bed. . . . But on the set, *you're* the director. There can only be one. After all, I couldn't even be there if I wanted to be. And on top of everything, you'll be guaranteeing a secure production. We can all relax!"

And with that he collapsed back onto the bed, exhausted.

Actually this had all been a charade. The moment I had heard the offer, through Eva, I had wanted to do it. And it was more than normal, ego-driven behavior. I had the weirdest sense that it was my destiny to do it. It was my salvation from career boredom and midlife ennui. I could see everything before me—the cameras, the set, the actors. Even the script, which before had seemed a tad dull, if not mediocre, now seemed, if not a masterpiece, at least of work of substance and importance, a message that the world absolutely must have. And I was the man to be sure that it got it. . . . And beyond that, I knew that for many in my generation being a serious movie director was among the most highly coveted of all professions, even with all of Farnsworth's reservations.

So the first thing I did was check with Arthur to see if this was for real, knowing that the completion bondsman could nix such a change in a moment and withdraw the insurance policy from the film. And, technically speaking, I was still under his employ. But Farnsworth had already conferred with him and gotten his approval as he had from the two producers, one of whom, Volksbruner, had already gone back to his own country the moment there was the first whiff of trouble, and this was more than a mere whiff, and the second of whom barely spoke any English anyway, even *with* the aide of a translator.

After that I spoke with Donna and found, unsurprisingly since she was the star, that of course she had instigated the decision. She had called in advance from Germany to warn everybody that if somebody with security experience weren't installed at the helm of the film, namely me as director, she would quit and go home. She felt too vulnerable and would be too freaked out by her recent experience to work otherwise. No wonder everyone was so enthusiastic. When I pointed out the obvious to her, that I was unqualified, she laughed and said that was the last thing she was worried about. She, personally, didn't need a director. She had taken an acting class from David Mamet for that very reason. Apparently the playwright prided himself on making his students "director proof" because so many movies these days were helmed by clueless film school brats who knew less about dramatic art than a goldfish. I didn't know whether to be reassured or insulted by this but Donna certainly didn't seem concerned.

The only one who preserved the slightest bit of sanity about the whole thing and therefore thought it was nuts was my wife Samantha. She hadn't heard from me and was going out of her mind when she finally found out, thirty-six hours late, about my disappearance. She was about to get on a plane, when I called from the air base in Germany as soon as they would let me to tell her that I was all right. She was so happy she didn't complain when I said I was headed immediately back to Prague because I was worried about the fate of the movie. I called her again that night on my return from my hotel room at the Forum, which had miraculously been raised to a Castle-view suite on the same floor as Donna's. I didn't realize until the next day that these larger digs were not a reward for my heroism under fire but a reflection of my new elevated status as director.

"I know it's flattering and everything," she said after I had explained the substance of my discussion with Farnsworth. "But do you *really* want to do this?"

"I'm thinking about it," I said, playing it almost but not quite as modest as I had at the hospital. "It's worth a try. But I wouldn't be giving up being a detective or anything. In fact, Arthur says it's the best way for the production to be secure, with me on the set as director."

"Uhuh," said Samantha in that way she did when I made a pronouncement she thought was particularly loony. "Are you sure you didn't hit your head against a rock or anything?"

"Don't be silly. And don't worry about me making a fool of myself. The movie will direct itself. Even Farnsworth says so.

And as for that little terror cell, it's probably all gone. And their higher-ups, whoever they are, will move on to fresh targets more important than one little art film. I'm just making everybody feel better. And you'll be here soon to stop me from getting a fat head."

"If you say so," she said.

"I say so."

But what I didn't tell Samantha then was what I discovered under my pillow, stretching out on my king-sized bed that night while I was bidding her good-bye over the phone with a kiss. It was a plastic snake.

6

ONE OF THE MORE salient aspects of film directing, at least during the middle phase of what I later learned was a three-part process (pre-production, production, post-production), is that you have no time to agonize over anything, even terrorist threats. A bomb could be going off, the stock market crashing, your kid being arrested for felonious assault and your ex-wife suing for twenty years of back alimony with punitive damages, and all simultaneously, but your job was to get the movie finished.

So I put any thoughts of snakes on the back burner the following morning at six-thirty when I climbed aboard the picture van, taking my place in the front passenger seat where Farnsworth had sat. Behind me were Jiri, the director of photography; Alfons, the camera operator; Ivan, the location manager; Cindy Lemon, the script supervisor, in whom I now took more than a passing interest; another Brooklynite—they had just come off the same movie—Scott Fabricant, the sound mixer; Arthur, who had no reason to be there other than his usual state of extreme anxiety, in this case probably centered on my ability to handle my new job; and, of course, Eva, our irrepressible first A.D.

"Good morning, *sir*," she said.

"Good morning," I replied, easily repressing my natural neo-sixties impulse to disassociate myself from the class system by disavowing the "sir." Actually I kind of liked it. "Good morning, everyone," I added, turning to the rear and waving. They all waved back, looking at me with weak smiles that were obviously masking massive apprehension.

"Have you got your shot list?" said Eva, as we pulled out.

Shot list? What was that? I didn't have one, of course, but I had read the scene we were doing five times—it was only two and a quarter pages long—and assumed that was enough. I was wrong, apparently. "It's in my head," I said. "I'll write it down for you later." Eva did not look especially reassured. I had a quick flashback, appropriately enough, to one of my favorite old flicks, the Marx Brothers' *A Day at the Races*, in which fake doctors Groucho, Harpo and Chico are called upon to perform an operation but keep washing their hands over and over to avoid causing irreparable damage to their patients or, worse, their own exposure.

"We will discuss these shots," said Jiri, putting a kind hand on my shoulder. "It is your first day."

"Thanks," I said, nodding to him gratefully. I turned around, not saying anything else for the rest of the ride for fear of making a mistake.

The day's location was the National Museum, a grandiose nineteenth-century affair at the top of Wenceslas Square, that hub of modern Prague famously overrun by Soviet tanks in 1968. Now the whole upper part was being overrun by our film crew, nearly a dozen trucks ringing the museum with black cables running everywhere. I was supposed to be the general leading these troops to victory and I didn't know a fucking thing. Jiri, the cinematographer too seemed worried. "Is very big," he said, gesturing to the cavernous main room where we now stood. A giant travertine stairway in front of us led up to an expansive balcony filled with baroque statuary surrounded by murals of angels on clouds. "I do not know where put lights. Where you want to play scene?"

I resisted the temptation to say wherever you want and backed up a few steps to survey the area. This was to be one of the key love scenes of the movie. Goran has left Donna here to tour while going about some business at a literary magazine he edits. By the time he returns, he has decided to marry her and proposes to her right here at the museum. "Why don't we do it there?" I said, pointing to a remote part of the balcony. "That way we can see Goran coming from a distance, watching her romantically, while Donna stares at one of the statues. Also he'll be walking across this." I nodded to the ornate floor. "American audiences love inlaid marble. It makes them think they're in Europe." I don't know where that last notion came from, but it seemed to please Jiri, who probably didn't have much of an idea what Americans liked anyway.

Then I remembered my other job. "Eva!" I called out.

"Yes, sir." The A.D. came running over.

"Make sure Ms. Gold is all right. We're supposed to have two armed guards around the makeup truck and two on her trailer. Make sure they're there too. And make sure she's always accompanied by one of the pairs when she walks between the two or to the set."

"Yes, sir," she repeated and started relaying my orders in Czech over her walkie-talkie.

"Wait a minute," I said. "Do it in person. Those things are never secure. From here on in, use cell phones. The only people listening in on them are on our side."

"Yes, sir," she said and headed off at a brisk pace.

Jiri looked at me impressed. "You make decisions quickly," he said. "You should have no trouble being director."

I was beginning to like this guy.

But within minutes we had a problem. "I am sorry, Mr. Wine," said Ivan, who had hurried over when he heard about my choice. "But we do not have permission to shoot on the balcony. Mr. Schlick did no pay for it."

"What does Schlick have to do with it?"

The location manager stared at me, momentarily surprised I actually didn't know. "Mr. Schlick arranges everything on the Czech side. The foreign producers give him money, what you call a flat fee, and he, as you say in your country, takes it from there."

"Don't the producers tell him what they want?"

Ivan shook his head. "They do not know how things work here. They do not know what people are paid or what they really do. That is why Mr. Schlick has a good business."

"So no balcony, huh?"

The location manager smiled. "I will see what I can do." He took out his cell phone and started dialing. I glanced over at Jiri who was watching all this and signaled for me to follow him a few feet away.

"Don't worry," he said, nodding toward Ivan who was now smiling at me and giving the thumbs-up while talking on the phone. "He already had it. He just wanted you to be in his debt. . . . Remember, Moses . . . may I call you Moses? . . . When you are here, you are on bridge between West and Byzantium . . . Russia. People think differently. . . . By the way, I imagine you want to do closeups first in love scene, while actors are still fresh." He did everything but wink at me.

"Absolutely," I said and walked over to Eva, who had returned from makeup. "Get the first team," I said, using the term Farnsworth employed for the lead actors, the "second team" being stand-ins for the mind-numbing procedure of setting lights. Possibly because it was my first day, the two stars responded quickly and in a short while we were up on the balcony rehearsing, but I was having trouble concentrating. My old professional instincts had taken over and I kept scanning the opposite side of the balcony for snipers instead of watching the performers in their intimate embrace. Not that it mattered. Right in the middle of Goran saying, in his gravelly voice, an oddly seductive mix of Bob Dylan and Charles Boyer, "Please do not go back to America, my darlink. I vant to spend ze rest of my life mit you," Donna broke off and exclaimed, "I can't take it!" running off down a corridor behind the statue of Aphrodite I had chosen, perhaps too obviously, as the background for the scene. I had no choice but to follow.

"I can't play a love scene with him!" she said, when I caught up with her at the cul-de-sac. "He hasn't taken a bath in weeks. He's got cooties in his hair and his breath smells like a backed-up garbage disposal!"

"Europeans," I said. "They're not as into hygiene as we are."

"I know it sounds sick, but I preferred Latif."

"It does sound sick."

"Yes, but at least he bathed. And he was always swallowing peppermints."

Then I took a flyer. "Why don't you just pretend it's him?"

"He's a terrorist!"

"So use it. It'll give the scene some . . . ," I searched for the right actory phrase, ". . . emotional verisimilitude. It's the kind of thing . . . Meryl Streep would do. Utilize her life experience like that."

Donna frowned, thinking. "She would. You're right." I made a note, from here on in, to write down everything I heard over the earphones.

"Why don't you give it a try? Meanwhile, I'll make sure Goran takes some of these." I pulled a pack of Certs out of my pocket and put my arm around the actress, escorting her back to the set before she could object and musing how detective-director might *not* be such an usual hyphenate, after all. Deceiving the people you were working with was the stock-in-trade of both professions.

I told Farnsworth as much when he called me on the set from his hospital bed immediately after we shot the first scene. "I knew we made the right choice," he said. "So how'd it go?"

"Okay, I suppose. Except I got a little embarrassed when the script supervisor . . . your friend Cindy . . . said I was . . . what do you call it . . . 'crossing the line'? My camera angles would con-fuse the audience and make them think the actors weren't even in the same room. Anyway, she corrected it."

"I told her to look out for you. . . . But don't worry about that 'line' stuff," said Farnsworth. "Godard didn't know a thing about it when he made *Breathless*, and he was anointed a genius because they thought all his mistakes were on purpose. . . . I've got something actually important to tell you, but hold on a minute." I waited while Farnsworth said a few words to a nurse about changing his bedpan before he came back and asked, "Are we on a secure line?" and then answered for himself "Of course not. The only secure lines in the world belong to George Bush and George Lucas. Anyway some CIA suit named Cornwall showed up in my room about an hour ago. He was filled with questions about you, wanted to know if you were impersonating a CIA agent. I said no, you were impersonating a director. Just kidding." He must have been honking that Demerol again. "So *were* you impersonating a CIA agent?"

"Only for a short time. So Latif and his crew would take me along with Donna."

"I guess in the current climate they're taking it kind of seriously. He kept asking why we're letting someone like you direct a movie, so I said you actually knew a lot about it and that in fact you were a good friend of Academy Award nominee Harry Chemerinski." I wasn't sure it was a good idea to bring Harry into this, but I let it pass. "It's against the law, isn't it? Impersonating a CIA agent."

"Probably," I said, wondering how they knew.

"I haven't told anybody else. Not even Arthur. But I sure hope they don't shut us down. That would be a shame."

"It would," I said, but I didn't have any more time to talk. Eva was signaling me for the next setup.

⬞

WE HAD DAILIES—the showing of the previous day's raw footage—at the Filmovy Club that night at eight-thirty, a half hour after wrapping. Most of the crew department heads were there, but blessedly, not the actors. As director, I sat in the front row next to the editor, a big-boned woman named Linda Fisk whom I had never met before. "Get used to me," she said. "We'll be seeing a lot of each other," and waited with a yellow pad for me to say which takes I favored. They came from several days back now, just before the camera truck was hijacked, when Farnsworth was on two feet and running the show. Still, I made my selections, basing them on a mix of his original choices recorded by the script supervisor when the shots were made, my instincts, whatever they were, and Linda's advice. I wasn't a fool; as editor, I weighted hers most heavily. She had made a lot of movies before and Farnsworth and I had made a grand total of none. Even so, she had the grace not to parade her superior knowledge and even tried to make me think some of her ideas were my own. I had to smile. I used the same strategy in my own work to co-opt egotistical lawyers.

The program of dailies was short, but it ended dramatically with a wild image of the camera truck careening down the street. It was the kidnapping itself on film, recorded accidentally and erratically as the camera, jolted out of position, spun around on its axis. You could see Goran and Donna with terror in their eyes, Farnsworth himself, in dread, making his way to the cab and then, for a split second, a hooded figure visible standing by the bridge, seemingly dressed top and bottom in a heavy white down suit, signaling to the truck with what looked like semaphore paddles. "Who's that?" I said, loud enough for Jiri, who was sitting three rows behind with his operator, to hear me.

"The abominable snowman?" said the cinematographer.

"Looks like the Michelin man." That was Arthur, trying to be clever. By then the film had run out and we were sitting there with the lights on, a group of locals already clustered at the back, waiting to use the room for a screening.

"Better give that last clip to the police," I said to Linda. "But make me a video copy first."

"I already did," she said.

She was another good one, I could tell immediately, like Jiri. I remembered once at the Farmer's Market, Chemerinski was going on about how the majority of people working on a movie wanted the director to succeed but there were always a surprising number who secretly or not so secretly wanted him to fail for reasons ranging from low pay to plain, old-fashioned jealousy. The trick was to sort out who was on which side before they could do serious damage to the production, or worse in this case.

I didn't pay much attention at the time, as I didn't with much of Harry's palaver, but now I was grateful for it. I tried to think of some other tips he might have had as I sat there in my suite that night, finishing my shot list for the next day. But I couldn't think of a bloody thing. I was having enough trouble staying awake. Farnsworth may have thought directing was not such a big deal, but it was about as exhausting as anything I had ever done, bone-wearying work that was a lot more taxing physically than intellectually with hours spent on your feet, worse than tailing errant spouses or reviewing endless tape from a hidden video camera in a child abuse case. And this had only been my first day. And on top of it, I had my other job, that little life-or-death matter. I had been doing my reading for that as well, slipping in bits of *The Protocols of the Elders of Zion* between setups. A production assistant had downloaded a copy, which I told him was research for the movie, and I had made my way through the first half-dozen of the twenty-four sections plus an introduction. The latter informed me that the book, once virtually unknown in the Muslim world, had in recent years become a regular Middle Eastern best-seller, right up there with *Mein Kampf* and a sprightly number called *The Matzohs of Zion* that details how Arab children are habitually ground up by Jews to make their unleavened bread. But I didn't know how any of this connected with the rabbi's screenplay, which I still hadn't read, or any of the untoward events of the last few days. I was also troubled by why the screenplay was in the rabbi's hands when he died. Was he such a devoted artist he wanted to clutch his work to the end? Not even as an incipient director/*auteur* could I believe anything as sentimental as that. More likely it had been placed in his hands to deliver someone a message or to implicate someone. And the word "Kaprova" . . . was it written in Rabbi Herzog's own hand or by somebody else? If that too was a setup, to use a term that now had a dual meaning for me, for whom was it intended? Someone I didn't know, perhaps, or even, as unlikely as it seemed, for that supposed intimate of the late Mohammed Atta, not to mention various anonymous agents of the Iraqi intelligence, *moi!* I had no immediate way of knowing. And certainly now, near collapse and barely able to keep my eyes open, it was unlikely that I could figure it out. I was about to give up altogether, leave my shot list dangerously short (I would tell Eva I intended to be an "economical" director and not waste film like so many of those notorious Hollywood profligates) and go to bed, when there was a knock on my door.

"Hello . . . are you awake?" It was Donna. I opened the door to find her standing there in the kind of silk robe I associated with old movie stars like Deanna Durbin, always imagining them to be apricot although they were filmed in black and white. The color of this one was something close to that and it was cinched tightly around her waist, revealing her body in a way that made you want to wrap your arms around it. "Do you mind if I come in?" she said. "Ever since we got back, I've barely been able to sleep. And the few times I do, I keep having nightmares that they're coming to get me all over again and I wake up in seconds. And that guy doesn't help much." She nodded to her room right down the hall where the bodyguard in front of her door was slumped on a camp chair, snoring away.

"Sorry about that," I said, backing away and letting her into my suite. "We'll get somebody more responsible tomorrow. Would you like a cognac?" She nodded and I went to the minibar.

"I'm scared, Moses. There were four of them weren't there, at that warehouse. But only three died."

"That's right," I said. She was repeating something we had already both reported to the U.S. authorities in Germany. There was no reason, I thought while handing her the cognac, to trouble her with the new information about that possible fifth accomplice, the "Michelin Man" in the white down suit.

"I don't know what to do," she said. "I called home—my shrink says I should come back, it's too dangerous and anyway what do I need to be in a movie directed by a private eye for? But my agent and Nick say I should stay and finish. Except I don't count Nick because I know why that slime bucket doesn't want me home." She grimaced and knocked down the cognac in one gulp.

"Another?"

She shook her head. "I don't want to show up in makeup with a hangover. I've got a five A.M. call." She put the glass on the coffee table and began to pace around the living room, starting to work herself up all over again. "But how am I going to sleep? I can't go back in there by myself. I'll just have another horrible dream and . . . you mind if I stay here on your couch?"

"Of course not. But why don't you use my bed? *I'll* take the convertible."

"You sure?"

"Absolutely," I said, opening the bedroom door for her. "They changed the sheets this morning."

"Thanks, Moses. You're a really nice guy—you know it? And I think you're going to be a good director. Maybe better than Farnsworth."

"I wouldn't bet on it. I've only done it for one day. . . . Get some rest." I shut the door behind her.

Indeed my second day wasn't as easy. It began simply with a few pickup shots of Donna I missed the previous afternoon. Then she went off garnet shopping with Harriet Whelan and two security guards, promising to stay on the main streets, while I worked with Goran and some local day players on another scene. His character had just been elevated to Minister of Culture of the Czech Republic and the point was to show the bohemian writer was discontented in his new official role, relegated to making decisions about visiting choral groups and the like. But as soon as we started to rehearse, it all seemed rather dull to me. It wasn't Goran's fault—he never read a line badly—or even the fault of the day players who, although they could never be mistaken for Laurence Olivier, were decent enough. And it *certainly* wasn't the directing. So it must have been the script. I told Farnsworth as much when I called from the set on my cell.

"Don't change a word," he said emphatically from his hospital room. "That's not your job. It's supposed to be boring. He's *bored* with being Minister of Culture." He said all this before I even had a chance to state my case, as if Cindy had called ahead to warn him. That would have been a first—the girlfriend protecting the wife's screenplay.

"But does it have to *be* boring to show boring?"

"It has to be what it has to be. You're a detective. What do you know about it?" he said, predictably changing his tune the minute I criticized his work.

Just then Fule and Pisek, the two Prague homicide dicks, entered the room, stationing themselves in the back and staring at me with their hats in their hands.

"Maybe we should shake the scene up a little. Bring something into it."

"Like what?" said Farnsworth. Now he was sounding hostile.

"I don't know. Maybe Goran gets arrested or something."

"Arrested? For what? What does that have to do with the story?"

"Look, someone's here now. I'll talk to you later. And don't worry about it," I added, "I won't change anything without your permission," although, from what I knew of directors, that was stone-cold bullshit.

I hung up and walked over to the cops. "Gentlemen, I take it you're here to see me, unless you're fans of the cinema. But if that's the case, there are probably better places you could be."

"Excuse me, Mr. Wine," said Fule, the short one. "But I hope you would not mind but to accompany us to police headquarters."

"Excuse me, sir, but that's not possible. As you can see, I'm directing a movie here."

"We just have some questions to ask you."

"What about?"

"About your role in the death of Rabbi Herzog."

"What role?" I looked back at the crew, several of whom were staring at us. "I don't have any role in that."

"According to Mr. Chaim Edelbaum and Mr. Yehudah Finkelstein of the Belzer Hasidic sect, you were rushing down the stairs of the rabbi's office building a short time after he was murdered. You even tried to cover your face in order not to be recognized."

"Then how do they know it was me?"

"They have seen you on your website. There are many pictures there."

My website? I barely remembered I had it. Like so many others, a few years go I had been told it was absolutely necessary for my business and it had ended up being a useless money pit. Last time I looked it had thirty-eight hits. Now, it seemed, there were thirty-nine.

"Do you mind if we speak privately for a moment?" I said. The detectives nodded and I led them into the next room, which was being used by the sound crew and was empty at the time. "Look, I'll go down to your station if you want but I can tell you everything right here on the record. You obviously know who I am, that I'm a private investigator and, yes, it's true I went to see Rabbi Herzog the day he was murdered." Fule nodded to Pisek who took out a tape recorder, switching it on. "Of course I had nothing to do with his death," I continued. "I was there to interview him in the guise of a *Variety* reporter to try to understand why he suddenly denied permission to this movie to shoot a scene at the old Jewish Cemetery. I didn't call the police because I didn't want my cover to be revealed and I assumed you would find the body in a short while anyway. Now, through an unusual set of circumstances you are more or less familiar with, I have become the director of the film. This leaves you with several choices. You can arrest me for leaving the scene of a crime. You can have me deported back to America. Or you can allow me to stay here and do my job."

"Why should we be interested in that?" asked Fule who looked as enthusiastic for this last proposal as for an all-expense-paid vacation in Mogadishu.

"Because it seems a terrorist cell has infiltrated the cast or crew of *Prague Autumn* and it would be your best way to find out about it." I had no idea if this was true, but I imagined it would get their attention. And the minutest change of their expression told me I was right. "In fact," I went on, "if you arrest me, you will only alert them, so why take the chance for little old me, who means nothing in this case. . . . *And* you already know I'm willing to cooperate. My editor sent you rough footage of the kidnapping without your asking. Of course, I'll stay in contact with you on a daily basis. I'm only asking to be treated as well as your normal undercover operative in an average suburban mosque." At this point the two homicide cops began conversing in Czech, obviously trying to decide how to handle my offer. Like any good poker player, I knew it was time to up the ante. "Oh, and I'll need a photocopy of the rabbi's screenplay, the one about the *Protocols of Zion*. . . . And I'll hook you up for an interview with Wolf Blitzer when the case is solved!" That last angle got them. Everybody in the former Warsaw Pact loved being on CNN.

That night the screenplay was hand-delivered to me at my

hotel room by a uniformed officer of the Prague force who made me sign for it in triplicate on smudgy carbon paper that looked as if it were left over from the days of the NKVD. It was no time to wallow in my glorious manipulation of the Czech police, however, or their manipulation of me, which was as likely the case, because my suite was already occupied by people dealing with a weightier matter—the closing down of the film altogether. I had my first inkling of that further calamity after Fule and Pisek departed. I returned to the set to find Jaroslav Schlick and Anna Rockova standing by the camera with Arthur. The Czech producers and the completion bondsman all had grim faces and at first I thought they were about to fire me, but they had bigger game—they were about to fire everybody. Well, not fire them exactly but put the film on ice until some problems with the financing got sorted out.

"It is not such big problem, Moses," said Schlick, putting his arm around my shoulder in a Godfatherly way. "When the great Yugoslavian director Kusturica made his masterpiece *Underground* here in Prague, he had to stop production seven times to go back to Paris and get money. And that film won the Palme d'Or."

"You expect me to go to Paris and raise money to make a movie? What's going on here? I thought this film was financed."

I looked at Arthur who seemed even more sheepish than usual. "It is," he said. "I mean was. The money just never arrived."

"Whose money?"

"Volksbruner. He was supposed to send four hundred thousand this week."

"What happened?"

"We can't get hold of him. His Berlin number doesn't answer and the fax machine is always busy."

"Does Farnsworth know about this?"

There was a moment of uneasy silence before Anna stepped in. "We did not want to disturb his convalescence."

"Well, I'm going to disturb it," I said, taking a few steps away, dialing my cell phone and explaining the situation to Peter.

"That lying swine Volksbruner! How could I have trusted that fuck?" he blurted out in response, his voice nearly carrying across the room to where everyone else, including the actors, was now watching and listening. "I put him in my house! I loaned him my Beemer! I—"

"Cool down," I whispered. "Keep your eye on the prize."

"The guy's such a freak," he continued, equally vehemently but this time at a volume that was for my ears only. "He looks like Rumplestiltskin with his belly sticking out of those used designer suits. You know when he was born? Nineteen forty-two. Right in the middle of the big show. He claims he never met his father but Ellen thinks he was one of those *lebensborn*, you know . . . those experimental babies Hitler bred for their pure Aryan blood."

"And he came out looking like Rumplestiltskin?"

"So what? They made mistakes, plenty of them. And it explains his twisted personality. . . . The whole thing's just weird. Some German claiming he wants to finance a movie about reconciliation from the Holocaust and then sandbagging us on the money at the last minute."

It *was* weird, I had to admit. "So what do you think we should do?"

There was a moment's silence. Then I thought I heard him conferring with his wife, who must have been in the room with him, before responding. "Find out from Schlick how much we need to keep going."

I turned to the producer and asked him. After consulting briefly with Anna, he said, "Seventy-five thousand U.S. dollars to continue until Friday, including the catering."

"He's overcharging for the catering," said Farnsworth before I could relay it to him. "But tell him I'm paying it personally today."

"You're what?" I said. "Are you crazy?" I didn't know a lot

about filmmaking but I certainly had picked up that most hoary and immutable law of Hollywood: *Thou shalt not under any circumstances invest in thine own movies.* But Farnsworth was completely ignoring it.

"Yeah, sure I'm crazy," he said. "But we didn't come this far for nothing. What're we going to do? Send everybody home? I can't even get out of bed here for two weeks. Tell Schlick to call me with his wire transfer numbers. And start shooting." And with that he hung up.

"Okay, next setup!" I said to Eva after I had, still bewildered, passed on his message to the Czech producer.

"Weren't you going to make some changes to the script, sir?" she said.

"Not anymore. This boy is paying for the movie himself. He deserves to get it his way."

Actually, he was only paying for a small part of it, such a small part that I knew we would need another cash infusion in a matter of days. Someone was going to have to find Volksbruner. And then there was Takashima. He seemed to have vanished into thin air as well, although, according to Arthur, most of his money wasn't due until post-production. Still, even I knew that the prudent thing to do was to cut the budget and that is why I called the meeting that night in my suite of Eva, Jiri, Arthur, Cindy—who I assumed would be reporting to Peter—and Linda, the editor with her young assistant Danny. I asked for advice.

"You must cut pages, sir," said Eva with a shrug. "It always happens."

I looked over at Linda, who concurred. "The script is a hundred and eighteen. You could lose twenty and have enough for a full-length film."

"That's *so* brilliant," gushed Danny.

"It would save a week at most," said Arthur, unimpressed. "Two hundred thousand dollars. We need to cut more like three million." Where was all this money going, I wondered. I hadn't read any fancy special effects—plane crashes, flying wizards or alien invasions—in the script. There wasn't even a car chase, although perhaps there should have been. "But it's worth doing anyway," continued the bondsman, now addressing me directly. "I suggest you try. Meanwhile, I'll see if I can dig up a foreign sales deal for us." My blank expression made Arthur laugh for the first time since I had arrived. "I forget. You don't know what that is," he said. Then he explained that foreign sales companies were outfits that pre-sold countries—"territories"—to distributors before a film was completed and gave those advances to the movie company to finish their work. The problem was the commissions and charges on these transactions were so great that by the time the money filtered down to the production they were lucky to get 50 percent of the cash. Nevertheless, the trick for the producers was to *pre-sell* as few territories as possible to make their film so they could *sell* the finished version to the rest of the world later for enough to recoup their initial investment or even, miracle of miracles, make a profit.

"How often does *that* happen?" I asked Arthur.

"Don't ask," said the completion bondsman, checking his watch. "Nobody wants to know. Otherwise no independent movies would be made. . . . Well, good night, everyone." He stood. "It's almost eight on the East Coast and I have to call my mother. . . . Good luck with your cutting," he said to me before exiting. There was no point in trying to stop him. Arthur's mother was the most important woman in his life by far. I remembered a couple of years back he had agonized so painfully about putting her in a retirement home in New Jersey that he had almost ended up in the home himself, sharing the room with her. In fact there were *no* other women in Arthur's life, though I'd heard occasional stories of college affairs. Arthur was more like those movie business people whose life became so overwhelmed by the silver screen, especially the deal-making part, there was little time or emotion for anything else, even those romantic relationships endlessly portrayed by the medium for which they lived.

I sent everybody home after Arthur left and sat down to edit Peter and Ellen's script, but I started to feel guilty about doing it without them and turned to Rabbi Herzog's screenplay instead. But my eyes were already starting to close by page twelve. If I had any doubts about *Prague Autumn*, it was *Citizen Kane* by comparison to this self-involved drivel. So far the entire story consisted of an aging Deadhead sitting in a Mongolian-style yurt somewhere in New Mexico cataloging the collected banjo compositions of Jerry Garcia while commenting about the various takes in voice-over and then discussing his preferences over a joint with his ex-wife. This segued into a rehashing of their marriage, which had evidently not been a good one. They had been divorced for ten years though still living in adjoining yurts, raising an extended family of dysfunctional kids and eating in the same communal kitchen presided over by an angry Mexican with the name of Ensenada.

By now I was on page thirty-seven and I still had no idea what this all had to do with *The Protocols of the Elders of Zion— The Motion Picture*. In fact, I was beginning to doubt if that was really the title of the rabbi's movie. Perhaps it had been added on by another hand. Or the screenplay had been added to *his* title. Whichever way, the title page was typed in a face that was different from the script, indeed looked as if it had been printed separately on a laser printer, while the screenplay itself was originally outputted by one of those old daisy wheel jobs with the irritating paper rolls that repeatedly tore while you were breaking them apart. Even in photocopy, the pages appeared to be browning and I wondered if it had been written back in the eighties when those kinds of printers were in use or—if daisy wheels were still prevalent in Eastern Europe, which wasn't unlikely—it was a pastiche of some Czech's addled vision of America or a tale from somebody's even more addled youth.

Whatever it was, it "wasn't a movie," as they would say at the Farmer's Market. Of course they said that about films that had been nominated for Academy Awards. In this case they would have been right.

The next morning on the set I asked Jiri about the rabbi's script. We were standing by the catering truck, making our way through a pair of those behemoth-sized "Breakfast Burritos," filled with eggs, cheese, chilies, refried beans, leftover stew and everything else under the sun, the Czechs had learned to make from visiting American film crews. "Don't tell my wife I am eating these," said the cinematographer. "Her brother is a cardiologist. Actually, the same one as Rabbi Herzog."

"Your friend had a heart problem?"

"No, no, no. Is my English . . . I mean the same clinic. Shmuel was, what do you call, a vegetarian. He loved the works of Isaac Singer and copied his diet from the great author, including the blintzes. If only he could write as well. At least it was good for his heart. Not that it mattered." A deep sadness suddenly overcame the cinematographer, who stood there with the burrito in his hand, staring blankly through the window at our location for that morning, The Globe Bookstore, a bookshop and café created a decade back by young expats come to bask in the reflected glory of the Velvet Revolution. Now it was something of a local institution offering Starbuck's-like takeout coffee and free Internet connections. "Anyway," Jiri continued, "he did not write that movie about New Mexico. I can promise you that. The only script he has written is about a sixteenth-century rabbi in Minsk who has a crisis of conscience while leading the Passover Seder and becomes an atheist. He had been working on it for ten years."

Another commercial winner, I was about to say, but I bit my tongue. "Was it called *The Protocols of the Elders of Zion—The Motion Picture?*"

The DP looked at me strangely. "You are kidding, of course.

This is some kind of American Jewish humor. . . . It was called *The Fifth Question*."

"After the 'Four Questions' they ask on Passover?"

The cinematographer nodded, then frowned, groping for the English. "Why . . . on this night . . . do normally intelligent people believe this primitive bullshit?"

"Doesn't sound very sixteenth century to me."

Jiri laughed. "He used the old slang. . . . That was Shmuel's mission in life—to make people see that religion was dangerous folklore."

"But he was a rabbi."

The cinematographer laughed again, this time with a certain ruefulness. "It was a job. Here in Prague we do not give them up easily. And now it is our turn to do *our* job." He gestured to the set where Eva was signaling to us. "It pays even better than being a clergyman."

I wasn't so sure about that. So far I was still being paid my detective's salary, although I saw on the budget the director was supposed to make twenty-five thousand dollars a week. But given the state of the film's finances, I wasn't holding my breath.

Inside the coffeehouse/bookstore, the assistant director was in the process of placing the extras for the morning's scene—a poetry reading. Already I was worried. Who in the movie's audience was going to sit for that? "Let's cut the poem," I said to Eva. "We'll just shoot Goran and Donna in the crowd applauding and leave it at that." I would explain this to Farnsworth later. Time was money, after all.

"Excuse me, but did I hear correctly that you are cutting the poetry reading?" I turned to see a man standing before me with a sheaf of paper in his hand. It was Mr. Earring. "Do you realize I've been rehearsing this for three days?"

I glanced at Eva. "Didn't he already play a reporter? You can't be both a reporter and poet in the same movie."

"Why not?" said Earring. "Such things happen in life."

Just then one of the wardrobe assistants came up, holding out an orange jacket. "For the tour group at the concentration group. Or do you think red is better?"

"Orange is fine," I said, noticing a man sitting at a table in the corner. He was in suit and tie and was obviously not one of the extras for the poetry, whose attire ran to denim and turtlenecks "Who's that?"

"His name is Cornwall," said Eva. "From the U.S. Embassy, I think. He said he had something to talk to you about and I told him to wait until after the first setup."

"He's not from the Embassy, but I'll see him now. Tell Jiri what I decided about the reading and call me when the lights are ready." I started for the man when I felt a hand on my shoulder. It was Earring.

"So you're definitely not going to use my poem," he said. "I wrote it specially for the occasion. To give your scene a genuine power rarely attempted in these ersatz Hollywood productions."

"Look, there already *is* a poem in the script, which I'm cutting, and this is scarcely a typical Hollywood production. But I'm sorry about it anyway. Why don't you . . . give your work to the A.D. and I'll take a look at it later?" I gestured to Eva, who rolled her eyes at the ridiculousness of it all. "Just stick it in my bag," I said to her with a wink, feeling like I must now really be a director because I was turning into a perfect shit. Then I walked over to Cornwall, who stood to shake my hand.

"How do you do, Mr. Wine? Fred Cornwall from the—"

"I know. From the 'Embassy.' Why don't we talk somewhere private, Mr. Cornwall?" He nodded and I ushered him out the side door and into my teardrop trailer, which was parked just outside. "Sit down, please," I said, pointing to the tiny banquette shoehorned in behind the minute kitchen. Cornwall, who was about six-three, proceeded to wedge himself in with difficulty. "Sorry about the cramped quarters, but my star has the only

Winnebago in Prague. . . . What can I do for you? I understand you already spoke with Peter Farnsworth. You apparently had some concerns about my qualifications for the task I'm now performing. Let me reassure you—so do I."

Cornwall didn't smile, but nodded politely and looked at me thoughtfully, trying, I assumed, to size up how much I could be trusted.

"Let me reassure you about something else," I said. "There was a period in my life I thought you guys were my sworn enemy, even a pernicious evil. But those days are gone. So whatever you want to tell me, you can assume I'm on your side." As long as it doesn't compromise the film in any way, I found myself thinking. But there was no point in explaining that.

Cornwall studied me for another few seconds, before he spoke. "How many days do you have left?"

"Quite a few. Why?"

"We've received a report. We think there may be another threat to your production."

"What do you mean?"

"A shipment of C-4 explosives coming in via Turkey."

"How do you know it's meant for us?"

"I'm not at liberty to say."

"Then where did this report come from?"

"It's a new source. It has to stay confidential."

"Can you tell me if you believe it's credible?"

"We're looking into it."

"Well, then . . . do you think we should stop shooting the movie?"

"That's not for me to say. This is only an advisory. We were going to deliver it to the producers personally, but we've been having difficulty locating them."

"You too?"

There was a knock on the door.

"Who is it?" I said.

"It's me," said Arthur, letting himself in but stopping at the door. "Am I interrupting something?"

"I was just leaving," said Cornwall. "I don't believe I have anything else I can tell you at this point, Mr. Wine. Let me know what you decide. Oh, and regarding your visit to Westwood, it really *was* a computer error." He left his card on the table before shutting the door behind him.

The completion bondsman squinted at me. "Where's *he* from? The CIA?"

"You guessed it."

Arthur couldn't suppress a grin. "It was all over the set."

He sat down at the table and I told him what little there was to tell.

"I don't think we have to worry *that* much," said Arthur. "After all, he said it was a new source."

"Right . . . but maybe we shouldn't shoot out at the concentration camp. It's such a target."

"God, my mother will be heartbroken."

"She cares *that* much?"

"She was an inmate at Terezin."

I looked at the bondsman, who suddenly seemed deeply upset, on the edge of tears. "You never told me that."

"She met my father there. When she was fifteen. They were separated when he was sent to Auschwitz and barely survived the gas chambers. But they met again by accident after the war and had me only a year later." I stared in unabashed surprise at Arthur, who I hadn't realized was a child of the Holocaust. "But anyway," he continued, "it's the heart of your movie. You have to shoot there."

My movie? I still thought of it as Peter and Ellen's. "Here's a possibility," I said. "We're supposed to shoot at the camp next week, but I'll see if I can get it quietly switched to tomorrow. We can change the schedule on *all* the locations that might be targets. That should confuse whoever's out there . . . assuming it's not an inside job," I added, the obvious only then occurring to me.

But it didn't seem to concern Arthur. "Brilliant solution, Holmes," he said, his mood brightening considerably.

So did mine that evening when we were watching my dailies. To my amazement, the crew agreed they were quite decent, equal to some well-known directors they had worked with. "Quit brown-nosing," I said. "I'm not even *in* this business." But they insisted the performances were good and that Donna, particularly, and especially in that crucial proposal scene, had never been better and that I should get the kudos for that. Though I was still not quite convinced their vociferous praise was entirely candid, and I had no idea at that point just how misleading dailies could be, they sent me home with a smile on my face, a broad one.

Unfortunately, it was wiped off completely a few minutes after I got back to the hotel. A woman was waiting in the living room of my suite with her winter coat on and she didn't look happy. It was my wife.

"I came to surprise you," said Samantha, "but I guess someone beat me to it." She was staring coolly through the open bathroom door where a half-dozen pieces of the most chic and sheerest super-expensive women's lingerie—La Perla, I believe it was—were hanging from the plastic clothesline over the tub. That selfish bitch of an actress, I thought. She got so much per diem and she couldn't even bother to use the hotel laundry.

7

I CAN NEVER BE SURE, but I think it was that night Samantha got pregnant. Counting backward, the numbers checked out. But we didn't get to that for a while, of course. First there were some long, tense, silent and extremely frosty moments and, even though I was supposedly an experienced detective with trained deductive powers, it was a good half hour before the clouds cleared and I figured out that I was being had—that she and Donna had rigged the whole thing, stringing up the lingerie and messing up the sheets in the bedroom while leaving empty champagne bottles and glasses strewn around the headboard. (It was the heavy magenta lipstick smudges on the glasses that did it. They were over-the-top and caused me to break into a relieved grin and ultimately to receive a fervent embrace.) Apparently Donna actually *had* been there in my room when Samantha arrived, but Sam never even gave a moment's consideration to the notion that I had been doing the wild thing, or any *thing* for that matter, with the actress, that was how much my wife trusted me, even though Donna had been sleeping in my bed for a couple of days now.

But as we lay there in what was supposed to be post-coital bliss, an altogether different matter appeared to be troubling Samantha.

"I understand you've got a new career," she said.

"No, no. That's ridiculous."

"I wouldn't say that. I hear you're very good."

"Who told you that?" I asked rhetorically, knowing full well.

Who else was she talking to in the few hours she was in Prague?

She didn't even bother to answer the question herself. "Dichter was really happy with our work on the Harrison job," she said instead. "That's why I got out early."

"*Your* work. I didn't do any of it."

"I know. But you were there for the first week. Anyway, he's thinking of putting us on a retainer. That might not mean a lot to you right now . . . considering what you're so consumed with at the moment . . . but in the present economy . . ."

"It's okay, Sam. I'm not going to be a director," I said, touching her arm and trying to sound more convinced than I felt. "I couldn't even if I wanted to be. And I don't."

"You're sure about that? Because I don't want to feel down the line like I thwarted your ambitions or anything."

"The only ambition I have is to be an investigator with you. And I've already realized that."

"Well, that's good because I did some research on the plane." She started to sit up and reach for her briefcase.

"Later," I said, "please . . ." I was suddenly almost totally overwhelmed with fatigue. It was past 3 A.M. and I had been going full tilt for over twenty-one hours. I said good night and, not even bothering to suppress a yawn—I wouldn't have been able to anyway—flicked out the light and rolled over on my stomach. I fell dead asleep within thirty seconds. Unfortunately I was awakened all over again in exactly two hours and forty-three minutes. It was Farnsworth.

"I knew you'd be up," he said. "You have to be on the set in forty-five minutes. I understand you had a visit from Mr. Cornwall yesterday."

"News travels fast."

"He came to see me first. I told him you were the director now and had to make any decisions about shutting down the production. You didn't, did you?"

"No."

"Good. Because I finally got the e-mail reply from Milan St. Clair. I heard he was in Europe making the rounds, so I wrote him and, as luck would have it, it just so happens he's been in Prague for a while, meeting with the people from the Karlovy Vary Festival, I imagine, or some such. Anyway it doesn't matter. He'll be in our cutting room tonight!"

"Milan St. Clair?"

"Oh, silly me. You sound like such an old pro already I forget you don't know. . . . He's the head of the Sundance Selection Committee. . . . What a break, huh?"

"I suppose. Why do we need him?"

"To get in this year's festival, of course. It's by far the best way to find a distributor."

"But isn't Sundance in January? That's only ten weeks from now."

"We can make it. We finish shooting by early December. We have a cut by Christmas. It's not impossible. Lots of movies-of-the-week do it." He sounded like a man talking himself into something. "Anyway, it'd be a crime to miss this opportunity. I'll tell Linda to throw a couple of scenes together for St. Clair and you can put your, um, 'directorial stamp' on them when you get there from location, if you make it in time that is. You're shooting at that abandoned warehouse, right?"

"No, we're at Terezin."

"What? That's next week."

"We changed it. For security."

"Oh." His manic vocal pace suddenly slowed several RPM. "I hope I didn't screw things up by talking over the phone."

"Not even terrorists get up this early," I said, adding a quick good-bye and rolling my eyes for Samantha, who was already out of bed, heading for the shower.

TEREZIN WAS ABOUT an hour outside Prague along a road dotted with farms and small factory compounds. I had broken the protocol and Samantha and I were sitting together in the back seat of the van behind Jiri, Eva, Arthur, Ivan—the location manager—and Jana—our translator—who still looked as glum as when she had just broken up with her boyfriend.

"What was that research you wanted to tell me about?" I asked her as we drove north from the city.

"I was comparing your future locations with a map of Prague," said Samantha. I was about to ask her why when I caught that look she gets when she doesn't think it's advisable to discuss something in public. So I was on my own to retrace her process and figure out what she was thinking. But my wife was far more intuitive than I was and probably a better analyst too. Only two years out of Brown, she had gone straight from standard FBI training into the National Domestic Preparedness Office, giving her a lot more experience in this area than you could get in a lifetime as a private dick in LA. But I didn't let that bother me. I had long ago learned that the wise man knows to follow the lead of an intelligent woman. Only in this case, when I realized what she had in mind, the proximity of our locations to major civic monuments in Prague, many of them related, directly or indirectly to government agencies, foreign and domestic, I didn't like it.

"I hope you're wrong," I said.

"Me too."

It was starting to snow, the first of the year, as we pulled up giving the concentration camp an eerie foreboding quality that I knew would be good for filming, but I was filled with more than enough foreboding of my own. I already understood one thing about directing and that was that every shooting day would begin with a catastrophe. And it looked as if this was not going to be an exception. Several production assistants with extremely anxious expressions had immediately surrounded our van, gesticulating and shouting over each other in Czech. Jana pulled our door open and started to translate but Eva, not surprisingly, beat her to it. "Goran is in the hospital!" she said.

"Holy shit! Who did it?"

There was some quick back and forth in Czech. "No one," Eva continued. "He did it to himself. Drank too much schnapps in makeup this morning. Now he is in . . ." She didn't know the English word.

"Cardiac unit," said Jana.

In a way I was relieved. At least it wasn't terrorism.

"Now what're we going to do?" said Arthur, as we climbed out of the van into the snow flurries. "We've lost our leading man."

"Better not tell Farnsworth. There go his dreams of Sundance." And eight million dollars of Arthur's money, I didn't have to tell him, if the actor didn't get better soon. "Maybe we can shoot here another day."

But the words were scarcely out of my mouth when Ivan shook his head sternly while waving his finger. "Not possible. I spend all afternoon yesterday begging three bureaucrats at city hall to make the change. Even Schlick called himself for once, using the name of his old friend the Prime Minister's cousin. We cannot do this twice."

I stood there with snow falling on my balding head, trying to think of some way out of this. I was feeling bad, especially for Farnsworth, who had informed me when we had gone over the script together that first day in the hospital that this scene was the most important part of the movie to him, its emotional heart and the reason he and Ellen had wanted to make it. It began a few years before when Peter was invited to a television writer's conference in the Czech Republic. "I knew it would be boring," he said, "and it was. But I was depressed—the network had just canceled *Herman* without giving anybody warning, not even the goat—and it was a chance to see Prague. So Ellen and I ditched the panel discussions and ended up, among other things, on a tour bus to the Terezin Concentration Camp. Our guide was a seventy-five-year-old man who at twenty had been an inmate at the camp. He was a carpenter then and was forced to build a gallows to execute suspicious Jews. He was also required to participate in a game the Nazis set up, throwing naked inmates into an empty swimming pool and forcing them to club each other to death while the wives of the SS looked on from a balcony, like ancient Romans at a gladiatorial. But this man refused to fight his fellows and was trampled and beaten for his goodness, his bones broken and his chest nearly smashed in. Yet there he was, over fifty years later, leading tour groups to the very swimming pool where he had almost died, exuding compassion and expressing forgiveness. Ellen was very moved by this and she decided to write a movie about it for me to direct, something that I had always wanted to do. This man became the inspiration for Goran's father . . . and for the central scene of the movie when Goran takes Donna to see the camp."

Which now would not happen, I thought, peering out across the lawn by the former SS headquarters where the infamous pool was barely visible in the increasing snowfall. No Goran, no scene. I was about to give up and go home when Samantha came up beside me, sticking the hat on my damp head I left behind in my haste to get off the bus.

"Who's that?" she said, pointing to a long-haired, scraggly dude who was waiting his turn to take a piss in the honey wagon.

"What's his name, the Czech hair guy?" I recognized him from the makeup truck.

"Zdenek," said Eva.

"Zdenek," I repeated.

"Well he looks like Goran. Why don't you use him?"

"He's twenty years younger and about forty pounds lighter."

"So put some gray in his hair. And pad his stomach. Shoot him from faraway on a wide-angle lens and have him turn his back a lot. No one will ever know. Then you can do some head shots of the real Goran when he's feeling better, or if he doesn't, put his voice over it."

I turned to Jiri for his advice but he was already looking at Samantha, impressed. "She's pretty clever," said the cameraman.

And so thirty minutes later we were set up by the swimming pool, shooting the scene, first with Donna down at the bottom, moodily walking along the cracked wall with her fingers caressing the concrete the way I had remembered Monica Vitti doing in some old Antonioni movie, and then with the wadded-up Zdenek, stationed as far away as possible on a hill behind the SS headquarters, staring off into the clouds as if communing with the ghosts of his ancestors. I read Goran's dialogue over the shot to time it out as narration. We did it twice, but on the third take, Alfons, the operator, stopped midway, said something in Czech and stepped away from the camera.

"He says there's someone extra in the frame," Jana translated for me. I looked in Zdenek's direction and couldn't see anyone else in the stark landscape. But then I squinted and began to make out the outline of a figure at the crest of the hill. It was standing further back than Zdenek and quite a bit to his left, but still close enough, I imagined, to be encompassed in the extreme wide-angle shot. If it had a head, it seemed larger than normal, tilting to the side and bending forward as if straining for a better view. Was it the hooded man? If it was, he must have been wearing white again, rendering him almost invisible against the swirling flakes.

"Tell him to keep shooting," I said to Eva, who gave me a curious look as I gestured to the operator "We'll use it," I added with a smile. Then I backed up slowly, mingling for a moment with the sound crew, and then, with a nod to Samantha, disappeared around the side of the former SS headquarters. I scampered up the hill behind the building. When I got to the top I was out of breath, but I didn't have time to rest because standing not more than thirty feet in front of me was the man himself. He had a black kerchief partly obscuring his face and he wore cross-country skis with poles, but other than that his entire body was clothed in a white down suit and hood whose bulbous, tire-like filling indeed made him look like the Michelin Man.

We stared at each other—his dark, brown eyes peering out above the kerchief—for about ten seconds before he spoke. "You come here for a story that never happened," he said slowly and deliberately with a thick accent. I couldn't tell where it was from or even if it was real. "Abandon your film or face disaster," he added. Then he turned around and started to ski away.

"Wait," I said, and began to run after him, but he was obviously a practiced skier and far too fast on snow for anyone on foot. Within seconds, he had vanished down a gully that led straight out of the camp into an open forest. I stood there wondering what he was there for, why he had come to taunt us, or if he was merely watching, but one thing had become clear. There had to have been a leak from the inside, one of the government ministries involved with location permits or, more likely it now seemed evident to me, someone from our own cast or crew.

But I decided not to make a big deal of it and returned to the set via Zdenek, who never said anything to me about the skier as I gave him some directorial instructions made up, I assumed, as so many of them were anyway, on the spur of the moment to make people think I was doing my job. In this case, though, my motive was more to distract attention from our mysterious visitor than to impress others with my artistry. It seemed to work, because everyone was anxious to get going, if only just to stay warm. Nobody had any questions about where I was except for Arthur, who came up and, in a nervous whisper, asked what was going on. I told him it was nothing and that we had to hurry up and shoot before we lost the light. Frankly, I was too busy asking myself questions. I had no idea whether the guy was truly gone or whether he was hiding out behind some rock at the other end of the gully, waiting to return and pick us off one by one at point-blank range like Rabbi Herzog or whether he had other means at his disposal, some C-4 perhaps, to blow the makeup truck and all its inhabitants to the far side of Bratislava. Not until we were on the way back did I say a word about our visitor, and that only to Samantha and then only obliquely because we were not alone in the van.

They dropped us at the Filmovy Club where Linda had set up a cutting room on the third floor. And to my surprise, I thought we were arriving early enough that I actually *could* put my "directorial touch," whatever that was, on the edited footage before the arrival of the Sundance guy. But that was not to be. When we entered the room, Farnsworth himself was already there. The cast of his shattered leg propped gingerly on a chair and his shirt bulging from heavily taped ribs, he was sitting across from the computer editing monitor with a pair of crutches across his lap, watching Linda, who was about to replay the scenes she had just cut. Ellen was there too, standing just behind him. She didn't seem particularly happy. "I told him he was crazy," she said, "but he unhooked the traction himself when the nurse was out and insisted if I didn't bring him over here, he'd never hook it up again."

"Hey, I promised you—I'll be fine. Don't worry," Farnsworth said. Then he turned to me. "And you don't worry either. I'm not going to change a thing." He gestured to the computer editor.

"No, no, no. It's okay. It's your movie." What did I care? I hadn't edited the scenes anyway, not that I could.

"Well, if you say so," he said and signaled to Linda to let her rip, but just then the phone rang.

Danny, Linda's assistant, picked up. "St. Clair's here," he informed us. "He's downstairs."

"Shit, he's early!" said Farnsworth, twisting around toward the elevator in such a sudden way I was afraid he was going to injure himself again. "Should we let him up?" He checked his watch. "Fuck, what're we going to do?"

Milan St. Clair—pronounced Sinclair, like the oil company—proved to be one of those ubiquitous show business Brits who turn up everywhere from the receptionist at a porno company to the head of HBO. This one was in his early thirties and wore a "distressed" leather jacket that probably came from one of the more expensive stores in Aspen.

"Sorry I'm premature," he said when he entered. "But I'm on a schedule and I did want to squeeze you in. I quite enjoyed your television series. What was it? Something about a pig?" He was staring directly at Farnsworth.

"A goat."

"Right . . . fire away," he said to Linda.

She clicked her mouse and the cut movie appeared on the monitor. I don't know what I expected, something from earlier in the schedule probably that Farnsworth had directed himself, but it was the very proposal scene, my first day, with Donna and Goran mooning at each other in a way that had seemed cornball to me at the time but here was tarted up with jazzy cross-fades and schmaltzy temp music that sounded like the theme from *Dr. Zhivago*. I was trying to read St. Clair's reaction when his cell phone rang.

"Excuse me," he said, jumping up and going off into the next room to take the call. "My apologies again," he said when he came back. "Family emergency. I have to get the night flight to London."

"Is there anything we can do?" said Ellen.

"No, no, no. An elderly relative. Just need to do a bit of hand-holding." He frowned for a second, started out, then turned back to Farnsworth. "Well done, by the way. I must confess to some trepidation when I heard it was Donna Gold in a Holocaust film, but you've done brilliantly with her. No *Casino Nights* here." He tapped Peter on the arm. "Congratulations—another *auteur* is born. We'll definitely consider your movie if you're kind enough to send it to us."

Farnsworth looked like he'd just won the Nobel Prize. "Oh, we will," he said.

"I'm off then. What happened to your leg?"

"Automobile accident."

"Sorry about that. Look after yourself." And then he disappeared, abjuring the elevator for the more rapid stairs.

Farnsworth made an excited fist as soon as the Brit was out of earshot. "We're going to be in competition!" he said.

⚏

"Cocksucker didn't give me any credit," I later said to Samantha. We were returning to the hotel in the backseat of the Tatra. "He didn't even apologize. All he said was keep up the good work."

"What do you care? I thought you didn't want to be a director."

"Well, he could have at least . . . I don't know . . . acknowledged my contribution."

"Poor bastard's digging himself a hole as big as Hades."

"Because of a little money? I'm sure he can afford it." Actually I wasn't so sure. Only moments after St. Clair's departure and flush with visions of Sundance glory, Farnsworth had picked up the phone to Schlick and told him to expect another wire transfer. Apparently the Czech studio chief was demanding two hundred thousand more to continue for the next week and, with Volksbruner and Takashima still AWOL, it was up to Peter to come up with it. Now he was on the way to financing his own movie big-time.

She didn't say much more, and neither did I, until we were back in the suite looking at a tourist map of Prague. Samantha had put little dots in red ink next to each of our future film locations and arrows pointing at the nearest major sites of the city like the Castle and the neo-Italian Renaissance concert hall called the Rudolfinum. "So you don't think our little movie is enough?" I said.

"It doesn't seem like a sufficient target to merit all this attention. It's not the next installment of *Star Wars* or anything. It doesn't even have distribution. And with all due respect, Donna Gold is not Julia Roberts. I don't see why anyone would really want to kidnap her."

I saw her point. Were we being used as some kind of decoy? That would explain the mysterious appearance of the Michelin Man at Terezin, as if he were trying to remind me of his presence so I would alert someone. But what I didn't understand is why anyone would be interested in a Czech target either. I mean it was a fascinating culture and all and it had played a pivotal role in the downfall of the Soviet Union, but that was years ago. And now that Slovakia had declared its independence, it was just a minor Eastern European country of seven million with no particular enemies except disgruntled tour operators and people who couldn't stand heavy food, definitely not enough to merit a terrorist attack.

"What about this?" said Samantha, pointing with her pen to a location near the top of Wenceslas Square.

"The National Museum?" I said. "We already shot there. You just saw the cut footage an hour ago."

"No, no. Not there. Just beyond, past the opera house." She was indicating a larger building farther down the square. It had a number next to it and I looked it up on the map legend.

"The Czechoslovak Parliament?" Who would be interested in that old communist warhorse?

"Not any more it's not," said Samantha. "Since 1995 it's been the headquarters of Radio Free Europe."

Bingo! Suddenly I was back in Los Angeles at the Federal Building on Wilshire, suite 1700, the last conference room at the end of the corridor, listening to those bizarre questions from Special Agent Fiona Lucas. Have you met Mohammed Atta? When were you last in the Czech Republic? What about the headquarters of Radio Free Europe in Prague?

"How'd their old Parliament become an American broad-casting station?" I asked Samantha, looking down at the spot on the map again with the misleading number. It was cheek by jowl with one of our locations, a warehouse, not so much as an alley between them. Could this be an accident? At the very least I would be reckless to assume so.

"I read it was a gift to our country from the Czech govern-ment, probably to get our help in joining the European Community."

"Very generous of them," I replied, sitting down on the edge of the bed. "I hope it worked." When were we shooting at that warehouse? Thursday. But with our recently jumbled schedule, and since I hadn't chosen the locations myself in the first place, I didn't have any idea what scene it was. And I didn't want to draw anyone's attention with a question. I would have to find it myself on the production manager's revised board and made an excuse to call Eva and have one delivered to my room right away. A photo-copy was slipped under my door within twenty minutes.

"Forty-seven," I said, locating the scene number and com-paring it with the script. " 'Interior—Her Bedroom, Refugee Camp—Evening . . . Small and austere. The two lovers sit anx-iously on the solitary cot, unsure of their separate destinies.' " I looked up at Samantha. "Now that's weird. You would think we'd be shooting that at Barrandov. It's already rented for the entire schedule and there's plenty of room on the sound stage. Whose idea was it to use a warehouse next to Radio Free Europe? It's a waste of money too. Maybe I should change it."

"You're the director," she said.

I chose to exercise my authority by leaving it alone for the moment and, since we had a day off from the production the next day to allow Goran, whose prognosis was good, another twenty-four hours of detox, to pay a visit to our nation's embassy. The last time I had been to one was about fifteen years ago when I was pickpocketed in Rome, an embarrassment, admittedly, to a private detective. They were extremely cordial then, replacing my passport in less than an hour. But this time my encounter was noticeably more frustrating.

Ms. Zlatkova, the receptionist in the former Schoenborn Palace, an ornate baroque edifice of four wings and three courtyards with over a hundred rooms decorated in stucco and damask, designed in its present form in 1715 by the architect for Prince Charles of Lichtenstein and later inhabited, quite briefly, by the ubiquitous Franz Kafka, was not what could be described as welcoming. "We don't have a Mr. Cornwall here," she said, glancing past Samantha and me without even the traditional "I'm sorry" to her next customer in the vast entry lobby guarded by a dozen Marines holding assault weapons with laser sights.

"Yes, you do," I insisted. "Maybe that's not his real name, but that doesn't matter. Here, take my passport and tell him that Mr. Wine is here and would like to talk to him about the schedule. He'll know what I mean, whoever he is."

"And whom shall I tell then?" she asked, not even bothering to raise her eyebrows. She had the same constipated smirk I recognized from the clerks at the Russian émigré shops on LA's Melrose Avenue.

"Tell whoever . . . excuse me, *whom*ever is in charge of answering questions for people who aren't supposed to be here." I dangled my passport in front of her like a piece of thinly sliced squid on the end of a fishing line. "You'll be glad you did," I added and she finally snatched it up, motioning to another receptionist to take over and disappearing through a secure door that opened with a pass card.

Two minutes later she was back with the same sour expression, but better results. "You were looking for Mr. Jasperson, I believe. He's in our Commercial Services Division."

"You're so right. That's what we're here for," I told Ms. Zlatkova as we followed her across one of the courtyards. "Set up an import business, bring sausages to Prague. 'Send an organic

salami to your boy in the High Tech Army.' Think it will fly?"
She didn't laugh.

Jasperson/Cornwall had a spacious paneled office on the
third floor with carved ornamental moldings and an endless view
of terraced gardens with orchards leading up to what looked like
a Renaissance gazebo. Government jobs might not be the high-
est-paying in the world, but you couldn't knock the working con-
ditions. "What's your real name anyway?" I asked after we were
settled in and I had introduced Samantha.

"Does it matter?"

"No, I guess not." I then proceeded to explain to him my
concerns about the warehouse location.

"Whatever you do, don't move it," he said.

I stared at him in puzzlement. "But I just said it's right next
door to the headquarters of Radio Free Europe."

"I understand. And that's the reason we don't want you to
move it."

Now I was really confused. "Why?"

Jasperson/Cornwall looked briefly back and forth between
Samantha and me. "I suppose I can tell you because it's been in
the newspaper. The Czech government is no longer happy about
the presence of Radio Free Europe in downtown Prague. They
want to take back their old parliament building and put our headquarters out in the countryside someplace, where if someone
wanted to bomb it, they would only kill a bunch of cows . . . or
better yet ship the whole operation back to Munich where it
came from. But we can't let them get away with that, can we?
Anymore than you would want to shut down your film because of
a two-bit terror threat or a failed kidnapping." He looked at me
with something approaching a knowing smile. "The stakes have
become too high to give in to fear. The State Department has
already registered a protest. . . . So it should be obvious that any
kowtowing to this attempt on the part of their government, such
as changing a movie location because it might be dangerous or

*en*danger the offices of Radio Free Europe, is, to use the parlance of my profession, counter-indicated."

I didn't know what to say. I saw his point. There I was, Moses Wine, the People's Detective, sleeping with the enemy again.

But I also saw the Czechs' point. Wenceslas Square, where the headquarters sat, was the Times Square of Eastern Europe, filled with cars, pedestrians, theaters, restaurants, department stores, souvenir stands, hamburger joints and clip joints, all the flotsam and jetsam of modern life—a small universe of collateral damage should RFE be attacked. And what a plump target it was—the very epicenter of the War on Terror, beaming its message of democracy and freedom, however sanitized, across the Middle East, Central Asia and the Indian subcontinent.

And, like it or not, it was my ultimate decision whether we would shoot next door, unless I relinquished control of the film to its original director. But Farnsworth had wrenched his leg again that previous night getting into the cab home. He had returned in excruciating pain to his hospital bed to be mercilessly tongue-lashed by his nurse, as Ellen had told us, for having set his convalescence back as much as three months, according to x-rays, in the pursuit of a dubious placement at a film festival. He was lucky, she further said, to have avoided a third operation and was secured more firmly to his bed this time where he was resting in a Demerol-induced stupor, his wife having authorized whatever dose necessary to keep him immobile. I wondered if she knew more about Cindy Lemon than she was letting on.

In any case it would be useless to contact Peter, I thought, as I returned to the hotel by myself to prepare my shot lists for the week, Samantha having joined up with Donna and Ellen for a girl's day off at the Janak Institute. Cynical as my wife appeared to be about them on the surface, she had jumped at the opportunity to try the good doctor's treatments. And besides she would get another chance to chitchat with Donna, who had already told her she got special extra shots from Janak, whatever they were. I would leave that to Samantha to find out. So I sat alone at the desk in my suite. But before I began the lists, I had a nagging need to reassure myself about the warehouse, so I called Eva to ask about the sudden change of locations, why we weren't shooting the love scene at the studio anymore. She didn't know where the order came from and suggested I call Ivan. I tracked down the location manager on his cell phone. He told me it had come from above, from Schlick himself. I dialed the producer at his office in Barrandov. He was gone for the day to his country house, but Anna Rockova took my call.

"Unfortunately, Mr. Wine," she said, "when you started to shuffle the schedule, we lost the location."

"But I thought we had the use of the sound stage for the duration of the production."

"That was before poor Mr. Farnsworth began to finance this movie by himself. Since then we have had to make certain cutbacks. . . . And so, at the last moment, a request came in from an Albanian advertising company to use that stage for a lingerie commercial. They were willing to pay cash."

"Albanians make lingerie commercials?"

"It's a new world, Mr. Wine."

A new world indeed, I thought, and hung up the phone with a vague feeling of dissatisfaction. I had my answer but I didn't. And I didn't know what to do about it, so I tried to shrug it off and concentrate on the shot lists, but the phone rang before I could get to the first setup on day one.

"Hello."

"Can you hear me, sweetie?" It was Samantha, in a whisper.

"Yes. Where are you?"

"The women's steam room. I have to talk fast before someone comes in. You'll never guess who I just saw getting a shiatsu massage—Milan St. Clair. Why do you think he lied about having to leave for London?"

"For Farnsworth's sake, I hope he wasn't lying about Sundance too."

"If you hurry over, I think you can follow him on the way out. He just went in for a facial. Sorry. Gotta go." And she clicked off.

I jumped into a cab and hustled over to the Institute on Kaprova, positioning myself under the arches across the street just about where I had first seen Latif. Sure enough, in about ten minutes, St. Clair emerged. I followed him as he strolled a few blocks and descended into the Metro station at Malostranska, bought a ticket and then headed for the corridor to the A line toward Skalka. I bought one myself and continued after him, getting on the same car as he did and sitting down about five seats away from him on the opposite side. As we pulled out, he appeared to be staring straight at me without a flicker of recognition—he hadn't been paying me the slightest attention in the cutting room anyway, not even dreaming that I could have been, of all things, the real director—and sat there unperturbed for a couple of stops before standing again to change trains at Muzeum for the C line to Haje. This time I sat even closer to him, three seats away in fact as a test of my anonymity, which I passed with flying colors, and, even though the efficient Prague Metro is one of the city's more pleasant legacies of Communism, was starting to feel bored after another twenty minutes riding and was wondering why I had even followed this dude when he stood a final time and get off at Roztyly station.

That Scrabble winner proved to be one of those grimy Eastern European neighborhoods that put you in mind of earnest documentaries on toxic waste. I couldn't imagine what a tony character like St. Clair was doing there when he turned into a four-story apartment building with windows so caked with film they looked like the scrim from a forgotten shadow play in the slums of Djakarta. I waited for a few seconds then went into the small entryway after him. There were eight slots for the apartments listed on the wall by the stair, but only two of them had names in them. And I recognized one of them right away—Jana Staronova, our translator. Was Milan St. Clair the boyfriend who had been causing her such pain?

It didn't take me long to find out as I stood under the second-story stairs, listening to their conversation through paper-thin walls.

"I told you not to come here again," she was saying.

"But I had to. I love you."

I heard a snort and then maybe something being thrown. "If you loved me, you would have taken me with you last year."

"I'll take you this year."

"You are lying and you were lying last night. Besides, I do not want to leave. I am working on a great movie."

"Nonsense. It's terrible. I told you I saw some of it. That love scene in the museum—I've never seen anything so ludicrous. It's totally amateurish junk!" That dirty two-faced motherfucker, I thought. "That Farnsworth can't direct his way out of a paper bag," he continued. "I'm beginning to wonder if he even wrote those TV shows himself. But I'm sure this is all his wife's work, considering the subject matter—those Jews always going on about their shitty little Holocaust as if they were the only people who ever suffered. I bet he doesn't have any idea how many innocent people died in Rwanda in the last decade." That stung. I didn't either. "Now put that down and come here, Jana. You know I love you."

Then there was silence. I had to restrain myself from breaking in and waited for another twenty minutes, which stretched into thirty and then into forty. Obviously, St. Clair was getting what he wanted. At length, some music came on, Eurorock with French lyrics. Then I heard some laughter and what might have been the clinking of classes. Outside it was beginning to get dark. They were clearly in for the night. I gave up and headed back for the Metro, feeling mightily depressed and not knowing which bothered me more, the assault on my directing or the casual anti-

Semitism, hopefully the latter. But in an odd way the sonofabitch had struck home. We *were* obsessed with the Holocaust. And in my case, I wasn't sure why. I was born after it was all over and none of my immediate relatives, at least ones I knew about, had been affected by it. Horrific as it was, and it *was* horrific, I had no direct connection to it, no easy explanation for my fixation other than it was possibly the most despicable series of events that had ever happened. So, I couldn't honestly say I suffered from Survivor Guilt. I suffered from something more like Survivor Guilt Envy.

8

"I THINK MY MOTHER has cancer, but she won't tell me." Arthur was pacing around my suite that night while Samantha and I tried to calm him down with a homemade martini from the minibar. "It's something in her voice. She went in for an MRI last week."

"Why don't you go back and see her?" said Samantha.

"She wouldn't let me. She'd be so upset if I left this movie, even for a day."

I was about to tell him as diplomatically as possible that he could leave for a *year* if he wanted to—he didn't seem to be doing much of any significance, now that I didn't have any time to play hearts—when the phone rang. "What is your purpose for living?" came the voice at the other end. I immediately recognized the peculiar distorted accent of the Michelin Man. Was I listening to a synthesizer? "Do not bother to have this call traced," he continued before I could formulate a response. "I am talking to you on a stolen cell phone which will be thrown into the river at the end of our conversation and, yes, I am standing by the river you know, watching the boatloads of narcissistic tourists sail by in their drunken stupors, oblivious to the world's suffering."

"You sound judgmental, Mr. . . . ?"

"Answer my question. What is your purpose for living?"

"Beats me," I said. "I've been trying to figure that out for a long time myself." I glanced at Samantha and Arthur, who were frozen in place watching me. Sam gestured toward the extension, wondering if she should pick up, but I shook my head at the risk.

"So you have no purpose. You are simply another Western

materialist, going on from day to day, advancing your status and acquiring more goods."

"I wish I were," I said, unable to resist wising off, even to a terrorist.

"And yet you are making a movie about this so-called Holocaust, preaching reconciliation between religious and ethnic groups without the slightest mention of God or any spiritual or philosophical values beyond the most vague bourgeois liberalism, which is scarcely a principle at all. This seems like pointless self-indulgence, wouldn't you agree?"

"Whom am I speaking with? I don't think we've been formally introduced."

"It does not matter. I am one of many. And you have not heeded my warning. You have not stopped the production. If you do not want a disaster in which many people will die, meet me tomorrow night at nine by the steps of the Loreto Church. And come alone. Do not bring your wife, who I see often works with you."

"How do you know that?"

"From your website," he said. "I also learned she is twenty years younger than you are. Perhaps you should consider another visit to the Janak Institute while you are still in Prague, for one of their longevity treatments." And then he hung up.

That website again, I thought. First the Hasidim, now this sheik or whatever he was . . . I promised myself as soon as I got home I was going to deep-six the fucking thing—if only I could figure out how. But that was the least of it. This bastard seemed to know everything I was doing with or without the site. I wondered if he even knew I had been off eavesdropping on Jana and St. Clair and been privy to that humiliating evaluation of my work. I hoped not. But I did know the chances of following one of the key prescriptions Farnsworth gave me on directing—given to him, he said, by Chemerinski himself—which was to get as much rest as possible, even get in bed by ten, was virtually impossible. The next time I was likely to get a good night's rest would be either five years after this movie was finished or when I was blown to smithereens, whichever came first.

"That was him, wasn't it?" said Arthur.

"Just checking in, " I said, trying to make light of it. "Seeing if we made our day . . . Arthur, you really *should* go see your mother," I continued, escorting him to the door. "You don't have to be embarrassed about being a nice Jewish boy. We all are in the end. And her health is more important than any movie. Who knows if we'll even finish this one? Then how would you feel?"

"Why? Why're you saying that? What'd he say?"

"Go to sleep, Arthur."

It was clear by the next morning he wasn't heeding my advice. He was sitting right back in his old place in the van, heading for location. That was the first time I met Horst. He was sitting next to Arthur. "I am Horst," he said. He was a spectral figure, dressed all in black with a long topcoat, starched shirt and jackboots that made him look like an SS officer who had escaped in a time machine to contemporary Prague with everything but his hat and epaulets. "I work for Karl Volksbruner, your producer. He has asked me to come here from Berlin to supervise the budget." He handed me a business card in German and English. It was hard to tell if it had been printed an hour before or a year before. It was hard to tell *who* this guy was.

"Supervise?" I said. "What for? There's nothing to supervise, at least nothing from Volksbruner."

"Not any longer," said Horst, tapping an attaché case that was, not surprisingly, also black. "I have brought per diem for the crew. I understand they have not been paid." He opened the case, which was filled with a number of crisp new euros, though, I guessed, not quite as many as the U.S. dollars in the briefcase chained to the Uzbek at Barrandov. But they were more than enough to impress our gang. They certainly weren't going to ask any questions about his identity, especially Alfons, our camera operator, who eagerly recorded the occasion, as he had several others, with a portable camcorder he kept in his jacket pocket. He even encouraged Horst to reopen the case, asking the German to explains its contents to me all over again, as "insurance" that nothing had gone wrong with the first take just as if this were part of the actual movie.

Alfons also videoed, at my request this time, the three hundred or so geriatric extras filing into the auditorium at the venerable Charles University, which was our location for the day. The scene was a symposium at the international social psychology conference Donna was putatively attending when her romance with Goran began. The oldsters themselves were supposed to be playing delegates to that conference but they looked like the least likely psychologists I had ever seen, more like lonely retired apparatchiks in ill-fitting suits out to scarf double lunches from the catering truck. Someone was cutting corners somewhere. But I still wanted to make sure, if I could, that the Sheik or his minions weren't among them, having abandoned their burnooses for threadbare babushkas or ill-fitting toupees, and were hiding an unpleasant surprise beneath one or the other. So I asked Alfons to record each of them as well, so I could review them later, and added a couple of security guards into the mix, while Ivan set the lights with the gaffer.

As this was going on, Horst came and sat down next to me near the center of the amphitheater. "So . . . Mr. Volksbruner would like to know if you are having any problems."

"What do you mean?"

"I understand there were some . . . how should I call them . . . threats . . . made to this production."

"I thought Volksbruner sent you here to oversee the budget."

"There is no use for a budget without security," he said. "Have you . . . for example . . . been approached in recent moments by parties you might consider to be suspicious?"

"Suspicious might be an understatement."

Just then Donna walked up. "This is awful. I hate it. I look like a stewardess." She was gesticulating in disgust to the navy blue suit she was wearing that was her costume for the day. I could see what she meant, but it didn't look so bad to me and I doubted if anyone in the audience would even begin to notice. "I'm not going to wear it," she continued. "Just don't tell the Armani people. They'll never give me free samples again."

I was about to tell her not to worry when I realized she was no longer paying attention to me. She was suddenly focusing straight on Horst.

"You know *him?*" she said with disdain.

"Yes. This is Horst. He works for Mr. Volksbruner."

"I don't care who he works for. I want him banned from the set. Immediately! I want him off the production!" Donna spat the words like an old-time star in a Bette Davis movie and I almost laughed. But I could see she was serious.

"What's up?" I said, standing and escorting her down the steps to the dais where we could speak confidentially.

"That creep was around the hotel last night. He said he was giving out per diem to the crew."

"Well, he was."

"That's not all he was giving out. Or taking. When he came to Tina's room, he gave her five hundred euros and just stood there. Then he sat down on her couch. He wouldn't leave."

"What'd he want?"

"To get into her pants, dummy. When were *you* born? She threw him out on his ass. What does he think this is? Some kind of on-location prostitution racket?"

I glanced up at Horst who had not moved from his position and was staring down at us implacably. "Don't worry. I'll handle this," I said to Donna, feeling momentarily competent. I had been wondering if he actually worked for Volksbruner or, if he didn't, who he might be. I turned to Eva, who was a few steps away with the sound crew. "Get me Karl Volksbruner's number."

Three minutes later I was standing in the far corner of the

auditorium with a cell phone, ringing Volksbruner in his Berlin office, at least I assumed that's what I was doing, it having been nearly two weeks since any of us had exchanged a single word with the producer. In fact, I didn't know why I was even calling him a producer. As far as I knew, he had never even raised ten cents for the production; at least the mysterious Mr. Takashima had paid some of Goran's salary before disappearing into a Zen garden on the far side of Kyoto. Everything I had been shooting had been financed from Farnsworth's own fraying pockets.

"*Hallo,*" a tentative female voice finally answered after several rings. It was high-pitched and barely audible with all the wariness of someone avoiding a string of vicious creditors.

"Hello, this is Moses Wine. I'm calling from the production in Prague."

"Prague?"

"Yes. You know, the movie. Who is this?"

"Frau Volksbruner."

"How do you do, Frau Volksbruner? I'd like to speak to Mr. Volksbruner."

"Herr Volksbruner sick."

"I'm sorry to hear that."

"I speak . . . little English."

"I see. . . . Well does he have someone named Horst working for him?"

"Horst?"

"Yes, a man named Horst is giving out money in Mr. Volksbruner's name. I just wanted to know if he . . ."

"Herr Volksbruner sick."

"Yes, you said. I wanted to know if . . ."

She hung up.

I walked back and sat down next to Horst, who had not moved. When I asked a second time why he was there, he avowed once again that he worked for Volksbruner and was there in his capacity as the film's "comptroller."

"I didn't know films had comptrollers," I said.

"You probably call it a production manager or some such."

"I see. And was that the capacity you were acting in last night when you refused to leave the hotel room of our makeup artist Tina Kerides?"

"I think Ms. Kerides got the wrong idea. I wasn't trying to be forward or proposition her or anything of the kind. I was merely asking her the same sort of questions I asked you—whether she had encountered anything suspicious in recent days."

Yeah, like you, I thought. But then I wondered what the hell this guy was really doing. If he didn't work for Volksbruner, who was he? And where did he get those mint one hundred euro notes he was passing around like business cards at a car lot? But before I could come to conclusions about any of this, or even get any theories, Eva arrived. We were ready for the first shot. "Don't go away," I said to Horst as I headed after her.

He nodded perfunctorily, but when I looked up again, in the midst of composing the master shot of the symposium, from the eyepiece of the Panavision camera, he was already gone, his seat taken by a fat lady eating a sausage with her hose rolled below her knees. "Where did you get these bonzo extras?" I yelled at Eva in frustration. "This is supposed to be an international conference of *intellectuals*, for crissake. Don't you have some people with beards and glasses? . . . Fix it!" I added and then I stomped off in my first director's sulk.

But I wasn't really sulking. I was pretending so no one would notice when I took fifteen or twenty minutes off to find Horst. Unfortunately it wasn't enough—he was nowhere to be seen. And when I returned, the extras situation hadn't improved much either. I counted a paltry five new guys with beards, three of them obviously fake, but they would have to do. I didn't have a choice.

I glanced at the script again. Answering an audience question on responses to grief, panelist Donna was to reveal that her only child had died of leukemia. This would, of course, bring a tear to the eye of the most important member of her audience, Goran. On the page it seemed the most manipulative point in the movie, but I knew it was important to the writer—a moment of personal pain meant to demonstrate that we all had our own individual Holocausts to live through and that these could, if met with understanding and love, lead to mutual forgiveness. The question was how to show it, how to bring forth what Ellen had written. Corny as it was, I decided to place Goran dead center in the audience, so it would seem as if Donna were speaking only to him. As for the dreaded extras, I would move the camera back to the rear of the auditorium and film them on the widest possible lens to make them look like indistinguishable specks, the way I remembered the pilgrims in *Gandhi*. Then I would clear the set and work personally with Donna on her close-up for her speech, giving it intimacy as if it were a love scene while flattering her to build her confidence and helping her to concentrate to deepen her performance.

Maybe I was getting cocky, but I thought it all worked pretty well. I told Samantha as much when we sat finishing our dinner that night. "But I still can't understand why they're scrimping so much on extras when there's a six-million-dollar budget," I continued, as much out of directorial pique as investigative curiosity. "You'd think they could hire a few lousy college professors. It couldn't cost much around here. Or even those pretentious assholes from the Café Slavia."

"Somebody's siphoning somewhere," said Samantha.

"But who? And why?"

She didn't answer. Then, with a sudden intensity, she said, "I don't want you to go, Moses." I stared at her, momentarily confused by the non sequitur, but the way she was looking at me told me we had only now, with dessert in front of us, reached the true subject of our conversation. "Don't go," she repeated. "Please." She was obviously referring to my rendezvous with the Michelin Man at the Loreto, which was, according to my watch, still some thirty minutes off.

"You know I can't stop myself, Sam. It's who I am. If I didn't go, I'd shrivel up and become some desiccated old fart even Janak couldn't help."

"You're not alone now."

"But you do things like that too. It's our job."

"The times are different, Moses. The world is crawling with wannabe kamikazes. Besides, it's not what I mean."

"What do you mean?"

She looked at me with the agitated expression of someone who didn't really want to say what was on her mind, perhaps because she was embarrassed by it. "Suppose I were having a baby? How would you feel then?"

I sat up straight in my chair. "What? Have you missed your period?"

She shook her head.

"Well . . . ?"

"It's just something I feel. I know it's a cliché, but women have intuitions about these things."

"Cliché is right. I think you've been sneaking off to that gypsy with the ouija board we saw on the Charles Bridge."

"It was tarot cards," she said. She didn't so much as crack a smile.

I studied her a moment, then laughed nervously. "So why are you drinking?" I asked.

She pushed her wine glass away. I noticed for the first time she had barely touched it.

I sat there a moment, feeling a welter of conflicting emotions, all of them premature because this was all based on "intuition" anyway. Then I checked my watch again. "Look, I better get going. I don't want that bastard to be there ahead of me."

"I'll come with you."

"No. You know he said to come alone," I said, standing. "Besides, if you *are* pregnant, that would really be stupid, wouldn't it? Don't worry. I promise I won't take any unnecessary risks. I'm too old for that." I gave Sam a peck on the cheek before starting out without giving her a chance to protest.

I had been to the Church of Our Lady of Loreto before, over a lunch break in the shooting, because it was a future location for the love scene between Goran and Donna on their first night out together. The crew assumed we would be using artificial fog to enhance the romantic atmosphere along the stairway approaching the church where the leads would be walking. They wanted to know where I was placing the camera so the machines wouldn't be visible. I, of course, could only guess but I was smart enough to take Jiri along to cover for me.

I wished I had the cinematographer with me this second time as I drew near the extravagant eighteenth-century rococo structure built in an area just north of the castle. By day, the neighborhood was much frequented by tourists, but now, at night, it seemed deserted except for a couple of drunks standing in the doorway of a beer hall. I turned a corner at the narrow street leading up to the church and hesitated at the top of the stairway itself. Its heavy black granite railings were dotted with about a dozen statues of angels, their faces smiling almost erotically in the lantern light as their wings cast eerie jagged shadows across the cobblestones. I stopped behind the first of them and peered down the steps along the façade of the church to the gate of the cloisters when I heard what sounded like footsteps somewhere behind me. I spun around quickly for a look, but there was no one there. Then I heard a voice, scratchy and metallic as if it were being broadcast.

"You have not come alone," it said. I turned around again, searching for the source as the speaker continued. "You cannot be trusted. From now on there will be no negotiations, only actions." At that point I found it, a small broadcast device wedged into the gaping mouth of the third angel. But at that very moment there was a screech from the opposite side of the square as an automobile, with its lights off, sped off into the night.

I started to run after it, but, knowing that was absurd, slipped out of sight as soon as I could behind the last of the statues and then ran as fast as possible along the back side of Our Lady of Loreto, staying on a dirt path by the church wall to deaden the sound. I wanted to see if I could catch up with whoever was following me, hoping and praying it wasn't my wife.

It wasn't. It was Horst. I saw him walking along at a brisk clip in front of the beer hall where I had seen the drunks. He was trying to appear anonymous with a slouch hat and the collar of his long black coat turned up, but I recognized him right away and dashed up to him, grabbing him firmly by the arm and spinning him around toward me. He stared back at me with a mixture of embarrassment and dread.

"I think you owe me a drink," I said.

9

"How long have you been a member of the BND?" I asked him, studying the picture ID card from German Federal Intelligence, the *Bundesnachtrichtendienst*, he had just handed me with some reluctance after I threatened to report him to the Czech police, Interpol and the CIA. "How long?" I repeated.

"In the BND?" He reached for his ID.

"Yes, of course. What have we been talking about?"

"Twelve years I suppose."

"You suppose? You don't *know?*"

"Twelve years."

I nodded and returned his card, signaling to the waiter to bring us two large glasses of Staropramen. It was one of that brewery's pubs, although one of the more depressing ones, a dank place with long wooden tables and a rank odor that smelled suspiciously of stale vomit. "So you're bugging my hotel room," I said.

Horst shrugged. "For your protection."

"Thanks. And for what other reasons?"

"They are confidential. You understand."

"Sure. I wouldn't dream of probing. . . . How about who you're protecting me from—can you tell me that?"

"I am not at liberty to say."

"You're protecting me from someone but you're not at liberty to say who it is? Why don't you just lock me up for life in a fallout shelter? It's cheaper and more effective." I gave the bastard my strongest look of disgust, but he scarcely flinched. In fact he smiled back contemptuously with that cocky attitude that was coming back in style for intelligence agents these days. Ten years ago, at the end of the Cold War, most of them were looking for a new line of work, skulking around like underfed calves at an empty trough, but now, with the War on Terror in full sway, it was a bull market for spooks all over again, even the German ones who had been the most ambivalent of all after roughly half the citizens of the Eastern part of their country got exposed as Stasi agents. No wonder this schmuck was so arrogant as to think he could masquerade as Volksbruner's "comptroller" and get away with it. "Why don't we do this?" I continued because he clearly wasn't on his own. "Why don't I just make some suggestions and you just nod your head yes or no? Then, if you're inspired and you feel it doesn't compromise you too much, you can fill in some blanks at the end." He didn't nod yes or no, but I went on anyway. "Some character who likes to wear a white down suit that makes him look like the Michelin Man is leading what appears to be a group—a cell, if you will—of Islamic fundamentalist terrorists that has, for some reason or other, probably because it has certain themes, or just that it represents Hollywood, which is said to be dominated by a *certain* group, selected the film *Prague Autumn* as its target. I don't know who this guy is but I suspect, since *you're* here, that his cell has its origins somewhere in Germany, probably Hamburg, if recent historical events serve. Am I correct so far?"

Horst didn't respond immediately, but then, almost in spite of himself, a tiny smile appeared on his face. "Almost," he said.

"Where did I go wrong?"

"It's Munich, not Hamburg."

"And this Michelin Man, do you know who he is?"

"Not really. No."

"Not really? What does that mean? Is he Middle Eastern, European . . . ?"

"Probably neither. Probably American."

"*Probably* American?"

"It means just that. We don't know for sure." Just then the beers arrived and the German quickly grabbed his and hoisted it in a brief toast before downing most of the glass in one gulp. "I don't know why I'm telling you any of this."

"Because you're protecting me, remember? The more I know the safer I am." Horst fidgeted in his seat. "So who is this American, if he is an American?"

He stared at me a moment, then said grudgingly, "Michael Lancaster, Princeton '87."

"You don't know who he is but you know he went to Princeton?"

"That is the way he signed his name in e-mails he sent to the *Süddeutsche Zeitung* demanding better treatment for guest workers from developing nations, as he put it. Also on some letter he wrote to the *Quarterly of Ethnic Studies*."

"And is there such a person?"

"Who knows?"

"But surely you checked with the university?"

"Yes, of course. Even the incompetent BND does that." He was starting to look sulky. For a moment I thought he was going to get up and leave.

"I'm sorry," I said, trying to head him off. "You've been very generous and I didn't mean to insult you or your organization." Then I offered him another beer, but he waved it off and sat there silently a while longer.

"I don't know why I'm hiding this," he said finally. "You could look it up on Yahoo in five minutes anyway. It was a famous case at the time. . . . There *was* a Princeton student with that name for two years during the eighties. He was quite brilliant, one of the best in his class in mathematics and languages, when it was discovered that there was no such person as this Michael Lancaster who was the valedictorian of some high school in Colorado and that his application to the university was completely fraudulent. Even his entrance examinations were taken under an assumed name. . . . He was, of course, after going through the proper channels, expelled from the school with formal charges filed with your state of New Jersey. But by that time he had already disappeared from the campus, disappeared from the world even. To this day, no one knows exactly who he was."

"And how do you connect this Lancaster with a terrorist cell in Munich?"

"The e-mails he sent to the newspaper were traced to an Internet Café at one time operated by a Latif al-Aziz, a Yemenite who was once implicated in a failed plot to blow up the U.S. Embassy in Kuala Lumpur and who is, I am sure, well known to you and Miss Donna Gold."

"Indeed," I said, but I was wondering, how this Lancaster could have been so sloppy as to have linked his e-mail to Latif. Horst didn't have an answer for that when I asked him, but the German agent was halfway out the door by then, worried and embarrassed that he had already told me too much.

Samantha had what seemed the most logical explanation for Lancaster's behavior when I returned later that night. "Like most terrorists, he wants someone to know he's there."

"Who? The preppies in his eating club?" I joked, but I knew she was probably right. A message was being sent, but to whom? And why? Or was this simply another disaffected young Westerner fallen for Islam, that haven for the morally pure that had swept up aspiring idealists from Cat Stevens to John Walker Lindh, not to mention half the point guards in my beloved NBA who I hoped against hope didn't take much of this seventh-century mumbo-jumbo seriously and were just in it for the cool names . . . or even the polygamy. But this Lancaster guy's Princeton pedigree and leadership position in a cell gave the whole thing a different cast that was at once more intellectual and more ominous. Somewhere in all this too was a possible explanation of the appearance of my name on an FBI search engine linked to a veritable who's who of world terror. Someone knew I was coming to Prague before I did. The question was who?

I could see that Samantha, who had seemed so relieved a short while earlier when I arrived safely, was troubled as well as we sat there in front of a laptop in our pajamas, combing through the letters section of "The Quarterly of Ethnic Studies" on the Web. At a painfully slow 28K connection we waited several minutes before the name "Lancaster" came up and I could scroll down to his brief letter, which was titled "Another Evil Empire?" "As your recent study validates," it said, "different ethnic and religious groups have excelled naturally at various fields of endeavor throughout history. But in the modern world this should not prevent us from taking concerted affirmative action, collective or otherwise, against their dominance in areas where the well-being of society is directly affected, such as the media where the undue influence of one group creates dangerous distortions injurious to the common good. Yours sincerely, Michael Lancaster, Princeton '87."

"What a perfect shit," I said, staring down at the online magazine, which was dated Madison, Wisconsin, Spring 2001 but just as well could have been Berlin, 1936.

Just then the hotel alarm rang. "Holy fuck," I said, springing to my feet with Samantha. "Now he's starting a fire!"

"How do you know it's him?" she said, as we ran to the door to consult the map of the emergency exits.

"I just know. . . . We better take the stairs," I said, opening the door and running with Samantha out into the corridor. It was already filling up with terrified people, tripping over each other and making mad dashes for the exit at the end. A siren went off somewhere, adding to the jangling alarm, and another group of people scrambled for the door, falling on top of each other. "One at a time! One at a time!" I yelled, pushing my way through, doing my civic duty and trying to organize everyone into a double line at the entrance to the stairs. It was the kind of situation during which I became preternaturally calm, particularly since my kids were grown. But then I thought, what if Samantha *was* pregnant, and suddenly felt a clutch in my stomach.

We headed down a couple of floors. Several others were emerging from their corridors and I recognized key members of our American crew—Scott, the sound mixer, and Peter's amiga Cindy, descending several steps in front of Linda, the editor, who squeezed my arm in reassurance as she passed. Her assistant followed, grinning sheepishly, then Arthur, who was on the edge of hyperventilating again. I continued down another floor, but then I stopped. The actors, what had happened to the actors? They, notably Donna, had already proven to be Lancaster's special targets. I spun around and started back up the stairs against the flow, climbing several steps at a time ahead of Samantha.

When I opened the fire door to the eleventh floor, I could hear a woman screaming, "Help! She's been bitten! Get her to a hospital! Help! Help!" It was Donna. She was standing in the corridor gesturing wildly through the open door of her room. I stepped forward to see Tina Kerides writhing on the bed, clutching her neck in agony. Standing next to the obviously wounded makeup artist was none other than Dr. Pavel Janak himself, who was topless in a pair of silk pajama bottoms decorated with Modigliani nudes. He was speaking urgently into a phone and not particularly pleased to see me. "Relax," he said to Donna. "I'm dealing with it." But the actress continued unabated, "There's a fucking snake in my room! A python! A rattler!" She gesticulated for the missing animal, which I later learned, after it was discovered in the seventh-floor laundry, was not plastic this time, but a definite living thing, one of the world's most toxic snakes, an actual taipan from Australia, whose venom was capable of killing twelve thousand guinea pigs in a single bite. Fortunately for Tina, she had been smart enough or terrified enough to pull the fire alarm in Donna's room seconds after the viper had gotten its fangs into her. That may have caused massive consternation in the hotel, but it ulti-mately got her to the hospital in time to save her ass.

Of course the movie star had been the target. The makeup artist had been sleeping in Donna's bed, I also learned later but guessed immediately, because she had switched rooms with the actress who was trying to hide, as it now turned out unsuccessfully, her affair with Janak. I wondered how long *that* had been going on. But I didn't wonder long. I was fixated on the mythical Lancaster. Whoever he was, he was one sadistic young man, angry about something I didn't understand. But whatever his motiva-tion, it was past time to put a stop to his murderous activities.

Farnsworth would have none of it. "What is this, *A Beautiful Mind II?*" he said. "I'm not going to let some Princeton maniac shut us down. He didn't even graduate."

"It's only a movie, Peter. It's not going to change the world."

"Well, in that case, why're you using so many extras? Don't you know what that costs me? You used three hundred yesterday. You could have done the same scene with forty if you had some imagination."

"I'm just trying to preserve the integrity of your vision."

"Don't give me that artsy crap! I'm hemorrhaging money here! But, in any case, we're not quitting, no matter what. I'm too deep into this to get out now. I'll get up and direct this thing myself if I have to!"

"Please don't do that!" said Ellen. There was something in the way she said it that made me wonder if she knew about Cindy. I was sitting in Farnsworth's hospital room the next morning at eight in an emergency meeting with him, Ellen, Samantha and Arthur. The one-time director was now strapped into a much larger traction device, which looked as if it was padlocked to his leg with a bicycle chain, I suspected on the orders of his wife.

"Well, I'm going to as soon as the doctor lets me," he replied. "And when he does, there's still going to be a movie there for me to direct. Even if Wine carries through on his threat and quits, we'll find a temporary replacement. . . . Which, knowing you, you won't," he continued to me. "More likely you'll be arbitrating with me for credit at the Director's Guild. . . . Now where did you say you stashed the actors?"

"U Karla, a small hotel on a cul-de-sac near the American Embassy. It's surrounded by a stucco wall and only has one entrance with a heavy iron door." Earlier I had told them the situation the previous night had become even bleaker when we were informed that those new owners of the Forum, the Libyan government, had kindly asked the production to check out of the hotel because our presence was endangering their other patrons. Eva and I had been up until 4 A.M., finding accommodations for the cast and crew. Most of them were placed at the Marriott but on a tip from Jana, our translator, we had secretly put Donna and Goran at the U Karla. "Of course, a snake could get in under that door," I continued, "But they could almost anywhere and it was the best place we could come up with under the circumstances."

"Where *did* he get that snake?" asked Farnsworth.

"According to the local police, a taipan was reported missing from the Prague Zoo six months ago."

"So this Lancaster lunatic must have been planning this for some time," said the director.

"Seems like," I said. "Speaking of planning, when did *you* decide to shoot at that warehouse next to Radio Free Europe?"

"I didn't."

I stared at him. "Wait. Run this by me again. Shooting in that warehouse wasn't your idea. Whose was it?"

"I was just told we couldn't film on the sound stage that day. . . . It was already rented by some . . ."

"Albanian advertising company."

"Right. For a lingerie commercial." He rolled his eyes. "Anyway, I gave the Czechs permission to pick a warehouse. It didn't matter which one. Sound can be a problem in those spaces, but this was for an intimate bedroom scene so I figured I'd be looping all the grunts and groans in post-production. My big worry was going to be getting Donna to be naked. It's against her contract."

"But whose idea was this particular warehouse?"

He shrugged. "I just got a memorandum."

"You never saw the place?"

He shook his head.

"Do *you* know who it was?" I asked Arthur.

The bondsman shrugged. "The location manager? Sometimes they get kickbacks."

"Or worse," I said.

"Don't even *think* about pulling the plug!" said Farnsworth with sudden intensity. It must have been the look in my eyes.

"Well, how about something simpler, switching warehouses?"

"Up to you," he said.

As it turned out it wasn't simpler.

We had a noon call that day and I took the opportunity to ride solo with Tomas in the Tatra out to the Barrandov Studios for an unannounced visit with Jaroslav Schlick and Anna Rockova. The Czech producers weren't particularly surprised to see me.

"Welcome, Moses," said Schlick, standing the moment I entered his large office, which had a conference table and two antique desks, one for him and one for Anna. The walls were decorated with posters for movies filmed by his company, mostly German and Italian productions, but a few from Hollywood. "That was a frightening, how you say, episode last night with the snake. Thankfully, there were only two more stolen from our zoo this year."

"Two *more?*"

"Yes. You did not know? A Malayan krait and a boomslang from Africa. The boomslang is not so bad, but the krait, well, they have a fifty percent rate of fatality even after the antivenin treatment."

"Would you like perhaps some coffee, Moses?" said Anna, doing her public female hostess number, though I suspected she actually ran the company behind the scenes.

"Sure . . . I mean, no. I'm already wired to the ceiling as it is. I actually came to find out who selected the warehouse location for Thursday."

"Yes, that is where we have a problem," she said, folding her arms as she emerged from behind her desk. "Since yesterday, we have not been able to locate Ivan."

"And it was his idea?"

"We are not sure. But he is the location manager. He will know. But he seems to have disappeared."

Schlick nodded. "Yes, it is his job, picking this warehouse, I am sorry to say, although I take full responsibility of course." He was beginning, for the first time, to be a tad on the smarmy side.

I looked at the two of them, suddenly remembering the nasty comments about the Czech studio chief's parsimonious treatment of his employees Ivan made at the Café Slavia. I didn't doubt they encompassed Anna as well. And I wondered if this was some kind of payback on their part, some attempt to blacken the reputation of an overly critical underling. Or, just as likely, had someone else exploited the location manager's anger at these same bosses and manipulated it to some treacherous purpose? As a foreigner, it would be extremely difficult ever to find out. "In any case, there's one thing we absolutely have to do," I said. "Find another warehouse to shoot in."

The two Czechs were oddly silent. "I don't know if this is possible," said Anna finally. "Have you spoken with your Embassy?"

I exhaled slowly. "Yes, of course, I spoke to them and I know they're against moving the location because it would be caving in to terrorism or some such, but I'm the one who . . ."

"I don't know if that is their only reason," said Anna. I stared at her. What was this about? But I had a suspicion I already knew and

I didn't particularly like it. "Perhaps you should speak with them yourself," she continued, checking her watch. "You still have an hour's time before the filming. Tomas will drive you. Ask for Mr. . . ."

"Jasperson," I said. "In Commercial Services."

Anna nodded. "I understand you have met before."

It didn't take long to get in to see Jasperson this time, and it wasn't just because I asked for a name they recognized instead of Cornwall. Perhaps Anna had called to say I was coming or, more likely, they were anticipating my arrival anyway, because I was sent up the minute I flashed my passport. The CIA agent was waiting behind his desk with his door opened. "Come in, come in. How are you?" he said, immediately shutting the door behind me with one of those foot pedals.

"How am I supposed to be?" I said, slumping down into the seat opposite him. "I haven't slept all night, I have to direct a movie in thirty minutes and now I hear, thanks to you, I'm going to have to have my cast and crew offered up as tomorrow's lunch meat for some vicious reptile called a Malayan krait."

"I don't know what you're talking about."

"Yes, you do. It's kind of obvious you or your people are trying to prevent us from moving our location from the warehouse next to RFE and it's just as obvious why."

"Why?"

"So that we don't alert some Arab terrorist cell led by some whacko in a white suit and you can catch them all red-handed with their scimitars up their asses."

Jasperson didn't say anything.

"So you don't deny it."

"What do you want me to say?"

"To begin with, who is Michael Lancaster?"

"How'd you hear about *him?*"

"A little BND agent told me."

"The one who calls himself Horst?" Jasperson could not hide his disgust at the talkative German.

"Bad tradecraft, huh?"

"You could say."

"Well . . . join the club. . . . Who's Lancaster?"

Jasperson went silent again.

"Come on. I already know he went to Princeton under false pretenses and got kicked out. What else is there?"

Jasperson hesitated once more before replying. "Don't know. Nobody does, as far as we can tell."

"What about his cell? How big is it?"

"Why do you want to know this?"

"Because I'm the one responsible on that set if something goes wrong, if those snakes run wild."

"That's not what he's planning," said Jasperson.

"Ah. Now we're getting somewhere."

"At least we don't think so."

"What *do* you think?"

He stared at me another long moment. "You know I can't believe I'm supposed to tell you any of this."

"If you don't, I still have the power to shut down the production. I'm the director."

"Oh, yes," he smirked. "What a mistake that was." Oh Christ, I thought, another movie critic. But then I realized I was just being defensive and this had nothing whatever to do with aesthetics and everything to do with *realpolitik*. "In any case," he continued, suddenly sliding a sheet of paper across the desk, which probably had been sitting there waiting for me from the outset, "before we can go any further, I must ask you to sign this document confirming that any information disclosed to you at this time be entirely confidential and never revealed in any form, including and especially in a book, without the written consent of the United States of America and its Central Intelligence Agency."

"Sure," I said, scrawling my name on the dotted line without so much as glancing at the text and shoving it back to him. "Disclose away."

"Twenty-one months ago, an Algerian named Ahmed al-Imami took a janitorial job at a warehouse belonging to the Zlata Storage Company on Wenceslas Square. Employment in such close proximity to the headquarters of Radio Free Europe is, of course, subject to more than the normal security procedures and it was discovered that this al-Imami had been for some time, under the pseudonym of Mohammed al-Jihadi, a member of a radical Islamic mosque in Munich. This in and of itself wasn't startling. Almost all the mosques in Munich could be described as radical and al-Jihadi, despite his name, was not a particularly militant member. Nor did he do much of anything to arouse suspicion at his job, until, about three months ago, our satellites began to pick up repeated telephone calls to an Internet Café in Munich."

"Once operated by Latif al-Aziz," I said.

Jasperson stared at me in irritation. "Damn those Germans have loose tongues."

"Maybe they just want to make your life more difficult. . . . Anyway, no doubt you put it together with the Michael Lancaster material, that e-mail to the Munich paper and the letter to the *Quarterly of Ethnic Studies.*"

Now he really looked irritated. "What else did they tell you?"

"That's about it." I stared back at him for a moment before I came to the obvious conclusion. "You're the Albanian advertising company," I said and added somewhat more tentatively, ". . . and Ivan, the location manager, is working for you. . . ."

"After a fashion," said Jasperson. Then he smiled. "Fortunately, they have taken the bait. Twelve days ago, only three days after the Zlata warehouse had the luck to be chosen as a replacement location for your movie with an announcement posted on the premises, Mr. al-Imami and a Turkish colleague began to dig a tunnel under the warehouse lavatory into the cellar of Radio Free Europe. Simultaneously, a transshipment of cyanide gas was detected at the Slovakian border, heading for the capital. We let it pass."

"You *what?*"

"We didn't want to create undue suspicion. We assume it should be relatively easy to intercept tomorrow when the cell members attempt to transport it through the warehouse tunnel into the radio building."

"And why are you so certain they're going to do it tomorrow?" Suddenly I was feeling an agitation that made all those venomous kraits and taipans seem like little harmless garter snakes in a kid's aquarium tank.

"Mr. Wine, I can't believe you even asked that question. You of all people must know the enmity this Lancaster harbors for you . . . people in the media. He wouldn't miss the chance to win the daily double, to hit Radio Free Europe *and* a Hollywood movie at the same time. That's why we set this trap in the first place. . . . But don't worry. We're ready for every eventuality. I can assure you that *all* the personnel at our disposal will be in and around that facility tomorrow. You may not know who we are, but we're there. All you have to do is go on with your business, make your motion picture and leave the terrorists to us."

He made it sound like a jingle.

10

"How do you feel about being part of a CIA sting?" said Samantha in a low voice the driver wouldn't overhear. I was riding back with her in the Tatra having spent the better part of the afternoon standing in six inches of mud in a rundown schoolyard where we were filming a soccer match between two teams of eleven-year-old boys, one of whom played Goran's son in the movie. I had just confirmed my theory—my wife was a former government employee, after all—that the reason they told me about the plan was so I wouldn't muck it up if I saw some strange characters wandering around the set the next day. She agreed but reminded me that the feds also wanted to avoid a lawsuit in case innocent people got hurt. "It's SOP at the Agency," she had said before inquiring about my feelings concerning the matter, which were somewhere between depressed and numb. It wasn't exactly a pleasant prospect being an also-ran at an Al Qaeda turkey shoot, if that's what it was, and to make matters worse, in that highly charged and most unromantic of atmospheres, I was still the one who was going to have to convince Donna Gold to take her knickers off.

"Take us to the Zlata warehouse," I said to Tomas explaining it was the building next to Radio Free Europe on Wenceslas Square. I was becoming progressively more anxious about the next day and I knew at the very least I should see the place in advance. We entered through an open loading dock on the side street. Several members of the art department—the decorator, the lead man and the prop man among others—were already there, putting the finishing touches on the small set. Constructed of three walls near the middle of the vast warehouse floor, it was meant to be the interior of Donna's cabin in a Yugoslavian refugee camp. Her character had gone there to cleanse her soul by teaching orphaned children after her traumatic breakup with Goran. But unable to stay away, the writer would make the mountainous trek here in an UNSCOM truck to find her and they would have a tearful reunion, ending up in this cabin where they would make love.

I stepped inside the open wall and walked up to the metal camp bed where most of the scene would be played. I was trying to distract myself for the moment with the comically absurd problem of getting Donna to flash some flesh. That afternoon Arthur had reminded me how important for the film's financial future this was, that the movie's commercially unappealing Holocaust theme could be rendered suddenly attractive by a fleeting glimpse of our leading lady's nipples. This was particularly true for certain foreign distributors apparently blessed enough to have seen the sacred boobs before in the uncut European version of the *Casino Nights* steam room scene.

"Is there anything else you need, sir?" said the decorator who had followed me into the set.

"Maybe some mosquito netting around the bed. That always gives it a kind of sexy intimacy." And maybe it would relax Donna, I thought.

"But isn't it *wintertime* in the mountains, sir?" The decorator looked confused, but I didn't respond. I was staring right past her at a Middle Eastern man in a janitor's uniform standing under a work light with an industrial broom in his hand. He had heavily lidded eyes and mottled skin as if he were the victim of severe adolescent acne or a firebombing. Was this Ahmed al-Imami himself? I assumed so and nodded to him pleasantly, but absent-mindedly, in order not to raise suspicion. He nodded back and began to push his broom before him, heading for the other end of the warehouse.

"Why don't we just say it's leftover netting from summer," I said to the decorator, pretending to shift my interest to other parts of the set until Imami disappeared from sight. Then I asked for the location of the men's room.

I was directed to a door beneath another work light and walked over to it accompanied by Samantha, who stood outside when I entered. I wanted to see if I could have a look at the tunnel, which had allegedly been dug from under there to the Radio Free Europe cellar. I wasn't completely inexperienced in the area, having seen a few built in Baja to run pot, coke and illegal aliens under the border. I remembered one in particular that ran from under a taquería in Tecate that was wide enough to handle a Volkswagen.

I began to tap around on the floor until I heard a hollow sound and crouched over a tile that seemed to have been recently dislodged under the sink. It came out rather easily and I peered down into a black hole about the size of a tennis ball but still plenty large enough, I imagined, for a solid dose of cyanide gas or a Malayan krait, for that matter. But when I poured some water down it, the liquid backed up almost instantly in a pool of greenish slime resembling motor oil. At that point I heard what must have been a signal from Sam, three light raps on the door in rapid succession, and quickly replaced the tile, wiping up the slime, or as much as I could get, with a piece of the scratchy toilet paper that hung above the lavatory on a rusty nail. Then I stood, while ostentatiously zipping my fly for the edification of another man in a janitorial uniform approaching the bathroom. This one wasn't Middle Eastern at all, but tall and muscular with a blond buzz cut and the kind of lantern jaw you associate with old Red Ryder cartoons. He frowned when he saw me. I thought I had seem him someplace before and then I realized he was one of the Marine guards at the embassy.

"All yours," I said, waltzing past him to Samantha and slipping my arm around her back. On the other side of the set I saw three other men I recognized as Marines dressed as janitors. The game, not unexpectedly, had been joined early, about twelve hours to be exact. "I think it's time to leave," I whispered to Samantha and then called out loudly to the crew "Great work! See you in the morning!" As we walked through the loading dock, I was starting to feel distinctly unnerved.

Back at the hotel, my agitation only increased. What was I doing, allowing this to happen? I was responsible for these people. They were my cast and crew, my friends and creative collaborators. How could I entrust their safety to the CIA, of all sclerotic organizations?

"I'm not going to get in that argument with you again," said Samantha, reading me well, as she usually did, and knowing that it had always been my contention that few American intelligence agents of my generation had, to exaggerate but slightly, triple-digit IQs. During the Vietnam era, the best and the brightest didn't join the CIA; they ran from it. "How old is Jasperson?" she continued.

"Forty, I would guess."

"So? He's young enough. He should be sufficiently competent, even by your theory."

I nodded, but I wasn't reassured. It was Lancaster who troubled me. Whoever *he* was, *he* clearly had a triple-digit IQ, probably one in the highest reaches of the ninety-ninth percentile. In fact it was obvious he was far more capable than any of his pursuers, whatever their abilities, in various police and undercover agencies. He had been able to elude them on at least two continents for the better part of two decades. Yet now, with his identity still unrevealed, one of these same agencies had supposedly been able to infiltrate his small hermetic cell, setting it and him up for decimation.

It didn't compute and because it didn't, I didn't sleep. I lay there in bed, staring at the ceiling, wondering why such a brilliant young man would be attracted to fundamentalist Islam in the first place. But I already knew the truth—breaking the bell curve at some distinguished Ivy League university was no inoculation against totalitarian movements. The history of the twentieth century was proof enough of that. And this particular fascism had the added romance of seeming to help the world's oppressed.

To Samantha's displeasure, I got up and dressed at four-thirty. By 5 A.M., two hours before my director's call, I was on my way back to the Zlata warehouse. A second group of nearly a dozen new "janitors" were already at work, swabbing the floors and cleaning the windows. They were trying hard to look busy, but with their fresh workers' uniforms and scrubbed faces, these guys were obviously Marines to me and I thought any self-respecting terrorist could see them from a mile away. But then maybe that just made us a more appealing target.

I made my way past them to a room in back earmarked as the star's dressing area. Donna, who had the earliest call as she almost always did, was there with Tina who, although restricted by a thick bandage from the snakebite wrapped all the way around her neck and down her left shoulder, was gamely applying mascara to the actress's eyes.

"Moses," said Donna, "thank God you're here! Do me a favor, *please*." She was staring straight ahead so the makeup wouldn't run but I could see her watching me carefully with her pupils slid to the side. "When we get back to LA, don't under any circumstances tell anyone what happened. . . . I mean with Pavel. If Nick hears a word of it, I'm going to end up in palimony court with one of those ghastly photographs on Page Six, which I know they deliberately take from the wrong side."

"My lips are sealed," I said.

"And one other thing . . . The set absolutely *has* to be closed today. It's hard enough doing a love scene without fifty horny stagehands slavering for a peek at my jugs. Not that I'd ever allow them on screen anyway. The ones in *Casino Nights* weren't even mine. They belonged to a body double from a Culver City out-call service."

Just then Goran stormed in. "Son of a Slovenian Whore, what is going on here? We are surrounded by soldiers. They stop me on the way in for identification. Bloody fucking Milosevic. I thought he was in The Hague!"

"They're Americans," I said. "They're here to protect us."

"Lying sacks of shit! They did nothing in Sarajevo!"

"Soldiers?" said Donna, sitting up in her chair and inadvertently knocking the mascara brush out of Tina's hand. "Why the fuck is that? Why didn't you tell us?"

The actors were both staring at me as if I had been cheating them at poker for two years.

"I'm sorry," I said. "I should have told you earlier. Maybe I thought we could all just do our work and let the military take care of it."

"I do not like military," said Goran. "I do not like secret agents. I do not like police. I have enough of them in Yugoslavia. Is *your* job to supply security here. We know you are not really *director!*"

"Okay, okay," I said, carefully explaining to them, point by point, the situation as I knew it. "So," I concluded, "you can either go through with this movie, take the inherent risk and shoot here today, or pack it up. It's up to you guys. But personally, I wouldn't blame either of you if you decided to call the first cab and hightail it to the airport."

I waited for them to mull their responses but the actor snapped back immediately. "Why you talk this shit? Since when does Goran Babic let fascist fundamentalist communist imperialist reactionary pseudo-revolutionary bullcrap stop expression of his art?"

"Right!" echoed Donna, somewhat more ambivalently than her leading man, who now wore a broad grin. "But remember what I told you. It's got to be a closed set. This isn't a porno."

"I'll see what I can do," I said and walked out onto the warehouse floor.

Thirty minutes later we had built an enclosure of screens around the three-sided cabin, affording the actors a modicum of privacy while leaving a small slot open so that Jiri and I could set up the camera some distance off and film the love scene on a telephoto lens like voyeurs. It seemed like a reasonable and discrete way to handle things and I called for the actors. Before they arrived, however, a fight started breaking out, but it wasn't over getting a better view of Donna's privates. Our new English-speaking "janitors" had barred our Czech-speaking crew from using the bathroom—I had a pretty good idea why—and the Czechs weren't happy about it.

"Where's Jana?" I said, looking around for our translator, whom I hadn't noticed anywhere that morning.

"Don't worry. I'll handle it," said Eva, ever eager to appear indispensable. She walked over and mediated the situation within minutes, sending the disgruntled crew off to use the facilities at the McDonald's on Wenceslas Square.

A short while later we were shooting the scene. But I wasn't concentrating. I was thinking about Jana. I had sent a production assistant looking for her with disturbing results. She had checked out of her apartment and had her phone disconnected. Even her pager had been shut off. It seemed as if now she *and* Ivan had gone missing? Was there a connection? Or had she run off with Milan St. Clair? The last time I had seen her was two nights before when she had found that last-minute reservation for our actors in the secluded hotel near the embassy. It had seemed fortuitous at the time and we were all grateful under the circumstances. Now I wasn't sure what it meant.

"Should I keep rolling?" said Alfons. While maintaining eye contact with the lens of the camera he was operating, he tapped me on the shoulder, finally breaking me out of my reverie.

"No, no. Of course not . . . *Cut!*" I yelled, trying to sound as if this was the way I planned it all along.

"That was sensational," said Arthur, clapping me on the back and pointing to the video monitor. "How did you get her to do that? The foreign sales guys are going to have an orgasm!" I nodded noncommittally. Whatever Donna had done or shown, I hadn't seen it. Over my earphones I could hear her telling Goran to adjust his hand for the next take so it would cover her cellulite.

The rest of the morning was uneventful. The Marine guard, now augmented to over two dozen men and women, waited in readiness, but no terrorist group or anyone at all suspicious appeared. Even Imami seemed not to have come to work that morning. I found this more than a little bit perplexing but it didn't seem to trouble Jasperson, who arrived at the lunch break to assure me that everything was on track and that they had, as promised, intercepted the cyanide shipment on a two-lane country road fifty miles from Prague. It was clearly heading for the capital. He said a few words in private to the first lieutenant and vanished again. I sat there a moment, picking at my goulash, then picked up my cell phone and called Samantha.

"Would you mind going over to that hotel, the U Karla, and having a look around? . . . Wait a minute. Meet me across the street from it. I'll be there in ten minutes."

"Don't you have a movie to direct?"

"I'll get one of the grips to do it," I said and hung up. Then I informed Eva I was going to scout a location and slipped out the side door, jumping into the front seat of the Tatra and taking the keys from Tomas. I told him to take an extra hour for lunch and drove off myself into the heavy traffic of Wenceslas Square. I didn't know precisely how to get there, but knew the hotel was across the river in the Mała Strana and practically next door to the embassy. So I pointed myself toward the nearest bridge, went over it and up a street called Letanska, which ran along the wall of some government buildings for a few blocks until it came out in the Malostranska, the last main square before the long uphill trek to the Castle. I knew the way to the embassy from there and

I zigzagged up a couple of narrow streets to that small plaza where the American flag flew over the former Schoenborn Palace.

In a few seconds, it was looming in front of me, a mere two Marines now manning its vast entrance area and steps. The bulk of the squad was obviously off guarding our production and Radio Free Europe. I started searching for the U Karla, which I found almost immediately. It was a small low-slung building that looked like a rehabbed coaching house from the sixteenth or seventeenth century, not more than thirty yards from the side gate of the Schoenborn Palace. I parked on the sidewalk in the European fashion and was heading for the front door of the hotel when I heard a familiar low whistle behind me. It was Samantha, leaning against a tree with a guidebook in her hand, pretending to look like a tourist. I went over to her.

"It's locked," she said. "There are people inside but they won't answer the door."

"A hotel that won't answer the door?" I glanced over at the U Karla. From this angle it wasn't much, the size of a bed-and-breakfast with four or five rooms at the most. That was how Jana had recommended it to us, a discrete place that hardly anyone knew about, great for the actors' privacy and safety. Some safety. It was at that point that I saw two guys with ski masks in a window. They saw me and quickly pulled a shade. I reached for my cell phone and dialed Jasperson to warn him his elaborate little sting was about to be fatally stung by the most disenchanted Princeton dropout since Fitzgerald, but all I got was voice mail. So I hung up and called Eva, told her to notify the Czech police that if they didn't haul ass over to the Hotel U Karla, the U.S. Embassy in Prague would turn into the next World Trade Center.

I clicked off when I noticed a man standing across the street, right in front of the embassy steps, watching me. He was wearing a long threadbare topcoat and had a grunge-type watchcap pulled down to his forehead. The rest of his face was obscured with a brown scarf ostensibly twisted at random around his neck but allowing only a pair of deep-set eyes to peak out between the ratty wool of the scarf and the equally shabby yarn of his knitted hat.

"That's him," I said to Samantha under my breath. "I know it's him."

I stood there a moment, scarcely moving, then started to walk across the street. "Don't come any further," he said as I approached the opposite curb. "Or you will cause more problems than you already have."

"What's going on here? What're you planning?"

"You should read your Austro-Hungarian history. In 1657, when the Count Colleredo-Mansfeld lost his leg at the battle of Lutzen, he had a special underground passageway built for him from the Schoenborn Palace to its horse stables."

"And what's it being used for now, Lancaster? Snakes? Explosives?"

"Lancaster?" he said with a laugh. "What a dull name that is. It's so normal, it almost sounds made up. I mean not so average as Smith or Jones but ordinary enough not to arouse suspicion or be remembered."

"What's your real name?"

"Harry Lime," he said.

"Very funny, Lancaster." I glanced over at the Marines who were standing at attention on the Embassy steps.

"My name is not important. What is important is the battle against corporate global hegemony, American cultural imperialism and Zionism." He turned and started walking swiftly toward the alley on the other side of the embassy.

"Stop that guy!" I yelled to the Marines, who snapped awake and turned toward me in suspicious confusion. "He's a terrorist!"

The Marines looked at each other. One of them went inside for orders. They weren't about to take my word for it, but by now Lancaster was rounding the corner. "Wait for the cops," I said to

Samantha, glancing back nervously at the hotel before taking off after him. He wasn't on skis and I could at least try to catch up with him this time. I broke into a run as I reached the alley, plunging through it and turning uphill toward the Castle. Lancaster was still in view, hurrying along the sidewalk past the curio shops, but not going so fast that he would lose me, as if he were taunting me, the older man, to catch up with him. I drew closer at the top when he approached the gate to the Castle itself, a dozen or so of the guards in their royal blue uniforms doing a formal tattoo for the delectation of the international groups clustered by the entrance. Lancaster pushed through with the crowds into the compound, but I followed after him, edging through the multitudes filing toward St. George's Basilica and on into the Golden Lane, a row of terminally quaint Lilliputian houses where, needless to say, Kafka had also lived. A large throng of tourists was lined up in front of the author's house, number 22, waiting to go in and completely blocking the way.

I was unable to get to Lancaster directly, so I slid behind a tall group I assumed were Scandinavians, outraged a couple of older women from the American Middle West by waltzing in the side door of the building, which was exit only, and then raced up some rickety stairs and came out in Kafka's second-floor bedroom. Then, to the consternation of a guard, I opened the window, stepped on the bed and half-jumped, half-plunged like some idiot teenager into a mosh pit, landing partly on Lancaster and partly on some tourists, falling to the ground while grabbing at the younger man's scarf and yanking it off him, sending his watchcap simultaneously flying from his head. People yelled and screamed and surrounded me. But I was paying them no mind because I was looking straight up at the charming visage of Mr. Earring himself in all his neo-grunge glory.

"Trying to arrest me?" he said. "You don't even have jurisdiction. You're more pathetic as a detective than you are as a director." I reached my feet but he started to back up, slipping behind the milling crowd, which was eyeing me angrily, blocking my path. "And don't think because you've seen my face you know who I am. It doesn't even begin there."

"Where *does* it begin? I'd really like to know that."

"Don't even try to figure it out," he said. "You're wasting everybody's time, especially mine." He pulled out a little plastic device with "Hello, Kitty" embossed on the side out of his pocket. It was no bigger than a cigarette lighter—in fact it could have *been* a lighter, except for the minute antenna wiggling out of the top, which made it more the kind of knickknack common to Gaza City and Ramallah than to Tokyo or Osaka.

"Don't do that. Please," I said.

"Why would I listen to you?" he responded. "You are everything I detest." And he cocked his finger on the metal switch. I lunged for him but it was too late. A distant whooshing thud, like a pile of bricks coming down, went off from the direction of the U Karla. It wasn't much—in fact it was later revealed that only two officers of the Prague police force received minor wounds when the bedroom wall of Donna Gold's suite collapsed decimating the sixteenth-century covered bed and matching bureaus—but in the present climate, any explosion was enough to scare the wits out of everyone, especially the crowd at the nearby Prague Castle. A stampede had been set off with masses of guidebook-carrying, souvenir-toting tourists running pell-mell down the Golden Lane, trampling everyone and everything under foot. I was one of those swept up and I ended up on the ground again, wedged against the wall of Kafka's house, looking downhill in desperation for Lancaster. I saw nothing but a cloud of dust and receding heels.

11

IN HOLLYWOOD they say no one ever tells you that you're fired. That would be too embarrassing, too confrontational. I had learned this from the horror stories of writer friends at the Farmer's Market who told me of times when they had worked on a script for six months or longer before learning someone else had been hired to replace them, sometimes their best buddies or ex-lovers, even ex-wives, but something like that had never happened to me personally. I was in another, more respectable business. But, as it turned out, once I joined theirs, I didn't have to wait half a year to suffer my humiliation. I suffered it the next morning.

I arrived at the set as I usually did at the ungodly director's hour of six A.M. ready for the day's work, trying to make extra sure we would be able to make up for the shots we didn't get the previous day. The location had at my instigation been moved from the high-risk Zlata Warehouse back to the relative safety of the sound stage at Barrandov Studios and I walked into the make-up room to say hello to Donna when there was a weird silence, as if she didn't expect me to be there.

"Hi," she said finally.

"Hi," I responded, trying to sound ebullient on three hours' sleep. "Some day yesterday, huh? I was with police until midnight. It took me hours to convince them not to shut down the production." Actually, it had happened rather suddenly and I wasn't sure that I had anything to do with it. I had spent most of my time at their headquarters—a grim stone affair from the fifties that maintained its socialist-realist architecture of toiling workers carved in the façade as if to remind you that all this nasty Darkness at Noon stuff could rear its ugly head again and, if you didn't behave, you might end up sending desperate messages to the newly formed European Commission for the Prevention of Torture—answering questions about Lancaster and his cell. How did I know there could be a problem at the U Karla (I told them about Jana); what did I know personally of Lancaster (very little they didn't); was I certain that was a Mini he had driven off in the other night (I wasn't)? They already had a series of black-and-white stills taken by our set photographer and I was able to identify the lapsed Princetonian as Mr. Earring among the extras on our first day and on the day we shot at the Globe Bookstore. "Are you absolutely sure this is the same person?" one of the officers asked me. I think it was Fule. "Yes, I'm sure," I said. "I was rolling around on the ground with him with our faces three inches apart." "But you do not know his name," his partner Pisek said. "I mean the name under which he was acting in your production." I shook my head. "He was an extra. Directors don't know the extras' names. I suggest you contact the A.D. or Mr. Schlick's office." There were several other questions after that, most of them perfunctory. Then I was taken across the street to the old communist prison, which had been painted pink some years ago and turned into a discount youth hostel for the backpacking set. They ignored me as I waited there for hours while matters were "sorted out." Only at the end of this was I told, and then almost as an afterthought, that we would be allowed to continue shooting, if our government agreed. Why wouldn't they, I asked?

I was going to relate some of these details to Donna but something about the way she was looking at me, a kind of discomfort with my presence, made me change my mind.

"I . . . uh . . . is something wrong? I heard they got you a special suite at the Four Seasons. Was it okay?"

"Yes. Fine."

"Great. Glad to hear it. I'll make sure they have a secure phone put in and extra guards on both sides of the elevator."

Donna nodded, but she seemed even more uncomfortable. She shared a look with Tina. "Didn't Peter talk to you last night? He promised he was going to go over to see you after he visited me."

"He snuck out of the hospital again? Ellen is going to kill him."

"She was with him," said Donna.

"Oh," I said. "So it was okay with her. He must be better." I took a step backward, starting to get the picture. So it's over, I thought. Back to being a gumshoe.

"I just want to thank you for what you've done," the actress continued with an awkward smile. "You really were wonderful stepping in like that. Incredibly gutsy. And you're a real natural. If I had my way, you'd both continue. But a movie can only have one director."

"That's true, alas," came a voice behind me. I turned to see Farnsworth hobbling toward me on an aluminum crutch. "I thought it was going to be another couple of weeks, but the doctors say I made a record-breaking recovery. All I need is a year's supply of Percodan and I'm a hundred percent . . . joking." He put his arm around me and gave me an affectionate squeeze. "Sorry I didn't tell you myself, but I had to meet with Jiri and Eva and go over the shot lists for today. After that it was too late. I just want to thank you for everything you've done," he said, practically repeating Donna verbatim. Was this some kind of special movie business code for "Kiss off, sucker. We don't need you anymore?" "So what're you and Samantha going to do?" he continued. "Take a little vacation in Europe before you go home? Flake out in the Seychelles? I wish I could."

Take a vacation? Was I being fired twice here? "I thought, uh, I'm supposed to do security for the film."

Now the silence came from Farnsworth. After a couple of

uneasy moments he escorted me out into corridor. "The CIA is taking over protection of the production," he said finally in a low voice, having at last let go of my shoulder. "They're doing that on a lot of things now . . . the Super Bowl, the Olympics . . . I know we're nothing by comparison, but they said they want control and who are we to argue? And I suppose your showing them up had something do with it. Who knows? They deny it of course. But it is what it is." He looked at me for a reaction but I didn't know what to think. Getting the sack was always a surreal experience, no matter what the cause. "And I'm sorry, Moses, but we can't afford private security of our own anymore, now that that sleaze-bucket Volksbruner's dropped out of the picture. But it's no biggie," he continued, forcing a smile. "I had to cut the schedule too and we'll *all* be home in a couple of weeks. This will be a great story for the guys at the Market, not that those assholes will give a shit. Speaking of which Arthur says good-bye and thanks too. He had to fly off to Paris this morning to try to dredge us up some finishing money from one of those foreign sales thieves."

"What about Lancaster?" I asked and I could see Farnsworth frowning, searching for an answer, when Goran showed up, looking, as usual, as if he'd closed half the schnapps joints in the Czech Republic.

"My good friend," he said, throwing his arms around me in a bear hug. "I am so happy I did not miss you. Thank you so much. You were magnificent director! Fabulous! I will see you on my next trip to Los Angeles! Give my regards to your lovely wife."

Obviously I had been the last to know.

Well not exactly the last. Samantha, my lovely wife, was the last. "I don't feel like a vacation," I told her after I had recounted what happened. But my declaration was superfluous. She had already heard me saying good-bye to Jiri and Eva on the telephone. I would miss the whole crew, but them more than the rest; in fact I had felt surprisingly choked up by it all, unable to face the group personally, as if I had failed them in some way. In fact,

I found out during the process, I wasn't the only one who was fired, although I was the only one who would have called it that. The others accepted at face value the same story that Farnsworth had told his wife—Cindy Lemon had had a death in the family and had to return to America immediately. Actually the director had been consumed by guilt, as I later learned, and had, in the parlance of the movie business, "paid off " his script supervisor/paramour, who knew with how much, and asked her to leave. Ellen would take over Cindy's job herself. "Script" was definitely a below-the-line task, but there was no one else with the skills to do it available in the Czech Republic and who, in the end, had better knowledge of the screenplay than its author.

None of this needed a prolonged discussion. Samantha removed our empty suitcases from the hotel closet and started tagging them for home. We booked a flight for the next morning.

12

MY MOOD HARDLY IMPROVED when I got back to LA. I was in mourning for that accidental burst of creativity that had come into my life and now seemed destined never to return. And I felt trapped forever in the humdrum existence of a detective. This prevented me from taking satisfaction from the improved business climate that greeted our arrival. America was adjusting to terror and our voice mail had been filled with not one but five offers of work, including an industrial espionage case from an auto plant in Orange County, which came, miracle of miracles, through our website. Normally I would be in pig heaven with all this activity, but instead I acted more like a somnambulist, going through the motions and behaving as if I had come down with a severe case of anhedonia, that psychiatric condition that is defined as the inability to experience pleasure and had been, appropriately enough, I had once heard one of the wags at the Market say, the working title of Woody Allen's *Annie Hall*. Not even the news from Prague, which arrived in the form of an e-mail from Arthur, that Lancaster had apparently been killed, his Mini supposedly tracked by a CIA Predator across the German border into the Bavarian Alps where it was incinerated by one of the drone's missiles, did much to lift my spirits. To begin with I was distrustful of the report. (What Mini? And what was the evidence of his identity, assuming there was any? It couldn't have been DNA. They didn't even have an original source for comparison.) It seemed much too easy, as if those intelligence agencies, after decades of incompetence, were looking to shut the door on a matter that was embarrassing to them—though I had a suspicion that Lancaster, like one of his snakes, would slither under the door again. But most of all I felt left out of the action. This no longer had anything do with me and I wanted to be allowed to enjoy my misery in peace.

"Get over it," said Samantha, growing justifiably fed up with my behavior. "If you want to be a director, go to film school or something." Film school? I had never thought of it. But wouldn't that be going backward when I had already stood on a set yelling "Action!" and "Cut!" to a Hollywood movie star, at least a minor one, and a prize-winning Serbian actor who was acclaimed throughout Europe and had recently played Lear with some of the leading lights of the Royal Shakespeare Company itself? And even if I did swallow my pride and apply, what film sample could I possibly submit with my application? *Prague Autumn?* That was Farnsworth's movie. No, I was in the slough of despond and I refused to get out.

But gradually, and without Prozac, I began to rejoin the world of the normally neurotic. I went back to work and soon enough, in just a few weeks, I began to forget my short career in the cinema and all it engendered, or at least most of it. I was feeling better. And then something amazing happened, Samantha announced that her premonition was reality—she *was* pregnant, confirmed first by those handy home testers and then reconfirmed definitively by her gynecologist. We hugged and kissed and I spent the next days in another kind of daze, which led to a new feeling, for me, of harmony with existence. I was at peace with myself. I was to be a father again. It didn't matter what my occupation, I would be happy . . . until I got a phone call that wrenched me back into the movie world again.

It was from Arthur and at first I thought he was going to tell me that Lancaster was alive and had burned the negative and was coming after everyone associated with the film, but it was nothing of the sort, at least for now. Instead, the bondsman began by reporting in excited, almost manic, fashion that the production had wrapped and they had already returned to Los Angeles for a couple of weeks. They were editing away, and *he* personally had found the completion money, not with the French but with Kick Pictures, a small foreign sales outfit in the Valley that usually backed Kung Fu cheapies in Manila but had decided to upgrade their profile with an art flick. In return for the cost of post-production, about a half million, Kick Pictures was taking world rights to *Prague Autumn* except North America, not a great deal, Arthur admitted, but Farnsworth, who was tapped out and about to sell his house, was more than pleased. "At least he gets to finish his film," said the completion bondsman, who was no longer merely an insurance man but a full-fledged producer, Peter having raised his status in gratitude to fill the slot formerly allotted to the insidious Volksbruner.

"Congratulations," I said.

"I'm thrilled," said Arthur. "My first official producer credit on a movie like this. And it's coming out so well. It could really be an important film." He was kvelling so much I thought he was going to invoke his ill and sainted mother but then he got down to the true reason for his call. "Why'd you do it, Moses?" he said, his voice suddenly changing into something resembling a high school principal's.

"Do what?"

"You know what I'm talking about."

"Frankly I don't have the slightest idea."

"Lodge a credit complaint with the Director's Guild. It was greedy and rude. You're not a real director. What do you need that for?"

"I didn't do *that!*" I said, practically shouting into the phone. Half the world was about to blow up. People were scared of terrorists slipping into the country with dirty nukes in shipping containers and these dudes were worried about credit! That was Hollywood for you!

"Well, who else did?" Arthur responded. "And don't tell me it's the cast and crew. They don't know anything about these things and it wouldn't be to their benefit anyway. . . . And, by they way, Farnsworth's blaming himself for it. He says he planted the idea in your head." It was true. He had mentioned such a thing at our emergency meeting in his hospital room. But that was just a joke and I took it as such. "Moses, this could fatally endanger the distribution of our film. Harvey Weinstein and his kind don't like it when things like this happen. They don't smell Oscars. They smell lawsuits."

Oh fuck that, I thought. These people are impossible. "Look, I'll be glad to waive credit if that's what you want. I'll sign a paper or something."

"Too late. The Guild has already launched an investigation."

"Then what do you want me to do?" My voice rose to a near shout for a second time.

"I don't know. You're a detective. Find out who did it!"

I was about to ask what good would *that* do, when I realized I was talking to someone trying to get a movie finished, therefore temporarily insane. How quickly I had forgotten. There was no reasoning with a person in that condition and it was best to humor him like your average homicidal schiz in the locked ward of a forensic mental hospital. So I promised Arthur I'd look into it and true to my word went over to the Sunset Boulevard head-quarters of the Directors Guild to nose around.

I had always wondered why a creative organization of sup-posedly refined visual artists would be housed in such a banal-looking piece of urban blight. Constructed out of bronze glass like a branch bank and shaped like a missile silo, the DGA reminded me of nothing so much as the home base of some medium-sized Pentagon subcontractor. Indeed the reception I got that afternoon was entirely consistent with the most buttoned-up of corporations. I was shuffled by a series of anxious bureaucrats from the contracts department to the credits department to the communications department, ending up with a public relations woman whose sole job, apparently, was shining people on. Despite the fact I was one of the principals, not only would she not tell me the identity of the whistle-blower who instigated the credit arbitration, she wouldn't tell me *who* was going to decide it or even *when* they were going to do it. All she would do was assure me that *whatever* it was, they weren't going to do it the manner of the Writers' Guild, an organization she referred to as if their members were a group of unemployed Chechnyans conspiring to fire 160 mm mortars through the back wall of the DGA building. I was used to this kind of huffy attitude between the creative unions, having listened to the perpetual sniping between writers and directors at the table at the Farmer's Market, particularly over the "film by" credit, which appeared at the beginning of movies and ascribed their ultimate authorship to the directors even when someone else had made the whole thing up. I had always been on the side of the writers on that one, but now that I had directed I was feeling a little differently. How many writers had to deal with terrorists on the set? Directors should get some kind of extra credit for that. But just as I was about to concoct a speech to ingratiate myself with this woman by showing my great sympathy for the director's position and thereby possibly extracting some of the information she guarded so zealously, my cell phone rang. It was Arthur again. He sounded extremely contrite and about as anxious as I had ever heard him, which was saying a lot.

"I apologize a thousand times," he said. "You didn't do it. It couldn't be more obvious. But can you come over here now? It's an emergency!"

"What is it?"

"Lancaster! He's back!"

"How do you know?"

"A snake. We've been invaded by a snake!"

"Where are you?"

He gave me the address of their cutting room in Hollywood. When I arrived there, he was on the front lawn of one of those old craftsman houses of Franklin with Farnsworth, Linda Fisk and her assistant Danny. "It's in there," he said, pointing toward the house. "I think it's a fucking python!"

"Come on, Arthur. It's not that big," said Farnsworth.

"Have you called the police?" I asked. "Or at least the fire department?"

Arthur and Farnsworth looked at each other. Then Peter smiled over at Linda, as if to placate her, before he turned back to me. "It's not so easy," he said.

"What're you talking about? Just pick up the phone. I thought you had a poisonous snake in there."

"Well, we don't even know if it *is* poisonous," said Farnsworth.

"It's the first time I've seen a snake of any kind in an editing room," said Linda, who sounded irritated with her two bosses. "And considering what happened in Prague . . ."

"We can't jump to conclusions," Arthur chimed in, sounding more emphatic in his new capacity as producer than I had ever heard him.

"What're you talking about conclusions? You just told me on the phone that Lancaster was back."

"That may be, but . . ." He took me by the arm and led me aside. "Moses, we have to be discrete about this or we won't be able to finish the movie."

"I thought you already got completion money from that kung fu outfit."

"Kick Pictures." He nodded. "We have a contract, but we don't have cash in hand. It has to go through a whole banking process . . . loans . . . another completion bond . . . any bad publicity at this point could blow it right out of the water."

"That's why we need you," said Farnsworth, who had walked over to us. "To stop this bastard from sabotaging us, after the

CIA fucked up and he got away . . . I wonder what poor SOB they zapped with their missile. . . . Anyway, at least Lancaster's apparently back in this country. Now it'll be easier to find out who he is and bring the racist creep to justice." He put his arm around me in the same way he had when he fired me. "We have to have you back on the team, Moses."

"But we can't pay you," said Arthur.

"What?"

"There's no money left in the budget. *We're* both working for free."

"But you're the producer and the director."

Arthur and Farnsworth looked at each other again before the producer leaned in more closely. "We could offer you some small piece of the profits," he said, whispering almost inaudibly, I presumed so Linda couldn't hear. "Or course, we're talking about adjusted producer's gross after break-even including the normal recoupment costs, advertising and distribution fees not to exceed thirty-five percent foreign and twenty-five percent domestic."

"What the fuck are you doing?" said Farnsworth, staring angrily at his partner. "We've got a potential catastrophe on our hands and you're *negotiating?* It's true what they say. Living in Hollywood *is* like a terminal illness. . . . Please," he continued, turning back to me. "Help us. I've got to finish this movie. Just tell me what you think would be fair." He looked at me for the first time with an expression approaching despair. I almost felt sorry for the guy. "I'll sell my house, if I have to."

"I already told you that's ridiculous," said Arthur. "Investing in your own movie is crazy enough. Selling your house for it is certifiable."

"I'll do what I want," Farnsworth insisted.

"Okay, okay," I said. "I'll think about. Meanwhile, let's have a look at that snake."

I don't know why I was so sanguine about it, after what had happened to Tina Kerides, but I headed for the door and was the first one through after Danny. He showed me past a couple of cluttered rooms filled with reels of the work print to the actual cutting room where a long, fairly hideous red snake was indeed coiled up under the Avid computer, apparently asleep. Before I could have second thoughts, I walked into the kitchenette, grabbed a chef's knife and started lashing at the animal's head. It awoke and hissed at me and I jumped back, but I kept flailing with the knife, terrified that I would get bitten with its poison before I killed it, so I continued dancing around and blindly thrashing at the creature, intermittently striking it until I wore the serpent down and its guts started to spill out over the floor and it stopped moving. Then I gingerly scooped up its grizzly remains with an empty film can and dumped them in three layers of plastic bags. I later learned that these precautions weren't necessary when the reptile was identified as a Baja California rat snake, a not uncommon member of the benign colubrid family, which was, despite its menacing name, about as venomous as a cocker spaniel. Perhaps its appearance had been entirely accidental. But that was not an assumption I was prepared to make.

"The first thing you've got to do is move out of here," I told Farnsworth, after I had finished tying the bag. "But subtly, so Lancaster and whoever is working with him still thinks this is your cutting room. . . . The question is where. What about your buddies from the Market? Any of them got a space?"

"Chemerinski has a home office the size of Texas he never uses," said Farnsworth. "But he's too famous. Messengers are always going in and out. . . . Wait a minute. Stanley Vogel. He and his wife Eleanor have that basement with the windows all blacked out."

I knew exactly what he was talking about. I had met Stanley and Eleanor Vogel a few times myself over the years. On the surface, they were both fairly typical middle-aged writers—Stanley a novelist and screenwriter and Eleanor a journalist. But somewhere along the line, perhaps because they had no children, they got into the habit of lighting up a joint or two every night along with the *MacNeil/Lehrer Report*. Soon it was more than one or two, maybe like three or four or five. By the time Robert MacNeil retired, they had become serious home marijuana growers—not for profit (they were doing fine in their careers), but for their own delectation and as a kind of wry rebellion against their conventional lifestyles. Problem was the woman they hired to be their "agronomist," as they called her, got overly ambitious and soon there was enough grass growing in their basement to turn on the better part of West Hollywood. And then last spring, when Stanley and Eleanor were off in England retracing Wordsworth's steps in the Lake District, they received a nervous phone call from a neighbor describing lines of cars pulling in and out of their driveway at all hours of the night. The police were making inquiries. The panicked Vogels were on the next plane home with every one of the cannabis plants uprooted and chucked into a dumpster in the San Gabriel Valley within hours of their arrival. The gang at the Market thought this was hilarious and wanted to know exactly *where* in the San Gabriel Valley they could find this dumpster. I wondered whether, after all this, the couple would be willing to have their basement used for another high-risk endeavor; but Farnsworth was close friends with Stanley—they had known each other since Yale—and was sure he could persuade him to do it.

Before heading off to have the snake checked by a herpetologist at UCLA, I promised the producer and director I'd consider their proposal about rejoining the team. In truth, they knew and I knew that I was back in. I had clearly been infected by the moviemaking illness Farnsworth had described. I could only hope it wasn't terminal. Samantha must have thought it was because when I told her what happened that evening, she didn't seem happy about it.

"We've got plenty of work," she said. "And now you want to run around, trying to uncover Lancaster's identity. And for what?

The promise of profits on some movie that may never be released? And even then, from what I've read, you've got as much chance of getting your cut as qualifying for the decathlon in the next Olympics. On top of that, Moses, you're going to be a father again." She took my hands and looked me in the eyes. "You don't need to be placing yourself in unnecessary jeopardy. Let them call the FBI."

"They call the FBI, everything becomes public and they'll lose the financing for their movie."

"So what? People are in danger here."

"Look, I promise. I'm not going to put myself in jeopardy or anybody else. The minute I smell anything substantive, I'll turn it over to the authorities. For now I haven't done anything more dangerous than contact the Princeton Club of Southern California." Samantha stared at me, puzzled, and I explained that I had spoken with the club president, a Mr. Norbert Haley '56, concerning an "article" I was doing on the mysterious Michael Lancaster '87. Mr. Haley didn't remember who that was until I reminded him, but was perfectly agreeable when I asked if he could get me in touch with members of that class from the So Cal area who might have memories of the bastard.

I gave him my cell number and he called back the next morning when I was sitting with the crew at the Farmer's Market. I had arrived a few minutes earlier and was already getting worked over by the guys who, since Farnsworth wasn't around, wanted the real skinny on what had gone down in Prague. "I heard he's trying to get his film in Sundance," said Douglas Corfu.

"They've got a quota. They only take one Holocaust movie a year," said Chemerinski. "And that has to be from Bulgaria. . . . Now tell us the truth. Can Peter direct? Or did Donna Gold lead him around by his pecker until he didn't know which side of the camera was up?"

"Come on," said Stanley Vogel, defending his friend. "Peter's married. And this time for real." Obviously he knew nothing of

Farnsworth's dalliance with Cindy Lemon. Or if he did, he was covering up. "Besides" he continued, "it looks like our Donna has her hand on someone else's pecker." He was pointing to a photograph on the gossip page of that morning's *Variety*. It had the headline "New Beau for Gold?" and showed the actress in a slinky cat suit, her hand blocking the camera in the classic pose of celebrities not wanting to be photographed, emerging from a Paris nightclub with Dr. Pavel Janak. "Isn't he the quack with the longevity injections? You could boff every leading lady in Hollywood with that gig."

"Who do you think put it in the trades?" said Corfu. "Nick Hodgetts is going to shit a brick."

At that point Haley called me back with the names of local alumni. "Back in the P.I. business?" said Chemerinski as I jotted down the members of the class of '87. "We must be winning the war on terror. People are paying to have their spouses tailed again."

"Peace of Mind Insurance," I reminded him. "I'll put it on a bus bench." I nodded a quick good-bye to the gang and started to leave when I ran straight into Farnsworth coming the other way. His face was ashen and he looked like the proverbial infantryman who was just told his grandmother died.

"I have to talk to you," he said, pulling me toward the doughnut stand to where the others couldn't hear. "Sundance passed," he blurted out in agony, sighing before he added, "Please don't tell anyone."

"Don't worry. I won't. I'm a profit participant too, right?" I tried to laugh but it came out a dry chuckle. The director didn't think it was very funny either. He seemed on the edge of tears. "I have an idea. It's a long shot but maybe I can get them to reconsider."

Farnsworth stared at me incredulously. "You know Robert Redford?"

This time I *did* laugh. "No. But I know something he wouldn't want to *hear*." The director continued to stare at me.

"Cheer up," I said. "All is not lost," and clapped him reassuringly on the shoulder before heading off for my car.

I spent the rest of the morning in typical LA fashion, parked on the freeway about forty miles from my destination. So I did what I usually did and used the car as my office. My first call was to Milan St. Clair. I suspected I wouldn't get him immediately and I was right. It took three tries and only on the third one, after having mentioned the address of Jana Staronova's apartment and wondering aloud if Mr. St. Clair had received some tape recordings made there that contained, I was certain by mistake, some "completely inadvertent slurs about one ethnic group," did the selection committee chairman get off his endless series of "conference calls" to take mine.

The subtext of our conversation was the hard, simple reality of job preservation (his), so our talk was surprisingly brief and entirely cordial. The chairman of the Selection Committee immediately apologized, insisting there had been some misunderstanding and that, of course, a film of the quality of *Prague Autumn* would be welcomed, even solicited, by the Sundance Festival. How could they be without it? The only question was whether we would like it to be in competition or in the prestigious World Cinema category with other "important exemplars" of international filmmaking. He asked me to consult my "estimable colleagues" on this small matter and assured me that an official letter of acceptance was on its way "that day" by Federal Express. I relayed this information to Farnsworth a few minutes later and I don't think I have ever made anybody so happy. I caught him at the Vogels where he, Arthur and the editors were working to set up the new cutting room. When he passed on the news to the others, they let out a whoop that sounded like Times Square when the ball comes down. Farnsworth thanked me profusely. "I don't know how you did it, but you're a genius!" he said. "You more than earned your points. You should take them all. And the directing credit too, if you want it!" I knew he wasn't serious about the latter. I didn't much want the credit then anyway. The whole exchange, my having blackmailed St. Clair, even though I disliked him immensely, had left a bad taste in my mouth. Worse, I had this uncomfortable feeling that there was something missing, that I was living out in my small way the newly popular Theory of Unintended Consequences.

13

"I slept with him. . . . Well, I think I did. I was pretty gone on 'shrooms at the time. Your generation wasn't the only one who did things like that you know. Anyway, I don't know if I *really* slept with him, but he sure was my type—cowboy hat, wild hair, scruffy beard, bandana . . . just like Willie Nelson."

Willie Nelson? Lancaster was clearly a man of many disguises. But Vanessa Bamberger-Dougherty '87 (at that time just plain Vanessa Bamberger) had nodded confidently when she identified her mysterious classmate from the faded color production still I carried with me, even though the picture showed someone with a bald head, shaved eyebrows, spectacles and an earring (although the earring could have been worn by Willie). "It's his eyes," she said, pointing to his pupil, which was an unremarkable shade of brown. She also indicated that the photo reminded her of Lancaster's appearance when he wore a full bodysuit as Iago in a wretched student version of *Othello* at the McCarter Theatre. He was the only decent one in the production, according to Vanessa, and had considerable natural acting talent. I wasn't surprised. We were standing in the backyard of her immense Tudor estate in Bel Air while her young daughters bounced high on a trampoline the size of a three-car garage. It was the middle of the afternoon by then and, after interminable stints on the freeways, she was the third Princeton '87 I had met that day. The first two were a dot-commer turned restaurateur in Redondo Beach and a lawyer in the Oviatt Building downtown. They had little memory of Lancaster other than the *scandale* of someone bilking their way into their esteemed alma mater, which, the lawyer pointed out to me with pride, was cited this year as the nation's number one undergraduate college by *U.S. News & World Report.*

I grew impatient with the lawyer as he blathered on self-importantly, my mind dominated by visions of Lancaster's snakes slithering under his office door and by what the young man might be planning. Ever since I suspected he was back in the country, I had the distinct sense he was watching me, tracking my every move, but I had no idea how or why. I kept checking my rearview mirror as I drove out to Vanessa's place, though I didn't know who I was looking for, how he might be appearing. Once I thought I saw Mr. Earring riding behind me in a Volkswagen Jetta and I slowed for a better look, but it wasn't him. There were a dozen guys who looked like that in every coffee shop in LA. My nerves were completely on edge, as if I were somewhere on the higher end of the government's color-coded terror alert scale, but I couldn't remember whether it was supposed to be yellow or orange or green or red. Who could?

I kept at that state of high anxiety until I met Vanessa.

"What about Lancaster? Did you stay in touch with him?" I asked her, struggling to redirect the conversation from Willie Nelson. She apparently had a lifelong crush on the singer.

"How can you stay in touch with someone when you don't know who he is? Not that I know who *I* am half the time."

"What about where he came from? Did he ever tell you anything?"

Vanessa said nothing. She started to frown, giving her a suddenly thoughtful look like the intelligent young Princeton grad she was. She was an attractive woman with close-cropped flaxen hair and angular features. "'Never grow up in a yurt,'" she said. "'You'll never get over the hurt.'"

"What?"

"He loved doggerel. He would repeat it over and over again. I think he made it up. 'Never grow up in a yurt. / You'll never get over the hurt. / Dah-dah-dah-dah-dah-dah-dah-dah / dah-dah-dah-dah-dah-dah-dah. . . .' I can't remember the rest. Actually, he was kind of annoying. Maybe I didn't sleep with him."

A few minutes later, I was reciting those words to Eva over the phone. I had awakened the assistant director at four in the morning in Prague but she responded to me with her usual obedient yet slightly ironic "Sir," as if I was still directing the movie and about to tell her about a sudden change for the next day's shooting. The word "yurt" had struck a familiar chord with me from the screenplay appended to the title page of *The Protocols of the Elders of Zion—The Motion Picture*. But perhaps more important, Lancaster reciting doggerel had reminded me of Earring's poem, the one he wanted to read for the scene at the Globe Bookstore. I wanted to know what Eva had done with it. It turned out she had placed it in my director's box at our Barrandov office. She would go out to the studio that morning and try to retrieve it, if the contents of my box had not been emptied when I lost my job.

I thanked her and drove over to the Vogels' house to make sure the editing room was secure. Jaibo Sandoval was seated at the top of the basement stairs playing a golf game on his laptop. Jaibo, a retired cop from El Monte, was a black belt in *krav maga*, the self-defense system invented by the Israelis in the 1940s when the British forbade them to bear arms, and I often used him to do guard duty when a little muscle might be useful. "*No he visto nada de serpientes,*" I haven't seen any snakes, he said with a laugh. I grinned and walked past him down to the editing room where Linda was hard at work on the love scene at the refugee camp. "I can't believe you got her to do that," she said, gesturing to the monitors where every inch of a recumbent Donna Gold was on display as if she were posing for Penthouse. "I hope we can get her to sign off on it. Gary Greenhut thinks it will be very helpful."

"Who's Gary Greenhut?"

"The agent Arthur hired to sell domestic rights. They're down at the Petit Prince. They said if you came by to send you over."

The Petit Prince was a café on that part of the Sunset Strip populated by more Eurotrash than you could find on the length of the Via Veneto. It was as if after Fellini died the entire cast of *La Dolce Vita* was loaded on a plane to Los Angeles to be dumped only on this fifty yards of sidewalk with their shirts still unbuttoned to their navels and newfound cell phones growing out of their ears like the trunks of a twisted elephant. Arthur and Farnsworth were there when I arrived, sitting with a young guy in a black Prada suit, dark Ray Charles glasses, thick cosmetic suntan and a short haircut with bangs that made him look like Caligula reborn in the mailroom of ICM. "You must be Gary," I said.

"None other!" He jumped to his feet, extending his hand and speaking in a staccato accent that sounded like a cross between Rodney Dangerfield and Jackie Mason. "And I am sure you are Moses Wine, the renowned private investigator and sometime film director who gave us the most revealing and seductive shots ever of the luminous Miss Donna Gold."

"Entirely an accident," I said, shaking his hand. "I didn't even know the camera was running."

"You are too modest, sir. As we all know, the job of the motion picture director is to provide a comfortable creative environment for the other artists to express their unique imaginative capabilities. And you did that extremely well in the short time available, if I may say so, as well as, I understand, finding a mysterious method of correcting a gross oversight made by the Sundance Film Festival selection committee, apropos of which, as I told the gentlemen," he gestured to Arthur and Farnsworth, "I am recommending they elect to screen their movie in the highly influential World Cinema category. Much as competition is alluring, you cannot trust any jury to reward even the most obviously superior work and I have seen many masterpieces and near masterpieces overlooked for distribution because they didn't win a prize they so eminently deserved." The agent looked both ways, and then leaned in more closely, talking in a stage whisper. "Moreover we can mount a little campaign for the film that implies that, due to the seriousness of the subject matter and the present delicate international situation, we do not want to compete for awards and cheapen our message." At that point, I heard a blast of the *William Tell Overture.* Greenhut winked at us and reached into his pocket, flipping open the smallest cell phone I had ever seen and squinting at the mini-screen. "A junior acquisitions executive from Paramount Classics," he explained and stood up. "Way down on the food chain. She wants to see some footage from our film. Of course, we're not going to let her—she can only say no . . . in fact she wants to say no, so she can tell her boss she's seen it and turned it down . . . but we can't offend her . . . hello, Lisa." He faced away from us and took a few steps toward the restaurant. "Yes, I saw the Lynch picture . . . disappointing."

"He wants us to change the title," Farnsworth told me, eyeing Greenhut unhappily. "What's the matter with *Prague Autumn?* I always thought it had just the right touch of melancholy."

"That's his point, Peter," said Arthur. "It's a bit of a downer. And besides, Middle America's never *heard* of Prague. Right, Moses?" I shrugged, not having any idea *what* they knew. "He just wants to change the title, not the movie," the producer continued to his partner. "What about *Autumn Mist?*"

"Why even bother with *Autumn,*" said Farnsworth, "with all those depressing yellow leaves? Why not just plain *Mist?*"

"Now you're talking," said Greenhut, glancing back at us. "The shorter the better." Within seconds he was folding up his phone and heading back to the table.

"Like your phone call," said the director.

The agent nodded with a frown. "Unfortunately, as of now, I don't think Paramount Classics is in play. They've got a Bosnia movie. It's not the Holocaust, I know, but they say it appeals to the same audience. We have to change their minds. It's all perception." He sat down and studied us all thoughtfully before continuing. "I hope you don't mind my bringing this up, but there's some buzz about a terrorist threat to your film. We can't stop talk. The question is whether to encourage it. It's the sympathy factor versus the fear factor."

"I'd stay away from fear," said Arthur.

"Well, that means we ignore it," said Greenhut. "Still it may be our best card. Every movie needs something to separate it from the endless screenings at Sundance, not to mention Slamdance and the other mini-festivals for high school dropouts who stole their father's camcorders."

"If we were to play it up," said Farnsworth, looking doubtful, "what would we do?"

"I'll think about it," said the agent, again studying us before he went on. "There's another angle, if you'll permit me. I understand there's a guild arbitration over the directing credit on this movie. Maybe we could turn that to our advantage."

"I don't want the credit," I said.

"Suit yourself, sir, but we'd certainly be the first film with a co-director who's a private investigator."

"Oh, please," said Peter disdainfully. The arrogant bastard looked so appalled I almost started to change my mind.

"We'll discuss that later," Arthur interjected, immediately adding, "I don't think it's a good idea either," obviously for Farnsworth's benefit. I wasn't sure what he *really* thought but I didn't want to pursue it. In any case, at that point *my* cell phone rang.

It was Eva. She hadn't been able to fall back asleep and had gone out to Barrandov at the crack of dawn to find what I was looking for. Obviously she had been curious about what had prompted me to call her in the middle of the night. "I don't understand why you want *this*," she said. "It's like a silly children's poem." "I don't either," I said and then she read it to me: "Never grow up in a yurt. / You'll never get over the hurt. / Be raised in

Nebraska. / Or even Alaska. / But keep your casa away from Bogurt."
Bogurt? Was this some kind of joke or just bad doggerel? No
wonder Vanessa Bamberger couldn't remember it. "Do you want
me to fax it to you?"

"Sure. Thanks. Be well," I said and hung up. "Some poetry I
forgot in Prague," I said to the others who were staring at me
curiously.

"Poetry?" said Farnsworth.

"I guess you really *are* a shamus after all," said Greenhut, his
eyebrows rising just above his Ray Charles glasses. "But if you
would be so good, Mr. Spade, as to take a few moments off from
your investigation to lend us a hand on another matter." I
looked at him with growing trepidation. I had a pretty good
idea where he was going and I was right. "I understand from
these gentlemen that you have the best relationship among this
august group with Ms. Donna Gold. Would you be so kind as
to urge her to sign her concurrence with the nude scene because
if she doesn't, there is little hope this important cinematic
enterprise will be distributed and Mr. Farnsworth here will lose
his entire investment."

"So forgiveness for the Holocaust comes down to Donna
Gold's tits?"

"You said it. I didn't," said the agent.

And, as he so quaintly added, I would have to do this with
all due dispatch. The others explained the situation in more
detail: There were only eleven days left until the start of
Sundance. Most of the film had already been edited in the
breakneck manner of television movies, but there would be no
time to have a normal sound mix, to cut negative and to strike
answer prints. We would have to show the film double-system
on a special two-track projector outfitted to run that way. The
grease pencil marks for the optical fades and dissolves would
still be visible. Farnsworth and Arthur thought this rough-and-
ready approach might actually rebound to our favor, creating

low expectations as it had for other surprise indie hits like the *Blair Witch Project* and the *Buena Vista Social Club*. However we presented the film, we still needed Donna's signed permission to show it, at least in a manner that the likes of Greenhut would consider commercially viable.

Perhaps fortunately, I was unable to contact the actress right away because I had something more pressing to deal with that evening—Samantha's first case of morning sickness, which had extended throughout the whole day. We were in the kitchen, discussing Lancaster's doggerel while she prepared a turkey *mole* from one of Diana Kennedy's Mexican cookbooks. Sam was stirring in the *chipotle*, asking me if I had considered that the casa referred to might actually have been Casablanca. "I mean everyone is supposed to know that was Bogart's most famous film. Bogart . . . Bogurt . . . rhymes with yurt," she continued before suddenly starting to gag. Her face turned several shades of green and she bent over the sink. It wasn't a pretty sight. I ran to the spice rack for some ginger, the only cure I remembered from my first experiences with nausea during pregnancy over two decades before, sprinkling it liberally into some herb tea. "You should run a search on Casablanca," she added before she gagged again.

"The movie or the city?" I asked, offering her the tea but she waved it off as if it were some useless remedy, which could only be selected by some member of my evolutionarily challenged gender. I clearly was not going to get an answer to my question, not immediately anyway.

I skulked off to the computer, muttering to myself about why I was attempting a tedious and probably fruitless search for Casablanca. It would more likely be the city than the flick, given the content of the poem, but where would it be located? As far as I knew, there weren't any yurts anywhere near the original city or anywhere in Morocco for that matter, although there had been in America, as I well recalled, back in the sixties and early seventies when a good portion of my friends were living in any kind of domicile from a dome to a teepee, as long as it wasn't a normal house with a roof. Yurts were high on this list, as I further recalled, and New Mexico was one of the centers of this pseudo-Mongolia. It was also the locale of the film script attached to *The Protocols of the Elders of Zion—the Motion Picture*. But a quick search on Casablanca, New Mexico came up negative. So I was wondering if I was going up the wrong road when, scrolling down the list of cities in that state, I realized my mistake. It was Casa Blanca, two words, New Mexico, a rinky-dink outpost somewhere between Indian Service Route 22 and Indian Service Route 24 about forty miles west of Albuquerque on the I-40.

"Don't go there," said Samantha, who had been standing over my shoulder for the last part of my search. At that point I hadn't even thought of going, but perhaps she knew me better than I knew myself. "He's just trying to set you up again, like he did at the church in Prague. Only this time you'll be out in the middle of nowhere. You'll end up lying under a saguaro with a Gila monster making lunch from your small intestines. And then where will our daughter be?"

"Daughter? How do you . . . ?" But I stopped, seeing Samantha eyeing me with the same weary impatience she had displayed at my offer of ginger tea. "Anyway, how could he be trying to set me up?" I continued. "He wanted me to get that poem in Prague, not in Los Angeles. I mean what if he's not even really here? What if we're just being paranoid? That snake wasn't poisonous. There's no proof he didn't die in that missile attack."

Samantha just looked at me. She knew Lancaster was alive all right, at least as certainly as she knew that the baby in her belly was a girl. How could it be otherwise? It was part of that feeling you lived with now, the yellow, blue, green and red alert of it all. And also just as certainly as we knew Lancaster was alive, we both knew he was planning something big, a finale for *Prague Autumn* or *Autumn Mist* or *Mist* or whatever it was going to be called, that was more dramatic and deadly than anything Ellen and Peter, who were the kind of filmmakers often accused of being "soft" in Hollywood—sitcom people, for godsakes—could possibly have conceived.

"Okay, go," said Samantha. "I guess you have to. I'll go with you if I can get some Diclectin in time."

"What's that?"

"The single drug for morning sickness that works. It's only available in Canada."

At that point the phone rang. It was Donna. "I hear you're looking for me," she said. I told her I had a request that was better made in person and asked her if I could come over that night. She told me she had a guest and that it would be inconvenient, but I said it was urgent and, after some persuading and promises of confidentiality plus the requisite amount of gushy flattery, she finally relented. Before she had a chance to change her mind, I jumped in my car and drove over to her place. It was a rambling Mediterranean affair on a cul-de-sac in the Hollywood Hills not more than ten minutes from my house. I was beeped in through the security gate and walked down a quarry tile path lined with red and white azaleas to the front door. Donna herself let me in. "Hi," she said. "What's the urgent matter? I'm kind of busy at the moment." She was wearing a pair of shorts with a tank top, which, because we were in the middle of LA winter, seemed grabbed in a hurry from the wrong closet. I followed her to the living room where her guest was waiting. It was Dr. Pavel Janak leaning against the mantelpiece and looking quite at home in a black T-shirt and jogging pants. I can't say I was terribly surprised. He shook my hand and, after a round of hello doctor and how are you's, everyone stood there, looking awkward, in expectation of my explaining my purpose. But under the circumstances, this seemed even less appealing.

"I think . . . ," I said at last, "it's better discussed in private."

"Anything you say to me, you can say in front of him," said the actress, smiling fondly up at Janak as she touched his arm. "It's the least I can do for Pavel, when he's finally come to California after so many years. And with our future in front of us."

Since it was obvious there would be no confidential communication here, I had no choice but to blurt out the whole embarrassing business. "I don't even know what's in the scene," I concluded. "But they seem to think they can't do without it."

"They're going to have to," responded Donna immediately. "I won't allow it."

Her boyfriend seemed puzzled. "Why not?" he said. "It's for the good of the film. And you don't want to seem stodgy, my dear. You're a serious actress. This is a movie about love. A little nudity won't hurt anyone. In fact its absence would probably detract from the reality of the movie. And if you're worried about offending me, don't. I will always support your art."

"Right," she said, momentarily confused and looking off to where I imagined the bedrooms were. "Nick never would have said that."

"Well, you've finally left Nick," said the doctor. "Welcome to the liberal European approach . . . *your* new approach."

"Okay, tell them to leave it in," said Donna, who was still staring off toward the bedroom. Then she snapped out of it and turned back to me. "I think you should know. The FDA has finally decided to approve Pavel's longevity formula for sale in the United States and he's moving here this year. We're going to get married. Hopefully, at Sundance . . . if the movie's a hit. If it's not, we'll just go do it quietly in a private ceremony on Mustique."

"Congratulations!" I said. "Both of you."

This news was met with astonishment and some levity the next day at the editing room at the Vogels. I had stopped there with Samantha on our way to the airplane to New Mexico to inform the powers that be that Donna had approved the nude scene. Sam and I were in a shaky mood when we got there, having just come from a Taiwanese acupuncturist a friend had recommended for the treatment of morning sickness. The old

Chinese woman, who barely spoke English, had significantly reduced Sam's nausea when, after removing the needles and touching my wife's stomach, she turned to us both and said, "Be careful next days. Much danger. Bad chi." Where did that come from? Did she know about Lancaster? Could she see what he was planning? Not being superstitious and feeling slightly ridiculous, I asked her directly but she didn't understand a word I was saying. We paid her and left.

On the way over to the editing we tried to convince ourselves that it was nothing, that the old woman was just reading our anxiety the way anyone would, but we still had that uneasy feeling when we arrived in the cutting room to see tears streaming down the face of a yet older woman, this one about eighty-five. She was gesticulating with two outstretched hands toward a computer monitor around which over a half-dozen people had been clustered watching the latest revised cut of the film.

"What a movie! What a movie!" she was saying in heavily accented Yiddish–English. "I couldn't stop crying. . . . Okay, too bad it doesn't have a little more suspense at the beginning . . . and maybe it's a bit long in the middle, you could lose a few things here and there . . . but still it's on the whole quite moving. I would give it two stars, maybe two and a half, on a scale of four."

"Moses and Samantha," said Arthur. "This is my mother, Frieda Sugarman."

"Pleased to meet you," I said, extending my hand. Her son may have been afraid she was dying of cancer, but from the strength of her grip, I had the sense this diminutive woman—she couldn't have been more than four-ten—was going to be one of the Future Centenarians of America.

"Pleased to meet you too," she rasped. "But I'd really like to know if you agree with me about the suspense problem at the beginning of the picture. It was a little slow-going, don't you think, until you discover the leading lady's grandfather was a Nazi." I wasn't nuts about her tact, but I had to admit her analysis was right on. "So maybe they should fix the first part," she continued, "make some cuts in the middle, especially that scene in the glass factory, which seems to be nothing more than local color, and then perhaps they could be in competition. I know their agent feels differently but . . ." She gestured again while nodding to Greenhut, who was perched on a table next to a fax machine. ". . . If you're at the Sundance Film Festival and you're *not* in the competition, someone will always wonder why." She had a point there too, I thought. "So maybe there's still time to make a few changes. It's not all written in stone, right? I want the best for my boy's film," she smiled, looking at Arthur. "I don't want him to regret later that he didn't give it his all."

"Thanks, mother," Arthur said. "But we really didn't invite you here for this kind of criticism. We just wanted you to see the movie."

"So I saw," she said. "It was good." She smiled politely over at Peter and Ellen, who looked as if they had just eaten a large portion of spoiled fish.

"I have an idea," said Samantha suddenly, "if you don't mind my butting in. I mean I'm not a professional or anything and I only saw an earlier version but . . ."

"No, no, go ahead," said Farnsworth, sounding about as enthusiastic as a clerk at the Motor Vehicle Bureau.

"Well, you know that scene at the end, when Goran goes to find Donna at the refugee camp in the mountains and you don't know if they're finally going to get together or not. You should put that at the beginning too . . . run it twice . . . so the whole story's a circular mystery. Then people will wonder what's going to happen. It will give you some suspense without changing what you have and seem modern at the same time, as if you intended it all along. And, after all, love's a mystery, right?"

She stopped and looked at everyone. They were all strangely silent—the director, the producer, the writer, the editor, the assistant editor, the agent and the mother.

"Well, it's an idea," said Farnsworth finally. "Let's give it a try. It might work. And maybe we *should* be in competition," he added, acknowledging Frieda with a nod.

"About time," said the old woman.

It was then that I told them about Donna giving permission for the nude scene and about her imminent marriage, which might or might not be in Sundance, after which Samantha and I said good-bye and headed off to Casa Blanca, New Mexico. On the plane south, Sam was still thinking about the film, wondering whether her idea for it would work.

"They seemed awfully receptive, don't you think?" she said.

"They're pretty desperate," I responded, but frankly it wasn't a bad suggestion, though my mind wasn't on the film. It was on the look in the eye of Samantha's acupuncturist when she warned us to be careful in the next days. "Much danger. Bad chi." If there was one thing I didn't like it was bad chi. I checked the passengers on our flight for someone who in some way resembled Lancaster. Then I made sure to buckle up before we landed in Albuquerque.

An hour later we were in the land of brilliant sunsets and cheap motels, turning off Interstate 40 and then driving along a low-slung mesa in a rented Dodge toward Laguna, a spot on the map only slightly larger than Casa Blanca, which itself appeared to consist of two small streets, one of which was a dead end. We continued along New Mexico 124 past another dozen miles of empty desert and then turned left onto an unnamed street, bearing left again on Indian Service Route 503 and then finally right on a second unnamed street. Up ahead, .3 miles, according to the driving instructions I obtained from my computer, was supposed to be Casa Blanca. But all I could see were acres of yucca, a broken corral and the rusted shard of an abandoned pickup. If you ever needed a definition of the "middle of nowhere," this was it. We had come a long way and wasted a lot of time and money for a middling postcard view of the American Southwest. But then I noticed something written on the door of the truck. OPERA HOUSE, 2.2 MI, it said in white spray paint. BEST PUCCINI AND VERDI THIS SIDE OF LA SCALA! An arrow pointed down a dirt road that looped around some lonely paloverde trees before disappearing down a narrow canyon lined with red rock.

Samantha and I didn't have to say a word to each other. If there was anything as strange as Lancaster himself, this was it. I backed up and we headed down this road, jouncing up and down on the ruts, until we reached the mouth of the canyon. It was a cul-de-sac. At the back of it, up against a rock wall and right next to a small one-story wood frame building that looked like a run-down general store, was a largish circular structure made of adobe and shaped like a sawed-off cone with a flattened canvas teepee for a roof. Though I had never seen a yurt before, as far as I could recall, I suspected I was seeing one then and it reminded me of nothing so much as those summer playhouses I used to go to as a kid to see productions of *Oklahoma!* and *Carousel*, hatboxes with cute little flags on top, so maybe it was appropriate that the schmaltzy masterpieces of Italian opera would be performed here. But where was the audience? It didn't look as if there were another human being for a thousand miles.

We parked outside and walked up some steps, several of which were broken, through an open door, which hung from one squeaky hinge, into the building. The lower part of the interior was set up as a theater-in-the-round with benches, most of them now also broken, encircling a small stage with a lighting bridge riddled with cobwebs. Above us was a platform balcony that ran for about two-thirds of the circumference. Still saying nothing, Samantha and I climbed up to it on a rickety Navajo ladder. This upstairs must have been living quarters of sorts because, hidden behind a paisley curtain, was a threadbare futon, an easy chair with springs coming out of the bottom and a battered sofa all covered with a thick layer of dust. A bookshelf stood against the wall with about a dozen mangy paperbacks still in place. I recognized dog-eared editions of Kesey, Castenada, Vonnegut and Marcuse, all signposts of my generation, and a *Farmers' Almanac* for 1979. Further along, past another curtain, was a second futon, a smaller one next to a chest of drawers with faded decals of sports stars on the side, Dr. J and Reggie Jackson, next to an old "No Nukes Is Good Nukes" bumper sticker. I opened one of the drawers and a spider crawled out. I was about to look into another drawer when I noticed a bulletin board leaning upside down against the wall behind the futon. I turned it over and started to examine the contents—a first-prize diploma at a high school science fair, a ticket stub to a Surf Punks concert and a faded Polaroid of a woman about twenty in a Mary Quant dress standing with a man in a dashiki. His face had been scratched out, but he must have been white because of the color of his arms. I was trying to detach the photo from the board when I heard footsteps below and stopped. I turned and looked down at a man with dark, mottled skin and a moustache, wearing a cowboy hat and a faded tribal serape. He was holding a shotgun, but it wasn't cocked.

"Can I help ya?" he said.

"Sorry. We were just looking around," said Samantha. We both walked over to the ladder and started down.

"We've never seen a yurt before," I added, dusting myself off once I reached the bottom.

"What's a yurt?"

"You know . . . kind of a Mongolian house. Shaped like this."

"Ain't no Mongolians around here. What'd you say you wanted?"

"We're opera fans. We saw the sign."

"Opera's been closed for about fifteen years."

"Sorry to hear that."

"Sign's been gone that long too."

I stared at the man who was peering at me suspiciously under his hat. "You're sure it's gone?"

"Uh-huh."

I was going to dispute him, but thought better of it. "How come the opera closed?" asked Samantha. A door swung open in the wind. I glanced through it, but no one was visible outside, at least that I could see.

"Owner went crazy. Took her own life after her boy went away to college. Right up there on top of the mesa, they say." He nodded through the window. "With a shotgun like this one," he added, wiggling his gun.

"Did you know her?" I asked.

"Before my time."

"Know anyone who did?"

He shook his head. "Everything's changed here. There used to be hippies living in teepees. Ranchers. Now it's tribal land. Mescalero Apache." He took a step forward. "Why you asking so many questions?"

"Just curious," I said.

"Uh-huh," he repeated. "Who are you?"

"I told you. We're opera lovers."

"No, you're not." He took another step forward. "You're a private dick. From Los Angeles."

"How'd you know that?"

"Fellow called to warn us about you. Said you'd be nosing around here."

"Who was that?"

"Don't know."

"His name wasn't Lancaster by any chance?"

"He didn't say and I didn't ask."

Just then I heard a click and looked to my left. Another man, also an Indian, was standing there, holding a .38.

"Well what *did* he say?"

"Said if I was smart I'd tell you to get the fuck out. He said you're working for that casino company. The one that's tryin' to steal our land and make a deal with the Zuni."

"We're not doing that, I promise."

"He also said your wife's pregnant and you shouldn't be draggin' her out here like this where she could get killed." He cocked his shotgun and trained it straight on Samantha. His buddy pointed the .38 at my head. They both took a third step forward as another two men walked in through a side door. Against the glaring backlight it was hard to tell if they were Indian or not, but it scarcely mattered. Even in silhouette I could see that they were armed. They muttered something indistinguishable and started advancing toward us. One of them poked the barrel of his gun toward Samantha's stomach. I instantly stepped in front of him, put my arm around her and began escorting her toward the door. The men came after us, but I kept moving past them, as if I didn't notice.

"We're on our way, fellas," I said, holding up my free hand and warding them off like a halfback. "Thanks for the hospitality and everything." I flashed a smile as broad as I could and held it. "Down with the Zuni. Long live the Mescalero!"

Then I pulled Samantha out the door, letting it bang behind me. We walked rapidly down the path and jumped into the rental car. "That sonofabitch Lancaster manipulates everyone," I said, gunning the motor and backing out as quickly as possible. "First the Arabs, now the Indians. Next it'll be the Eskimos."

"I hope this counts," said Samantha.

"For what?" I asked.

"You know. . . . 'Much danger. Bad chi.' "

"I wouldn't depend on it," I said. "Nobody even took a shot. That's not even a three on the chi scale." In the rearview mirror, I could see the Indians, staring after us. "I think that motherfucker's aiming for a double ten. I just wish I knew what it was."

Whatever level of chi we were at, it took a while for us to get our bearings again. It wasn't until we were on the plane that Samantha showed me a torn newspaper clipping she had taken from the yurt. It came from the *Albuquerque Journal* of June 7, 1977, and concerned the woman I now assumed was Lancaster's mother. HIPPIE SOPRANO TRIUMPHS AS TOSCA it said, going on to detail a "soaring rendition" of the Puccini opera, attended "regrettably" by only twenty-three persons, performed by the owner and lead singer of the Casa Blanca Opera House, Lydia Ellison, "the communard turned coloratura, now 31." If my instant math was accurate, that meant she had shot herself well before she was forty. I wondered if she had considered every finale of *Tosca*, when her character leapt to her death off a balcony, as a rehearsal.

Once we got home, it didn't take me long to learn more about the deceased singer. My first call was to my old friend Sherman who used to cover the commune movement for the Berkeley Barb and other 1960s underground papers, way back to the early days of the Merry Pranksters, the Paleolithic Age of American bohemia when hippies were still beatniks and Janis Joplin was in junior high in Port Arthur, Texas. Indeed, Sherman knew about a group down in Casa Blanca, New Mexico, a spin-off from a collective of disciples of the Guru Maharaji in Taos around 1968. About a dozen of them, who differed with the Guru on some fine point of spiritual doctrine he couldn't now recall, had moved down to Casa Blanca to live as one big family, which basically meant four men sharing eight women and a lot of peyote. They had stayed together for a few years, splitting up over a disagreement about starting a theater, although he wasn't sure if it was opera. He heard that three people had stayed on—a woman and two men—while the rest drifted away, including a woman he knew while an undergraduate at the University of Wisconsin named Sheila Novodor, the only person from the Casa Blanca commune he recalled by name.

"What happened to her?" I asked Sherman, hoping that this Sheila had been around when Lancaster was born. I wasn't sure that would help me find him, but it certainly wouldn't hurt.

"Last I heard, which was about ten years ago, she was divorced with two children, working as a social worker in Detroit."

After about a half hour of phoning and web searching, I managed to track down Sheila, whose married name was Banfield, on the night shift at an AIDS hospice in East Lansing, Michigan. Despite the popular conception that most sixties revolutionaries had long ago sold out for BMWs, a surprising number still worked for a better world, though in a less conspicuous manner. Sometimes I thought the idea that they had been corrupted was just a theory concocted for the comfort of those that were.

"Poor Lydia, she was always waiting for that boyfriend who never showed up," said Sheila by telephone that night after I had introduced myself and sent regards from her old friend Sherman. "She used to say he was browbeaten by his mother, but I said what man isn't?"

"So I take it this boyfriend wasn't the father of her son."

"I don't think so but who knows. It was either he or Mark, this guy who was at the commune for maybe a year before his trust fund ran out. But come to think of it her kid didn't look much like Mark. Mark was a blond and the boy had really dark hair, like his mother." Obviously, she had been around for the birth of Lancaster.

"Was the boy's name Michael?"

"Michael?" I could hear Sheila laugh on the other end. "No kid had names like that in those days. His was Sage, after where he was born, right behind a line of brush by the nude mud baths in Bandolier National Monument." I should have known better.

"Do you know what became of him?"

"No . . . he sure was smart though. Reading before he was four. And not just *Winnie the Pooh* and *Cat in the Hat*. But I lost track of him long before I heard what happened to his poor mother."

"So the name Lancaster doesn't mean anything to you."

"Just a city in Pennsylvania."

"What about Lydia? Did she have family?"

"She didn't talk about it, but I always thought she was a WASP, from someplace in New England."

"And the mysterious boyfriend?"

"Never met him. Though I did read one of his letters once. He was going on a trip to France, Italy and Israel and wanted Lydia to come with him."

"Why didn't she?"

"She was pregnant and wanted him to marry her first."

How bourgeois, I thought, but then I remembered the same thing had happened to me—only I *had* acquiesced and gotten married. So maybe I was just another bourgeois for all my rebellion, maybe we all were, and those gloating BMW drivers were right. After all, I had owned a Beemer myself for a while and even a Porsche. But then of course I realized we were all just a mishmash, sometimes wanting to save the world and sometimes wanting to get a piece of it. It was nothing less than common moral schizophrenia—the human experience. But Lydia Ellison's story was clearly something sadder and less rewarding emotionally and materially. She had resolved her dilemmas by blowing her brains out after her son ran away from home and into Princeton under an assumed name. It seemed obvious that the boyfriend was his father but the man's identity remained unknown to me. The question was—was his identity also unknown to Lancaster, or rather to Sage Ellison or whatever name appeared on his birth certificate, if indeed there was one? I tended to doubt that it was.

I asked Sheila Banfield a couple of more questions that night, but I had basically exhausted her fund of useful information, so I said my thanks and hung up. Samantha was already asleep and I was exhausted from flying to New Mexico, driving across the desert, running into some angry Indians and then flying back in less than twelve hours. I needed to get some rest and I switched out the light. But I knew I wouldn't be able to sleep.

Sage/Lancaster was watching my every move. I had already strongly suspected it, but proof of his presence confronted us as we headed back onto the main road that afternoon. The door on the abandoned pickup truck, which had initially pointed the way, had been freshly repainted with new lettering. THANKS FOR VISITING, it now said. SEE YOU AT SUNDANCE!

14

"NUCLEAR WAR? . . . There goes my career!"

It was Farnsworth who whispered those words to me and I remembered them well from the dialog bubble of the now-famous, mock-Lichtenstein cartoon that appeared on the cover of the *LA Weekly* around 1980. A gorgeous female yuppie of the terminally hard-hearted type was shown sobbing uncontrollably because Armageddon had arrived in such an untimely manner as to thwart her personal ambitions. It did seem depressingly appropriate to the current situation. We were standing in a seemingly endless line of movie industry detritus at LAX for the flight to Salt Lake City—studio execs and agents, filmmakers and film shakers, producers and seducers—waving their supercilious hellos and punching their Palm Pilots as they waited to have their bodies buzzed and their shoes inspected. Greenhut was positioned just behind us, determinedly clutching a carton of those miniature Evian atomizers, which he planned to give away as promos for the film, having added a label of our own to theirs that read: COOL OFF WITH THE MAKERS OF MIST—THE ONLY LOVE STORY AT SUNDANCE WITH EXCLUSIVE RIGHTS TO THE SECRET FORMULA OF DR. PAVEL JANAK! Apparently the romance between our star and the founder of the esteemed longevity clinic had generated enough heat in the gossip columns to create some buzz for our film, and Greenhut was riding it. The festival-goers might even suspect there was a hint of the good doctor's eternal youth potion lacing the Evian, creating a feeding frenzy for the atomizers and thus hyping the movie. "I'm not discouraging it," said the agent.

"You can put those there, young man," said Frieda Sugarman, motioning from the carton to her lap. She was sitting in one of the wheelchairs provided for senior citizens at airports and was waiting more patiently than the rest of us because, as she had told everyone, seeing the premiere of her son's film would be the apotheosis of her existence, restitution, not that any could ever be made, for the evil perpetrated against her in Poland almost sixty years ago. Ten minutes later, thanks to her, we were allowed to bypass all the other passengers to get on board, even those spoiled potentates who, to avoid simultaneous assaults to their knees and their status, had deemed it necessary to sit in first class for a measly one-hour flight.

At that point there were ten of us getting on the plane— Peter and Ellen, Arthur and Frieda, the two editors, Greenhut, Jaibo Sandoval, Samantha and me. Donna and her entourage would join us later at the condo, as would Goran, arriving from Europe. Takashima, our Japanese producer, was even flying in from Tokyo. I had brought Jaibo along to help with what was now my primary task, providing protection for this disparate crowd. He performed the double-duty of carrying the work print of the film to be projected in two of those large gunmetal cans known for generations as Goldbergs. As for myself, I had spent the better part of the last week, which otherwise had been almost eerily uneventful, trying to learn anything I could about Lydia Ellison and her son, when I was lying awake at night, worrying about whether he would burn down the cutting room with every-one in it or steal the film's negative from the lab. I called to warn *them*, but, given the temper of the times, they already had installed a double guard on their vault—all the laboratories had— just as the movie studios had added personnel at the entrance gates to inspect car bottoms for bombs with oversized versions of the angled mirrors dentists use to examine inaccessible teeth.

Meanwhile, I spoke with Lydia's few remaining friends and acquaintances, but I did not glean a lot more in the end than I had from Sheila Banfield. I did manage to locate the Mark (family name Detillio) who was the putative alternative source of Lancaster's—I should say Sage's—paternity. Mark had become a chef and lived up on the Russian River, where he operated an inn. He scoffed at the notion he could have been the father—he always used condoms, even on LSD, or so he claimed—and furthermore didn't remember much about the young child. Mark had left the commune when Sage was less than a year and a half, just after the women in the group had written a manifesto declaring the men equally responsible for child-rearing. The thought of changing diapers had sent him scurrying all the way across the country to New England. He did recall something strange about the boy, however, a small slate-blue birthmark at the tip of his coccyx. It worried the mother at first until she took Sage to see a doctor in Albuquerque who told her it was nothing to be concerned about and was just something called a Mongolian spot, a tiny blemish that occasionally appeared on babies whose ancestry could be traced to certain nomadic tribes. The relieved Lydia took this as a sign, Mark told me, to build the opera theater she had long been planning in the style of a Mongolian yurt. Mark thought that was a swell idea, but by the time she broke ground, he was already living in Vermont, hanging out with a couple of hippie guys who kept pestering him to help them start an environmentally friendly ice cream company. He thought they were dreamers and, to his undying regret, got fed up and split for California before Ben and Jerry shipped their first container of Cherry Garcia.

I heard more about the theater from Andrea Coyle, a woman whose name I had picked up from the review of *Tosca*, which said she had directed the production. That wasn't entirely accurate, she told me when I found her running her own real estate agency in Santa Fe. She was more like the stage manager, Lydia taking most of the control of the performance herself. "After all," Andrea said. "She was the only one who could actually sing that stuff. Except for the boy. He had a beautiful falsetto voice then." In fact, the realtor was quite transfixed with Sage, calling him an "extraordinary actor, almost a prodigy with the ability to mimic anything and anybody. I guess they call that 'born in a trunk,' don't they?" I allowed as they did, not wanting to split hairs with her that 'born in a trunk' simply meant born *into* the theater and did not necessarily imply great skill. But skill was apparently something Sage had because, according to Andrea, he was the reason for what small success the theater had, inspiring the good burghers of Albuquerque to make the one-hour trek to Casa Blanca to see a ten-year-old, dressed as an adult of either sex, play leading roles in *Rigoletto* and *Pagliacci*. It was something of a stunt, she said, but he could do it, holding his own with his mother, until one day his voice changed and it was over. Andrea ultimately had no idea what had become of the boy. Long before the coloratura took her own life, she and Lydia had had a serious falling out over programming, Andrea wanting to widen their dwindling base with a production of *A Chorus Line*, an assault to the artistic purity of her institution Lydia found abhorrent. The two women ended up not speaking to each other and, shortly thereafter, the realtor left, never to see the singer or her young son again.

When we reached the condo, I was wondering when I was going to see him again—or if I already had and didn't know it. For the second time in a week I had stood up in a plane, scanning the rows of industry types, trying to match their hollow faces to my memory of Mr. Earring. Indeed a dozen of them at least were wearing something in their ears—diamond studs, platinum hoops, vintage bottles caps—but none resembled the man I'd seen in Prague, not enough anyway. And who knew what he looked like now anyway? Sage, Lancaster, a onetime child thespian in a rinky-dink desert opera house—he could be anybody. I was beginning to fear my task was impossible, that disaster lurked around the corner and that I was an aging detective outclassed by a younger and prototypically insane ideologue of this rapidly less appealing New Millennium. And the punk probably had plans to kill us all and I didn't even know who I was looking for.

But I did my job anyway, inspecting the security of the condo with Jaibo, if you could call a nine-bedroom mansion built in a style reminiscent of Yosemite's Awahnee Hotel a condo. It was more like a set from *The Lord of the Rings*. I couldn't begin to imagine the nightly fee. Farnsworth, although in financial extremis, had been hectored into renting it by Greenhut, because, as the agent put it, the director wasn't a "fourteen-year-old neo-hip-hop rollerblader with twelve rings in his nose" making his first movie but a known Hollywood television producer, a show-runner even, with real credits. For him to hawk his film out of the back of a used Volkswagen bus would be a personal and strategic mistake, subject to ridicule that could be fatal under the circumstances. He had to show face, be a "player," to use that now somewhat outworn term, and make a splash by giving parties that would attract the movers and shakers, the big-time green-light decision makers, maybe even those undisputed mega-muftis of independent film the Brothers Weinstein of Queens, New York, or the man known to insiders in the more Bohemian bailiwicks of Utah by the wildly ironic nickname of "Ordinary," after a movie he had directed, but to the world as Robert Redford.

"Que huevos mas azules!" What bluest of balls, said Jaibo, who still liked to affect the street talk of his East LA childhood despite having obtained a Ph.D. in criminology from UC Santa Barbara. "Some *pinche cabrón* beat us to it!" He was pointing to the condo bedrooms where the "fucking cuckold" in question had put double locks and individualized security codes on the doors. I said it only made our work easier, not that if anyone had wanted to place a bomb or snakes in here it would have been that difficult. The high-priced log cabin construction of the condo was about as

porous as it got and the substructure of the building had so many openings—air vents and mud rooms for skis and snowboards—available to a python or an envelope of C-4, it would have taken an hour to count them. The same could be said of the Mary G. Steiner Egyptian Theatre on Park City's Main Street, where the film formerly known as *Prague Autumn* would be projected the next night as part of the main competition to what was already a standing-room-only crowd. A handful of professional guards from a company I did not recognize patrolled the area in discombobulated pairs who seemed to bear an unfortunate resemblance to the membership card checkers at the entrance to Costco. The festival people were trying to adjust for these dangerous times, upgrade their personnel, but there was only so much they could do or knew how to do.

We came to the end of the bedroom corridor, which opened onto the condo living room, an ad hoc cocktail party of over a dozen schmoozers having formed under the caribou head. Greenhut and Arthur were visible glad-handing some acquisitions people from Lions' Gate and a couple of wags from the indie film department of William Morris. "There's heavy want-to-see," one of them was saying. "How about want-to-spray?" quipped his compadre. "Everyone wants a dose of that longevity mist from the Czech doctor. Great title, by the way. Reminds me of the Eastwood picture. Sexy." Arthur winked at Farnsworth, who stood at the bar mixing martinis for a critic from the *Village Voice* and an Indian woman in a sari who was evidently a member of the jury. I learned this from Frieda, who, now free of her wheelchair, had sidled up to me with a martini of her own.

"I vant to be a player too," she said with a cackle and then told me that she had seen the movie by that name. "That's what I'd do if I were a writer . . . kill these people."

"Some of them *are* writers," I said.

It was then that the doorbell rang. Ellen opened it to reveal a uniformed courier from "The Go-Between," one of the more amusingly named LA messenger services, carrying several manila envelopes of a certain size that could only have been screenplays and some other "important-looking" letters and documents. The party-goers, each fearing loss of face if none of these missives were for them, acted blasé as Ellen moved about the room, distributing the mail, the bulk of which was delivered to the Morris agents and to Milan St. Clair, who had entered only minutes before and had spent the whole time talking on the phone and looking at his watch. Then, upon opening and reading what appeared to be a crucial communiqué, at least so he wanted the world to think, his brows publicly furrowed—the State Department perhaps, the British Home Office?—he immediately excused himself and left.

"You know what I heard?" said Frieda who was following my gaze as I watched through the window as the Brit climbed into a Land Rover and must have sensed my disdain—or shared it. "He's not even English. Just one of those fakes who spent two years in school there and kept the accent."

"Big surprise," I said, trying to sound blasé myself at the very moment I was startled to discover that one of the smaller envelopes Ellen was distributing was for me. That it was on the stationery of the Beverly Hills Hotel, of all places, filled me with a foreboding, which was not alleviated when I stepped aside to read its contents. MEET ME AT SLUMDANCE, 10P, it said in block letters. Slumdance? That was a new one! I knew Sundance was "dance" happy, what with the burgeoning Slamdance, the randy Lapdance and even Son of Sam Dance, all satellite festivals formed by defiant refuseniks from the slush piles of thousands of films submitted every year to the mother ship, but Slumdance? Why not Dime-a-Dance? That would seem a yet more subtle reference to the same class-conscious deprivation. But perhaps subtlety was not the point. It certainly wasn't in the signature because the note was signed *L* in a giant cursive flourish that was distinctly and no doubt purposefully Lancastrian.

"Don't worry. I'll bring Jaibo," I said to Samantha who had materialized instinctively at my shoulder with a foreboding equal to or greater than mine at the precise moment I opened the envelope. I folded the letter and looked out over the room. Donna and Goran, as if on a simultaneous cue arranged by their managers, had both just arrived and were pumping hands on opposite sides of the room. Pointedly ignoring the supposedly lowbrow actress, the *Voice* critic had cornered the Serbian star, slavishly soliciting his opinion of obscure Yugoslavian filmmakers all of whom seemed to be Goran's "great good friend."

I was already halfway out the door when Farnsworth came up to me. "I hope you're not too disappointed," he said. I was confused until I saw he was holding a formal letter from the DGA with their decision on the director arbitration. Why hadn't I received one? But I imagined it was waiting for me at home, I not having the foresight or even the desire to have it forwarded to me at the festival. "Of course there's a provision for an appeal," he continued. "But I beg you not to use it. It would be a terrible distraction for the production at this moment. And I'd be glad to give you any credit you want . . . like special security adviser or even creative consultant, if that's your wish . . . in the roll-up." In the roll-up? When ninety percent of the audience was already out on the sidewalk making dinner plans or desperately figuring out how to lose a bad blind date before it was too late? What a guy! I decided to let it go and clapped Farnsworth reassuringly on the back with only the slightest hint of condescension. This was his world anyway, not mine, or so I thought. "The pleasure's mine," I said and headed out the door with Jaibo, leaving the now solely credited director to his own ego.

A short while later we were walking down Park City's historic Main Street and the main drag of the annual festival, which transformed a mundane ski resort of six thousand persons into a teeming Baghdad-like cinema bazaar of over twenty thousand schemers, the vast majority of whom were selling and only the most miniscule minority, thirty or forty at best, buying. Even then, at a quarter to ten in the evening, fervent young men and women stepped out of doorways thrusting flyers in our hands like merchants in the Kasbah. See my film! Read my script! In an odd way it reminded me of the not-so-distant Prague where, in that city's also historic center students pressed handouts onto tourists advertising that night's concert at the nearest baroque church. Only in the Czech Republic the flyers would be for the Bach B minor mass and in Utah they would be for the latest tale of sexually ambiguous teenagers in Jersey City.

We continued on around the corner to Swede Alley—location of the combination city hall/police department and of the three-story clapboard building whose basement contained, at least this year, the migratory Slumdance Film Festival. We followed an arrow painted on a bashed-in garbage can down external stairs to a cellar door. Inside were several men and women— I guessed them to be in their early twenties—lolling around on bales of hay dressed like Depression Era hoboes. A sign above them, nonchalantly painted on a broken board, read, "Brother, can you spare a dime (to make a movie)?" Several aging Macs were positioned behind them on top of supermarket carts stolen from Ralph's and stuffed with tattered belongings in the tradition of the homeless but did not seem to be in use. We appeared to be the only visitors.

"Everything has lost its edge," said one of the men, rousing himself from what I hoped was not a drug-induced stupor and staggering toward us. He was a stout fellow in a Farmer John with a long, stringy rope beard that looked as if it were bought at a souvenir shop on Hollywood Boulevard. "Even the word edge has lost its edge," he continued. "You're too late for anything by the time you get there. So there's no point in going. Don't you agree?"

"Absolutely."

"Good. I could tell you were a man of discernment. But don't let that stop you from seeing one of our films." He gestured toward the computer bank. "You're not an acquisitions guy are you?" he added almost as an afterthought.

"Sorry," I said.

"The Sony Classics dude was supposed to be coming. . . . How about you, amigo?" he said to Jaibo. "Looking for some product for the expanding Latino market?"

Jaibo shook his head.

The man turned disconsolate. "Affirmative action isn't just dead. It's decomposed," he said, almost inaudibly. "But go ahead anyway. My mother always said, never insult anybody. You never know. Some day they may grow up and own a movie company." He waved us on toward the terminals and slumped down on the hay again in resignation.

I meandered over to the Macs, trying not to look too excited about the prospect, and in fact I wasn't. I was surveying, as covertly as I could, the rest of the wannabe underclass splattered around the room, trying to ascertain whether the woman in the patched gingham dress and stained kerchief out of *The Grapes of Wrath* was actually Lancaster in drag, when my eye was caught by something far more obvious, a conventional yellow pad propped against one of the computer terminals with the words SAGE PRODUCTIONS—LET'S ALL GO OVER IN A BARREL TOGETHER! printed in red ink on the bottom. I glanced at Jaibo, shrugged and pressed the on button, trying not to be overly concerned that the computer would blow up in my face. Lancaster had led me this far after all. He obviously had more ambitious intentions than to terminate me here. What good would I have been to him then? Soon, what looked like a video transfer of an old eight-millimeter home movie faded onto the screen. A naked four-year-old kid, probably Sage, was running around a desert landscape with some adults dressed in early seventies hippie garb rushing after him to keep him out of the cactus. A half-constructed yurt was visible in the background.

"Haven't seen that one before," said Farmer John, who had suddenly materialized beside me. "But eight-millimeter rules. I love the grain when you blow it up. The Zapruder film is on my top ten of all time between *Nosferatu* and *The Man Who Shot Liberty Valance*. You should see it on an I-Max screen. Aren't you going to use the pots?" He gestured to a set of earphones lying on top of the monitor as the image shifted to some extremely jiggly shots of a college graduation. A long line of mortarboard-clad students were happily grabbing their diplomas from a school official and waving to their parents but it was hard to make out their identities with their smiling faces bouncing in and out of the frame. "If it doesn't have sound of its own, we can pipe in some old Moby Grape records. It seems like the right period. Or some unreleased John Densmore tracks from The Doors at the Aquarius Theatre."

"No thanks," I said and lifted up the earphones, slipping them over my ears more to get rid of the guy than to hear some accompaniment for what I assumed to be a silent movie. I could see Jaibo rolling his eyes and muttering his favorite all-time phrase *"Hijo de la chingada,"* as if this particular son of a fuck took the cake, which he probably did. But the moment I had them on, another voice came straight at me, as if he were speaking from inside my head.

"Good evening, Mr. Wine, and thank you for coming. And thank you for taking such a great interest in my life history." The voice sounded tinny and distant, but I started to look around for its source anyway. "Don't bother," he cut me off almost immediately. "I am a more than a mile away. But if you're interested in how I am able to see you, I direct your attention to the video cam on top of the monitor. There is a microphone inside it if you would like to talk back to me, but first I would suggest you rid yourself of the buffoon in the clown suit and the Hispanic gentleman standing beside you."

I thought it over for a few seconds before turning to Farmer

John. "You're right about eight-millimeter. It's a heavy emotional trip. I better be alone so I can take it all in."

"I can sympathize," he said, backing away.

Jaibo rolled his eyes a second time, this time trying to suppress a guffaw, but he had already caught my drift and was easing over to the end of the computer bank without my having to say anything.

"I'm here, Sage," I said. There was silence on the other end.

"Please don't call me that name."

"Would you prefer Michael Lancaster?"

There was another silence.

"Why did you bring me here?" I said.

"Why do you think?"

"To stop the film from showing tomorrow night."

"It's useless to try to prevent what is about to happen."

"What's that?"

"Beyond your imagination."

"I don't understand." What was he talking about? Nuclear war? Chemical weapons?

"There's nothing you can do to change the situation."

"What if I got Farnsworth to cancel the screening and shelve his movie?"

"You couldn't even get him to share director's credit with you."

"But people's lives are at stake!"

"That didn't seem to persuade him in Prague. . . . Everything has been carefully established and is underway."

"What if I find you first?"

"So far you have not done a particularly good job of that."

"Then why did you bring me here?" I repeated, my voice suddenly rising in frustration. "To arrange for the production of *The Protocols of the Elders of Zion—The Motion Picture?* Surely someone with your intelligence doesn't believe that hideous old blood libel?" I knew the last two words were a non sequitur but I blurted them out anyway with an anger that surprised me, almost shouting the final phrase—*Blood libel!* Several of the would-be homeless were looking up from their hay bales with astonished expressions. But Sage—who undoubtedly had been dictating events, guiding them in an almost anal fashion ever since my first encounter with the LA feds and probably before, spoon-feeding information as he went—was perfectly calm in his reply.

"So you can inform others of who I am, where I came from," he said. It obviously had been his intention all along.

"How could I do that? Wouldn't I be dying in your action too?"

"I am confident that when you leave here, you will be immediately contacting the appropriate authorities."

"And what would you want me to tell them?"

He seemed about to answer, in fact he probably did, but for me time had stopped. The explanation was right in front of my eyes and I almost didn't want to hear more or was incapable of it. I was staring at the home movie on the monitor. The ceremony was over and the new graduates were celebrating with their families, picnicking and showing off their diplomas. One particular young man had doffed his mortarboard and was kissing his girlfriend, who was still in her cap and gown and, from pictures I had seen, was clearly Sage's mom Lydia. As for the young man— although the familiar, almost jovial, potbelly I had known for years was not then in evidence and the hair was certainly thicker and completely black, even at the temples—his identity was yet more obvious to me, so obvious in fact that my stomach turned and I could barely focus on the monitor as the last frames of the home movie faded to black and the face of Arthur Sugarman was obliterated by a stream of white eight-millimeter sprocket holes.

15

"GET AWAY FROM ME! I'm not gay!"

"I'm not either!" I said.

"Then what the fuck are you doing?"

It was a measure of how freaked out I had become in the few hours since I left the Slumdance headquarters that I was struggling to pull down Milan St. Clair's bathing trunks in the condo hot tub. And they weren't easy to get off. He had the drawstring double-knotted and was pushing at me with both hands, large amounts of water sloshing out of the tub and upsetting a bottle of cabernet to the consternation of those remaining party-goers who were still there going strong at two-thirty in the morning. I had come to the conclusion that I had to do this stripping after spending the better part of my time since viewing the movie telling what I knew to the local police, who themselves were immediately in contact with the FBI and the CIA, who then in turn spoke directly with me by phone from Salt Lake City and Langley about my allegations. Although they all took seriously my warning of a dangerous but unspecified threat to America's most famous film festival, no one seemed to know what to do about it. Was it sensible to evacuate Park City, create traffic jams, airport snarls, generalized panic in an era of terrorism, all because of a thirty-some-year-old eight-millimeter home movie, which, it went without saying, had no sound track or other elucidation of what was going on on it other than my own admittedly sketchy theories of vengeance for Lancaster's unacknowledged patrimony. And my references to what had transpired in Europe, the myste-

rious attacks on a seemingly insignificant art film in Prague leading to a military intervention, made the whole thing only seem
more convoluted and less comprehensible. Of course they had
assured me that they would look into the situation straight away
and act accordingly, but by the time I hung up with the various
government agencies it was almost one A.M. and I had the disturbing realization that far too much of this was going to be in
my hands. And, even though often I proceeded in life with the
self-confidence of a drunken gambler—witness the fact that I had
stepped in to direct a feature film when I wasn't even sure how to
focus a camera—at this moment I got heart palpitations.

The anxiety just increased when I returned to the condo to
find that Arthur had disappeared. That was the only word I could
apply to his absence because no one had seen him since eleven
o'clock that evening and no one had noticed him leave. Yet his
bed in the bedroom at the end of the second-floor corridor,
which was actually the smaller part of a master suite he was sharing with his mother, seemed untouched with not the slightest
dent in the fluffy down pillows or duvet. His leather toilet kit in
the bathroom was unopened; the fancy bottles of complimentary
Kiehl toiletries undisturbed on the counter; the contents of his
black Boyt suitcase not yet emptied into the distressed Mexican
armoire. Frieda herself was visible through an open door, asleep
on a king-sized bed, with her hair in a wool cap and the concentration camp numbers on her left arm peeking out under a laven-
der flannel nightshirt. This was the first time I had seen her little
tattoo and the sight of it made me sick to my stomach. I wondered
why she had never had it removed, but maybe that was fruitless in
the end. Forgiveness for the Holocaust, the subject of the very
film we were all there to promote, was nothing more than an
absurdly naïve and idealistic concept set up to be mocked by
present history, all history in fact.

I stood there with Samantha and Jaibo, taking deep breaths
and trying to figure out what to do. The pressure of time felt

enormous because I didn't know what the deadline actually was—the screening tomorrow night, breakfast tomorrow morning, ten minutes from now. It all seemed the same in the lexicon of Sage/Lancaster, who had not spoken a single word more after I had seen the image of my friend—his father—at which point the film ended, audio and video disconnecting simultaneously with a sudden final click. The Slumdancers stared at me in horrified fascination as I screamed desperately at the computer monitor to resume contact.

The most obvious move would have been to pursue Arthur but no one even knew the vehicle in which he departed, or if indeed he had left the condo on his own volition or had been coerced, which I assumed to be the case. We did know he had arrived that afternoon with Ellen and Peter in a Ford Explorer, which had been rented by Farnsworth and was now sitting in the driveway next to a half dozen or so other cars. Samantha had already interviewed everyone she could corral about the comings and goings of the producer/completion bondsman but they were all too self-involved to recall anything that didn't have to do with somebody's movie.

At this point, shrieks of laughter came from below and my rage began to boil over at the unbridled narcissism of it all, the inability of these creatures of the cinema to acknowledge the indisputable fact that the world as we knew it had gone down the drain and was headed for the sewers. That was the moment I made a beeline for the window and saw St. Clair in the hot tub. He was nuzzling the neck of a half-naked actress-model-whatever, simultaneously pouring himself a glass from the cabernet bottle that was soon to be spilled. His racist words in Prague coursed through my head mixed with Frieda's recent revelation that he wasn't a real Brit but a poseur, not unlike *L* himself. In fact, he was *L* himself, I was suddenly sure. Who else could it be?

So before it was too late, before he would suspect he was about to be unmasked and create untold havoc, I bolted from the room and demanded he tell the truth about who he was. "You're not even English," I said. "You're American!" And he looked at me as if I were crazy. Within seconds my hands were on his swimming trunks, pulling them down to display the only conclusive, or near conclusive, proof I knew of his identity, the rare Mongolian spot on the tip of his coccyx. But, alas, after the struggle and the dialog about sexual preference and a final yank, it wasn't there. All that was visible was a white, rather hairless and distinctly unblemished ass. For a split second I wondered if the blue mark had been surgically removed but by then I was being surrounded by party-goers who thought I had gone off the deep end of the hot tub. St. Clair was on his feet, standing on the step, screaming at me, unable to hear my apology over his own voice.

"What're you doing?" said Farnsworth, who ran over and started dragging me out of the tub. It was the first time I had seen him since returning to the condo. He threw a terrycloth robe around me and escorted me toward the dressing room door, whispering harshly in my ear. "Don't you realize the man sitting on the stone bench over there is Thomas Winterberg of Denmark's Dogma Movement, *the president of the festival jury?*" I glanced back at a lanky fellow who was drying his toes with a hand towel while staring at the proceedings with amusement.

"He doesn't look so upset," I said, but Farnsworth was having none of it. He pushed me through into the dressing room and locked the door behind us.

"Look, if you're still so angry about that credit thing that you're trying to torpedo our film, you've got to realize there's nothing I can do about it. The DGA has ruled."

"I don't give a fuck about movies!" I shot back at him. "In fact at this moment they're the last things I'm concerned about. And I'll tell you right now; you better cancel that screening of your little opus tonight or you'll have so much blood on your hands you'll regret you ever saw the inside of a multiplex!"

"Are you serious?"

"Couldn't be more," I said. And then I recounted my latest encounter with Sage, how I had seen the image of the twenty-one-year-old Arthur Sugarman on a computer screen at the Slumdance Film Festival and that that could only point to the producer's paternity and ensuing child abandonment that had created the chain reaction we were all living through. At first Farnsworth didn't believe me. Why would a guy like Arthur, someone known as the rare decent human in venal Hollywood, a normal schlepper who spent years toiling in the fields as a completion bondsman and was finally getting his chance to produce, have deserted a kid?

That had given me pause too, I admitted, but not for that long. The connections were only too easy to make. I pointed upstairs and Farnsworth immediately knew what I meant. He had imagination too. That was his job, after all, inventing stories, and most of the best of them started with a family. That was what they had always told me at the Farmer's Market anyway. I remembered Stanley Vogel singing a jingle about it once, "Oedipus-Shmedipus!" So Farnsworth, who, like Stanley, spent his life writing teleplays and screenplays, producing and directing, understood better than I did the missing link in this tragic chain. He was the creator of *His Name Was Herman*, after all, thirty some episodes with every possible permutation of family life. It was the old woman sleeping above us, the one with the tattoo on her arm. The young Arthur had fled his pregnant ladylove Lydia in order not to upset his Auschwitz-victim mother by marrying, or, worse, having a baby with, a gentile. We were involved in a tale, Farnsworth agreed with me, of second-generation Survivor Guilt.

He sat there without comment as I continued my theory of how the grown-up precocious offspring of the thwarted union of Arthur and Lydia had been seeking vengeance against both his runaway pop and the duplicitous tribe that spawned him using whomever he could, especially his natural allies, the unassimilated

Moslem masses of Western Europe. But it was almost as if all these failed attempts in the Czech Republic had worked in Sage's favor because now he could exact his retribution at the very apotheosis of his father's career at the Sundance Film Festival itself. And he could do it by himself, using the full brilliance of his intellect and his childhood acting skills. By then Farnsworth was slumped down on a wicker chair by the steam room door with a towel across his chest. Our discussion had left him drained, almost hopeless.

"Look, it's not so bad," I said. "There are other festivals. I hear that one in Telluride is pretty good. I know lots of people who go there. My ex-wife's been to it twice. She said they liked movies from weird places like Iceland. Surely, they'd—"

"We've already been turned down by them," he said. He stared at the tile floor a long while before emitting a sorrowful moan like an aging farm animal on its last legs. Then he stood up to leave.

I followed him through the door and along a breezeway, which led past the hot tub and back into the house again. For some reason the party had revived, a new infusion of revelers having augmented the initial group although it was nearly 3 A.M. and it had begun to snow outside, making the roads uninviting. The living room had filled up with people, many of them still in their parkas, dancing to a Santana album. In fact the whole place was jumping, like the parties you hear about, but never get to go to. I recognized Donna doing an erotic merengue with Janak, who stared at her with a bemused smile, and Goran, who had arrived and was demonstrating the fine art of mescal drinking for the William Morris crew and Takashima with his girlfriend/assistant dressed as Joan of Arc in a metal helmet and see-through chain-link tank top and St. Clair who was back with the actress-model-whatever and had apparently forgiven me—he even waved—and a bulbous triple-chinned individual with his shirt unbuttoned to the navel who looked for all the world like the infamous Harvey W., though I couldn't be sure. But if it wasn't he, it was one of the best celebrity look-alikes I'd ever seen. And the people around him were doing a brilliant impression of sycophants, importuning a worldwide distribution deal or at least lunch with Gwyneth Paltrow. In all this, I started searching for the great "Ordinary" himself—was that he in the worn Ralph Lauren bomber jacket and rumpled Madras shirt out of his own catalogue—when Greenhut came rushing up to us, his thumb thrust high in the air.

"We're the A list," he declared excitedly. "The place is crawling with acquisitions people! Auction, bay-bee!"

The agent drifted back into the crowd and I turned to Farnsworth, who had not changed his morbid expression for a second. "Look," I said, "there's still hope. If I can find the real Sage by noon or so, maybe you can still run it."

But the filmmaker just shook his head. He glanced over at Ellen, who was standing with the editors, for her agreement. They knew each other well and didn't need to communicate verbally at a moment like this. Their eyes locked in silent sadness, before he picked up an empty bottle of Cristal and started to bang on it with a fork, continuing until he got everyone's attention. Finally someone ran over and stopped the music. The party-goers all looked his way, waiting for him to speak.

"We're canceling," he said.

16

Trying to sleep that night was pointless, even for the paltry hour or two I had hoped to get. I already knew Sage had anticipated that Farnsworth—who gave the shocked assemblage the excuse that as the movie's director and primary investor he had had a change of heart and—apologies for the inconvenience—his work just was not ready for the public and he needed more time for his final cut—would ultimately do the right thing and pull the film from the festival. He had essentially told me as much, that he foresaw that withdrawal, over the Slumdance headphones and pretty much implied as well that he had planned for it. His catastrophic action was already underway. There was nothing I or anyone else could do about it.

So I lay there in the bed Sam and I were sharing in one of the smaller bedrooms on the third floor of the condo, not even bothering to shut my eyes. She wasn't sleeping either, even though she had been trying since midnight, and I worried whether this was healthy in her present condition. I also worried whether she should even have come, but I knew that if I were there without her, I would have been going crazy from loneliness despite the presence of a house full of people. As they had for so many, the cataclysmic events of the previous year had drawn those close to me even closer, made them even more necessary. Stretched out like two patients waiting to be wheeled off to the operating room, we stared up through a clerestory window where the increasingly thick snow swirled in front of an external floodlight attached to the telephone pole across the street. I was telling Samantha of my irrational attack on St. Clair, unburdening myself of the humiliation, when she asked me: "Who told you he wasn't a Brit?"

"What difference does that make?" I replied, but I barely finished the sentence. The question had been troubling me as well, especially since I was almost certain the disinformation did not come firsthand. The person who had told me this story had only just learned it and she had obviously gotten it from someone with an aim to distract or mislead, to point me in a direction that was away from Lancaster, not toward him. But the answer to that follow-up question was asleep, or supposed to be, on the floor beneath us and I was hesitant to wake up an eighty-five-year-old, although, from my experience, people in that age category rarely slept more than a couple of hours a night anyway.

"I'm going to have to go down there," I told Samantha when the faintest glimmer of pre-dawn light finally appeared at the edge of the shades. "I can't wait any longer. Will you be okay?" She was undergoing another bout of morning sickness.

She nodded, half-heartedly pointing toward her lifeline, the tall glass of ginger tea on the headboard. "Go. Just don't give her a heart attack."

But the old woman didn't express even the slightest shock when, sitting on the edge of her bed moments later—six fourteen in the morning according to the LED alarm clocks provided by the condo—I broke the news to her on her son's movie. "So what else is new?" she said. "This is what I have come to expect from life. Only the good things are a surprise." Then she added, tensing slightly, "How's Arthur taking it?"

It was the question I feared she would ask and I didn't know how to answer it. "I'm not sure," I said. "I haven't seen him," telling a half-truth that made me feel almost ashamed even though I told myself I had done it to protect her. She stared at me suspiciously and I had a strange sense of identification with her son that made me want to assure her that I had always walked in righteousness and deny that I had ever married a shikse—something that I actually had once done and regretted for reasons that had nothing whatever to do with religion. "Excuse me," I continued, fleeing from that uncomfortable emotion with all the force and rapidity my unconscious would allow. "I beg your pardon. But there's something else I wanted to ask you about."

"So ask," she said, but then something in my expression suddenly made her repeat, "Where's Arthur?" this time with greater agitation. I didn't answer. She stood up and started stumbling away from the bed, falling over her nightgown, gasping and crying out for her son as she headed out into the hall. I followed, afraid she was going to have that coronary or trip down the stairs.

"Please, Mrs. Sugarman." I took her by the arm. "It'll be okay."

"No, it won't. Something's happened to him. Stop lying to me!" she said, pulling away from me with surprising strength.

"I'll try not to. I just want to ask you one more thing—who told you Milan St. Clair was American?"

She stopped suddenly, clutching her ear. "Now look what's happened. I've lost my hearing aid!" She screamed out again: "Arthur!" and got down on all fours. I had no choice but to follow suit, getting down on the floor with her and searching about for the miniature device. It was hard to see anything against the patterned carpet, which was dark sepia with little nubs designed to conceal stains.

"Please tell me who told you?" I repeated.

"What? I can't hear you!"

"What's going on?" said Farnsworth, who had walked into the middle of the living room and was squinting up at us. From the bloodshot look in his sleepless eyes, it seemed as if he had been down there all night, or what was left of it, when the partygoers dispersed. Behind him, a couple of uniformed caterers were carrying in a coffee urn with the fixings, depositing them on a long table next to some pitchers of orange and apple juice and the unopened box of Janak/Evian atomizers with the now useless

MIST logos plastered all over them. In a second, another caterer entered with a large platter of lox and bagels.

"I thought everyone went home," I said.

Farnsworth shrugged.

"Arthur!" Frieda shouted again. It was beginning to sound more like a wail.

"Please, relax," I said, groping with my fingers for the hearing aid. But I realized, under the circumstances, she couldn't even hear that either.

"Greenhut invited everybody back for breakfast," said Farnsworth. "He didn't want any hard feelings. Bad for his business I guess . . . you need any help?" I shook my head. "I would have made the sonofabitch pay for it myself, but he went off skiing."

"Skiing?" I looked up from the floor at the very second my hand touched plastic. "The lifts don't open for two hours!"

"Yeah, well, that didn't seem to bother *him*."

"Why?" Now I was clambering to my feet. "He didn't go *cross-country* skiing, by any chance?"

"Yes, he did. I saw him. He's very good at it. . . . How'd you know *that*?"

But I didn't bother to answer. "This is yours," I said, handing Frieda her hearing aid. Then I raced down the stairs. "Which way did he go?"

"Just below the lodge." He pointed out the window, then looked back at me in confusion. "Are you trying to tell me . . . my agent is a terrorist?" It sounded like a bad joke at the Farmer's Market, but I didn't crack a smile.

"Why'd you hire him?" I asked.

"We didn't. He came to us," said the director, who now had the expression of someone suddenly considering hara-kiri. "He didn't have a lot of experience . . . but he was enthusiastic and we were having trouble getting someone for . . . such a . . . small picture." The last words sounded as if they were somebody's epitaph.

"Where's the mud room?" I said.

Farnsworth pointed to the back stairs and I ran toward them when I heard Frieda say, "You're going to catch cold." So I grabbed a parka from a peg and put it on over my pajamas while bounding down the stairs. "He's the one who told me, by the way. Greenhut."

"I'm sure. Call the police," I yelled out behind me. "And tell Jaibo to follow me with a skimobile!"

Though most of the skis lining the mud room wall were downhill, I found a pair of cross-countries in the corner and quickly slipped on its boots, which were about a size and a half too big. But they would have to do. I took the poles and pushed through the heavy door outside. A fresh pair of tracks, which could only have been Greenhut's—that is Sage's—led across the snow under the wires of the Quincy Lift where it disappeared in the gray morning mist. I pushed off to follow the narrow lines as quickly as I could, plunging the poles into the soft, evanescent powder, my heart rate starting to climb immediately. But I continued, traversing the wide trail beneath the lift toward the woods. Down below me were some stables and what looked to be the resort ticket office, another lodge and some other building I couldn't distinguish. But once between the trees, I couldn't see them anymore. It was difficult to see the tracks as well in the shadows of the low early light. I proceeded anyway, poling deeper into the forest, another chairlift visible atop a cluster of Douglas fir. Up ahead was a small shack of some kind, perched at the rim of a canyon. I was breathing hard now, struggling to get enough energy to go on. Sweat was pouring down my chest and back, soaking through my shirt and into the lining of my parka. I paused for a moment and looked down at the snow in front of me. It was stained with urine at the base of the trees as if an animal, a coyote or one of the eponymous deer of Deer Valley, was marking the path. I skidded around it and slid through a gully between some boulders, emerging in a small flat area before the shack. I could see a pair of cross-country skis leaning on the wall beside the door. I stopped and listened. It was silent other than the babbling of a brook at the bottom of the canyon. Then I heard a noise from inside, a low abrasive sound that could have been a guttural human groan. I released my bindings and slipped off my skis, then took a couple of steps forward to the rear window, which had three of its four panes boarded up with plywood. But through the one bit of grimy glass I could make out the supine figure of a man roped to the frame of a threadbare couch. His body movements were slow, as if he had been drugged, and his face was turned toward the wall, but from the full curve of the mound of stomach I had no doubt it was Arthur.

I was about to start for him when I heard a crunch in the snow behind me. I spun around to see Sage standing not more than ten feet away. The agent disguise no longer useful, he was back in his grunge/anti-globalist outfit, the Julius Caesar haircut gone, the Prada suit replaced by a wool plaid shirt with a North Face fanny pack. He held a Walther automatic in his hand.

"Hello, Sage," I said.

"Mr. Wine. I can't say I'm surprised to see you." The staccato Rodney Dangerfield rhythms were gone too, his voice returned to the measured tones of the Princeton intellectual.

"I see you've found your father," I said. "What are you planning on doing with him?"

"He will remain here, as we all will, so he can later learn about the fruits of his actions. What it means to have abandoned a child for such an appalling reason."

"What if it's not him? What if you've got the wrong man? Just because he was your mother's boyfriend doesn't mean . . ."

He raised the automatic, training it on my chest. That shut me up quickly. I carefully raised my hands above my head. I was starting to wonder where Jaibo was. I hoped he would arrive like the cavalry because I would certainly need him. But the only sound, other than Arthur's groan, was the brook.

"He's my father, alright. Would you like to see his Mongolian spot? It's considerably more visible than the one you were looking for on Milan St. Clair."

"Sure," I said. "Why not?"

He gestured with his gun and I began to walk slowly to the door of the shack. I pushed it open with my foot and entered. Inside was an abandoned warming hut, a rusted pot-bellied stove in the corner next to a broken coffeemaker. Old trail maps remained stacked on a shelf now covered with cobwebs. I looked over at Arthur, who still seemed drugged but had managed to roll over on his side with his head turned toward us. His eyes flickered open, then shut again.

"Wake him up," said Sage, motioning with the tip of his Walther to a bucket of snow in the corner. "It shouldn't be difficult. It's only phenobarbital."

I walked over to the bucket and scooped up a handful of snow, rubbing it on Arthur's groggy face. His eyes flickered open again and this time stayed there as they darted around the room in fright, first focusing on Sage and then fixing on me. "Oh, Moses, it's you. Thank God."

"Hello, Arthur," I said.

The completion bondsman nodded and shook his head, struggling to stay awake. "Who are you?" he asked, squinting curiously at the young man who had positioned himself by the door so he could see in and out and held his automatic in two hands, like someone who knew how to use it. "Some kind of terrorist? A kidnapper?"

"Tell him who I am," said Sage, brandishing his weapon.

"I'm sorry, Arthur. This is an awful situation. . . . This is your son."

"What?" said the bondsman, suddenly snapping awake as if he had just mainlined half the Dexedrine in a freshman dormitory.

"His name is Sage Ellison, AKA Michael Lancaster, Princeton '87."

"I don't have a son," said Arthur, who started straining fruitlessly at his ropes. Under the circumstances, I was unable to help him.

"If you would like to see our DNA markers, Mr. Sugarman, they are on the coffee table," said Sage. He nodded to three computer printouts arranged in front of Arthur. "The one in the middle is mine. On the right is yours and on the left are those of Lydia Ellison. I assume that name is not unfamiliar to you."

The bondsman stopped struggling with the rope as quickly as he had started and looked up at Sage in astonishment, studying him with intense curiosity while not bothering to glance for a second at the carefully arranged documents.

"She never told me she was pregnant," said Arthur.

"Stop lying, Mr. Sugarman."

"I promise you. I'm not."

"Of course, you are," Sage insisted. "My mother told me on numerous occasions when you heard about her pregnancy, you walked out. You refused to live with her because of who she was."

"What? That's crazy!" said Arthur.

"I couldn't figure out what she meant until I had grown up and discovered who you were and who your mother was. After that it was all clear."

"What are you talking about?" said Arthur.

"Auschwitz," I said. The bondsman stared me in bewilderment. "He thinks because of the Holocaust, your mother didn't want you with a gentile girl."

"But Lydia broke up with *me!*"

"Liar!" said Sage.

"My mother wanted me to go out with anybody—gentile, Jewish, Manchurian, she didn't care. She just wanted to have a grandchild. When I went out with a Kenyan dancer for two dates in grad school, I had to stop her from throwing an engagement party!"

This seemed to infuriate Sage more than anything and he

turned away from the door to aim the Walther directly at Arthur's head.

"Kill me if you want," said the bondsman, who was summoning up more courage than I thought he had, "but first I'm going to tell you what really happened between your mother and me."

"I'm not interested," said Sage, who took a step closer with his gun.

"Listen, please," said Arthur. "You should know who we were, where you came from, whatever happens." He looked up at the younger man, who seemed to be holding his breath, his finger curled over the trigger. "We met in college. We were idealistic young people, like you, in love with the arts. She wanted to be an opera singer and I wanted to be . . . you're not going to believe this," he added, glancing over at me, ". . . a movie director. It was 1968, remember, and the greatest hero alive was Jean Luc Godard. Isn't that right, Moses?"

"Him and François Truffaut." Arthur Sugarman, a director? It was about as logical as the dog at CAA.

"Lydia loved the idea—the two of us being artists together. She would talk about it to everybody all the time, make up stories for them about our coming lives, as if we were, I don't know, legends of some sort. . . . But I knew better. I knew I couldn't do it. I couldn't write. I couldn't direct. I had no talent for anything like that. So I secretly applied to and was accepted by the Wharton School of Business. Only I was scared how she'd react, so I didn't tell Lydia until the morning after we graduated. I guess I was right because she walked away from me that day and never spoke to me again. I had no idea there was a baby in her belly."

A slight tremor began to appear in Sage's hand. I wondered to what extent he believed what Arthur was saying. I did. It wasn't the kind of thing someone made up, certainly not someone like the completion bondsman who, in his own words, had "no talent for anything like that." I also wondered if it was time for me to move on Sage. But the young man was over twenty years my junior and a good three or four inches taller. And, as if anticipating what I might have in mind, he had swung the Walther in my direction.

"But if you *are* my son," continued Arthur, whose voice had dropped almost to a whisper again and was now staring down at the floor, "I welcome you. I never have had any children and whoever you are and whatever you've done, I'll do whatever I can to support and protect you."

He looked up at Sage again and smiled. The young man's face was beginning to crumble. It was as if he were staring into an abyss where the whole premise for his recent life, his anti-Semitic vendetta, was nothing more than a dark fairy tale he had told himself, perhaps abetted by his mother or his natural desire to protect her. He stared at his gun for a moment. Then he pointed the barrel toward his mouth.

"What're you doing?" I shouted. "Wait! You can't do that! What about your action? You have to stop it!"

I ran for him but he recoiled, shaking his head. "Impossible . . . too late . . . way too late." And then he blew his brains out, like his mother before him.

I looked from his bloody corpse to Arthur, who slowly slumped back onto the couch again in a fetal ball and began to sob.

"*Hijo de la chingada*, son of a fuck," said Jaibo once again when he walked inside two minutes later and saw the carnage. It was one of the most common of all Chicano curses, but in this case extraordinarily apt. "Sorry I'm late. Maybe I could have helped."

"Not in this case," I said, "but you can now. Take care of *him*." I gestured to Arthur. "And give me those." I snatched the keys from his hand and ran outside. And before he could even ask what I was doing, I jumped into the skimobile and took off, hitting full throttle and bouncing through the woods within seconds. There was no time for explanations and I was too pissed off at myself for not having seen the obvious. The answer to what

Sage had been planning, as Farnsworth or his Farmer's Market buddies might have explained in one of their movies or television shows, was "hiding in plain sight." And it wasn't until the young man had said it was already too late that I realized what it was.

I nearly upended a couple of ski patrollers under the Quincy Lift, but succeeded in reaching the condo in only a couple of minutes. I jumped out of the skimobile and dashed inside, running straight upstairs to where the buffet was. A handful of people were already present, munching bagels and sipping juice. But the box of atomizers was still there, seemingly untouched.

"Get out of the way!" I screamed at everybody who stared at me in confusion. Some of them must have been there the previous night when I pulled St. Clair's trunks down and must now have thought I was certifiable. But I ignored them and carefully approached the box, whose cardboard top was partially opened. I took a fork, pushed it back and began to count the canisters. Eighteen . . . nineteen . . . twenty . . . They all seemed to be there. Twenty-one . . . twenty-two. But no! The twenty-fourth was missing! "Holy fuck!" I shouted. "Did anyone take one of these atomizers? Put it back! Don't do anything! Whatever you do— don't touch it!"

Everybody looked at me puzzled. "What's the big deal?" said someone. "It's just a promo for another movie that will never be released." I couldn't tell who, because I was already up the stairs, running up and down the corridor, sticking my head in bedrooms, waking people, searching for the atomizers, warning them to stay away, until I reached the biggest of all the master suites on the third floor, the one with the most panoramic view of the ski lifts, which was Donna's. Her boyfriend asleep in the king-sized bed, she was standing in her nightgown facing the bathroom mirror. In one hand she held a brush and in the other, the last atomizer. The nozzle was pointed toward her and she had her index finger on the button.

"Put that down," I said.

"What're you doing here?"

"I said put that thing down!"

"What for? It's Pavel's formula. Why shouldn't I use it?"

"Put it down!" I reiterated.

"I will not!" she insisted.

"Yes, you will. Please. I beg you! It's dangerous!"

"Absolutely not. Now get out of here!"

She faced away from me and was about to press the button when I yelled, "I'm your *director* and when I say put it down, you better fucking do it!"

She stopped and stared at me in the mirror. For a moment I thought she was going to laugh. But then she exhaled and started preening herself as if she were getting ready for a closeup.

"Okay, have it your way," she said, placing the canister back on the counter. "You'd think it was anthrax or something."

17

"IF JEWS CONTROL THE MEDIA," said Chemerinski, "how come I can't get arrested?" doing his own ethnic variation on the theme of "Nuclear war? There goes my career!" It had been three months since I'd been to the Farmer's Market and the season had changed in that almost indistinguishable way it does in Los Angeles, the apples on display having gone from Fujis to pippins. Samantha and I were having a child—a girl, just like she'd said—and it should be no surprise that the thought of this normally joyous event sometimes depressed me. But I worked hard to overcome the negativity and by the night we felt the first tiny kicks in Sam's stomach, I had expunged most of the bad thoughts or at least suppressed them. I excitedly broke out a bottle of bubbly and a tin of Osetra to toast the auspicious coming of baby Frances Wine, named after Franz Kafka to honor the city in which she was conceived and called immediately "Frankie."

The gang at the Market pronounced that an apt name for a Jewish girl in these parlous times and toasted her as well with coffee and glazed doughnuts from Bob's. Then they got down to the serious business of grilling me. There had been a rumor flying around town since Sundance about my having saved Donna Gold from anthrax poisoning.

"And don't tell us about being sworn to secrecy by some agency of the U.S. government," said Chemerinski, who himself was the one to switch the subject from his personal ups-and-downs. "Back in the sixties you were thrown in jail by those same agencies more times than Jerry Rubin."

"Nobody's like that anymore," said Stanley Vogel. "Every ex-peacenik I know wants to join the CIA now, only they're too old." But he and Douglas Corfu were sure this whole anthrax business was just a PR stunt to get Donna a part on a new network mini-series on the Gulf War. Word was she lusted after the role of the nurse who thumbed her nose at misogynist Saudi laws by driving a convertible around downtown Riyadh and had instructed her publicist to do anything to get it, especially now that her impend-ing marriage to Dr. Pavel Janak had broken up. The story went that the good doctor, afraid of being tarnished by the criminal misuse of his product, had had second thoughts about the American market and retreated to Europe, leaving Donna behind. Actually it had been the actress herself who called the whole thing off. The trauma of what occurred had caused her to reevaluate everything in her life, including Pavel, and at this very moment she was staying at a cousin's house in a Minneapolis sub-urb, recuperating from a lengthy prophylactic treatment of ciprofloxacin and trying to decide whether she ever wanted to act again. When I last talked to her, she was considering getting a teaching credential.

As for me, they got it half right. I didn't want to join the CIA, or the MI5, or the Mossad. But I was certainly going to cooper-ate with them in preventing another anthrax attack, so, since no one had been infected in this case, I had agreed to keep my mouth shut while they investigated where the spores had come from. The first address was obviously Hamburg. Maybe, after that, other links would be made. It would be my small contribu-tion to the war on terror. The only people who knew anything about this were Arthur—who, quite understandably, given what he had gone through, had suffered a minor coronary incident himself and was now back in Philadelphia being attended to by his mother—and Farnsworth.

Peter was sitting across the table from me, not saying a word, as I fended off questions, trying to use what little wit I had among

ROGER L. SIMON

these entertainment professionals to obfuscate the situation. "Hey, I'm like a shrink," I said. "If I revealed my secrets, no one would ever hire me." Everyone laughed except for Farnsworth who grunted with self-pity. I cut him some slack, however, because I knew, from the few times I had spoken with him since the festival, that the writer/director/producer wasn't having the easiest time. The cancellation of the premiere of *Mist* had tainted his film, causing doubts about its commercial potential among the always skeptical acquisitions people, and he had to call upon an old friend to save the day by selling the movie off to a small distributor, who in turn sold it to a smaller cable channel that specialized in romances. The film would be seen, but the money wasn't much and Farnsworth had lost his entire investment, his life savings, in fact. To make matters worse, his wife had discovered a "love note" from Cindy Lemon in the back pages of his old director's shooting script and, despite Peter's sworn insistence that it had meant nothing, that it was a stupid mistake and that it was over now and forever so help him God, Ellen had walked out. I had heard that she had moved in with her college roommate and was considering going back to the faith and entering an orthodox women's yeshiva in Israel. In any case, the couple wasn't speaking.

"So what happened to *our* movie?" said Doug Corfu after they had given up pumping me for inside dope. It took me a few seconds to realize he was talking about the birthday videocassette I had carried to Farnsworth on location.

"I already told you fellas," said Peter. "I never saw it. It got misplaced in our Prague hotel room. I think the maid threw it out with all the back issues of *Travel & Leisure*."

"Jesus!" said Chemerinski, throwing up his hands in frustration. "And it had the truth about *everything*—Osama bin Laden . . . Saddam and that Atta guy . . . the Florida election. . . . You could have used it all in your new script. They'd be lining up for it."

"I'm not writing a screenplay," said Farnsworth, his voice

suddenly barely audible as if he were reluctantly revealing an extremely embarrassing personal secret. "I'm working on a pilot . . . about a family of space aliens who open a bed-and-breakfast in Sacramento."

"You're back in series television?" I asked him, somewhat surprised.

"A man's got to make a living." He took a deep breath and exhaled, then continued a bit more perkily. "Anyway, I'm writing it with Ellen. We're working on it together, sort of a reconciliation thing. But for obvious reasons, she made me promise I wouldn't direct it, that I'd never direct again. So if it goes forward, we'll be looking for someone to fulfill that role." He stopped for a moment and surveyed the table. Consciously or unconsciously, most of the group started preening. Even Chemerinski, with all his fancy feature credits, shifted in his chair as if he were anxious to direct a pilot, it was potentially big money after all, when Farnsworth's eyes settled on me. "Interested?" he said with a chuckle, but something in his expression made me think that maybe, just maybe, he was actually serious. Now the rest of the table was staring at me too. I read a mixture of emotions on their faces—astonishment, disbelief and that greatest of all demons, envy. I shut my eyes and leaned back, seemingly giving the matter careful consideration. Then I opened them again and faced Farnsworth directly.

"I'll think about it," I said. "But on one condition . . . I want final cut!"